Grave

of the

Leviathans

A COLLECTION OF HORROR

ELIAS WITHEROW

THOUGHT
CATALOG
Books

THOUGHTCATALOG.COM

Published by Thought Catalog Books®, an imprint of Thought Catalog, a digital magazine owned and operated by The Thought & Expression Co. Inc., an independent media organization founded in 2010 and based in the United States of America. For stocking inquiries, contact stockists@shopcatalog.com.

Produced by Chris Lavergne and Noelle Beams
Circulation management by Isidoros Karamitopoulos

thoughtcatalog.com | shopcatalog.com

First Edition, printed internationally and fulfilled by Amazon in select countries.

ISBN 978-1-965820-23-0

This book is for my daughter, Alison

You are loved beyond words

Our little sweet pea

One last thing
This book is not for the faint of heart

COSMIC RATS

Sandra went to the kitchen window and opened it, letting in the warm, sunkissed air. Her husband, Mark, had taken the tractor out earlier in the day and mowed the three acre field that backed their house. Now, as the evening sky slowly turned a deep plum shade, she breathed in the gentle breeze, listening to the trees rustle in the wind. She scanned the treeline that bordered the edges of the field, searching for her three children. They would be coming in for supper soon, laughing and prancing through the open field, their voices echoing into the sky.

Sandra stepped away from the window and pulled the roast from the oven, setting it down on the table as her husband Mark walked in, his face pulled into a grin as the smell of dinner wafted toward him.

"I'm starving and that smells *outstanding*," Mark said, going to the kitchen sink to wash his hands.

"Did you see the kids?" Sandra asked, wiped her hands on her jeans. Mark looked out the window and nodded.

"Yep, here they come now. Full speed ahead. They must have smelled the food."

Tucker, Kenny, and Jillian would be bursting through the front door at any second and Sandra knew it'd be a battle to get them settled and washed before dinner. Tucker was the oldest, at ten.

Kenny was six. And little Jillian was an innocent, sweet four. Now that school was out for the summer, the three kids spent most of their days outside, exploring the woods, splashing in the creeks, lost to imagination and fantasy.

Just as Sandra was setting a pitcher of iced tea on the table, the children exploded through the front door. A wall of noise erupted into the kitchen as the kids scrambled to kick their shoes off, charging the kitchen.

"Hands! Hands!" Sandra instructed, pointing down the hall. "Get in the bathroom and wash those hands, kids! I don't want your grubby little fingers anywhere near me, you got it?"

"I'm so hungry I could die," Kenny grumbled, his curly blonde hair tumbling toward his big brown eyes.

"Then go wash your hands, dumb dumb," Tucker said, always the obedient officer.

"My hands are clean," little Jillian said, holding up her hands for her mother to inspect.

Sandra laughed. "Honey, get in there with your brothers and scrub up. Your hands are filthy."

"We were digging holes," Jillian sulked, following Tucker and Kenny to the bathroom.

"Hurry up kids, Dad's starving!" Mark called after them, sitting heavily at the head of the table.

When the kids were washed up, they took their seats and said grace. Soon after, they were digging in with a passion. While they ate, Sandra noticed Kenny fidgeting with something in his pocket.

"What do you have there, Ken?" She asked.

Kenny yanked something from his pocket and set it on the table. "Me and Tucker found this when we were playing. Pretty cool huh?"

"I found it too," Jillian said, frowning.

Sandra leaned forward and picked up the little treasure. It was a wooden block, a little smaller than a baseball. There were little images carved on the sides. A star, a cross, a small flame, another cross, a rat or maybe a mouse, and then another star. The craftsmanship was incredible and it looked like something that might have been expensive at one point.

"You found this in the woods?" Sandra asked, turning the block over.

Tucker nodded, shoveling green beans into his mouth. "Yep. It was buried by a tree."

"We were digging to China," Jillian informed the table.

"Yeah, but I found it," Kenny emphasized. "It's mine."

Sandra handed the small block back. "That's a very cool treasure. You should clean it after supper."

"Duh."

"None of that," Mark said. "Your mom was just being helpful."

Kenny dropped his eyes. "Sorry mom."

Sandra smiled. "Finish your dinner, kiddo."

That night, after Mark and Sandra had put the kids to bed, they lay together in their bedroom beneath the sheets. Mark had opened the window and they lay in each other's arms, listening to the crickets and frogs converse outside.

"I'll be gone tomorrow," Mark said quietly. "I signed that renovation job today so Greg and I are going out to Wyattsville to start."

Sandra stared out the window at the stars. "Thank goodness. We could use the money."

"You can say that again."

Sandra turned to Mark, feeling the warmth of his skin on hers. "You're a hard worker, you know that?"

"I do, I do," Mark said, grinning in the shadows.

"You going to be home in time for dinner tomorrow?"

"I don't know. I'll try to be."

"What time is it, hun?"

"It's a little after midnight."

Sandra groaned. "Have we been in here that long? We gotta get some sleep. Jillian will be up at the crack of dawn, like always."

Mark planted a kiss on his wife's head. "Ok. Night, babe."

As she closed her eyes, she heard something through the open window. It sounded like voices. Little voices in the backyard.

She sat up. "You hear that?"

Mark looked up at her. "Huh?"

Sandra climbed out of bed and went to the window, peering down. Her brow furrowed. "What on earth...?"

"What is it?"

Sandra grabbed her bathrobe and headed for the door. "Tucker and Kenny are outside."

"What!?"

"I'll get them," Sandra said. She marched down the stairs and went to the backdoor. She opened it and strode barefoot out into the grass. Tucker and Kenny were about fifty yards away, standing in the field. It sounded like they were talking quietly. Both of them were in their underwear and staring up at the sky.

"Why are you two out of bed?!" Sandra called as she approached. "And what on earth are you doing outside?"

To her surprise, neither of the boys turned to look at her. They remained motionless, eyes cocked to the sky. Kenny was whispering something to Tucker, but Sandra couldn't make out what.

She grabbed Kenny by the arm and spun him to face her. She felt a cold fist of horror plow into her stomach and she gasped in shock, taking a step back. Kenny's eyes were completely black except for tiny pin pricks of light in the center.

"Kenny?!" She gasped. Tucker turned at the sound of his mother's voice and she saw, with the same icy fear, that his eyes mirrored his younger brothers.

"Can you see the stars, Mom?" Tucker whispered.

Kenny turned his eyes back to the sky, his voice a low rattle. "They're getting closer, aren't they?"

Sandra grabbed her two sons and shook them frantically. "Wake up! Tuck, Kenny, you're asleep, wake up!"

Suddenly their eyes returned to normal and they blinked. They looked at each other and then at their mother.

"Why are we outside?" Kenny asked, looking completely dumbfounded.

"Mom?" was all Tucker offered, his face a mask of confusion.

Sandra hugged her boys, rattled but relieved. "Oh my gosh, come inside, both of you. Are you alright?"

They both shrugged, staring out into the night. They looked exhausted, lost, and just as confused as their mother.

Sandra wrapped her arms around their shoulders and guided them back toward the house. "Come on, let's get you back into bed."

As they went, Sandra glanced up at the stars.

Once the boys were back in bed, Sandra crawled back under the sheets next to Mark. She pulled the covers up to her chin and stared at the ceiling.

"You ok?" Mark asked, sitting up.

Sandra continued to stare up at the ceiling. "Yeah. They were sleep walking I think. They seemed completely out of it."

"Both of them?" Mark asked. "What are the odds?" He sighed and rolled over, dismissing the whole thing. "Thanks for taking care of that."

"Mark?"

"Hm?"

Sandra bit her lip and then turned over, facing away from Mark. "Nevermind. Goodnight."

As she listened to Mark drift off to sleep, she couldn't shake the image of her sons' eyes. She had to have imagined it. It was dark out. She had just been tired and disoriented. For now, whatever it was, she decided to keep it to herself.

The next day, the kids seemed completely normal. Neither of the boys mentioned the incident from the previous night which relieved Sandra. She didn't want Jillian to start worrying that *she* would start walking around in her sleep.

After breakfast, she let the three of them go outside to play, but told them to stay within eyesight of the house. Mark had left before the sun came up and she hoped he was back for dinner. As the day progressed, she couldn't shake a feeling of dread and it irritated her and scared her in equal parts.

An hour before dinner, Mark texted her and informed her he would indeed be late and didn't know when he'd be home. Sandra fed the kids and sent them to bed around nine. When they were settled, she texted Mark and he informed her she'd be home around ten.

Sandra decided to wait for him in bed, laying on top of the covers in the dark house, praying the kids stayed down tonight.

She was looking at pictures on her phone when she heard it.

It was loud and singular, one massive *thump!* from downstairs that shot her up out of bed. She stood in the dark room, heart in her throat, waiting for a follow up. Nothing came. Clutching her phone, she creeped to the hallway and peered around. All the doors to the kid's bedrooms were still closed.

"Mark?" She called down the stairs, the first floor awash in total blackness.

No answer came.

She squeezed her eyes shut and forced herself to calm down. She was an adult and mother of three. Nothing should be able to scare her. Taking a deep breath, she slipped down the stairs. Nothing moved or made a sound and she started to feel a little silly. She walked into the kitchen and swept her eyes across every shadow. Again, nothing.

But then something caught her full attention and sent a lance of terror up her spine. Something or someone was standing outside on the back deck. She caught it for just a second, a fleeing shadow that jumped over the railing and went sprinting into the field where it vanished into the darkness.

Sandra caught herself on the kitchen counter and couldn't seem to get enough oxygen down her throat. Her eyes bulged and she clenched her jaw so hard she thought her teeth would crack.

She took a step back from the sliding glass door and let out a yelp of pain as she stepped on something. She looked down.

It was the small wooden cube the kids had found in the woods. She brought it up and studied the carved images, feeling her chest tighten. Slowly, she turned the cube over, examining the stars, the crosses, and then the rat looking creature. She went still. A small crown had been carved onto the head of the rat, a simple scratched image that looked new.

Still holding the cube, she looked out the glass doors, paralyzed with fear. She fully expected to see someone standing there, face pressed against the panes. She went to the door and made sure it was locked, relieved to find that it was. She was about to call Mark when a tiny voice cut through the stillness.

"Mom?"

Sandra jumped and then whirled to see Kenny standing on the opposite side of the kitchen, staring at her.

"Kenny! you scared me half to death! What are you doing out of bed?"

In the darkness, Kenny continued to stare at her, his voice soft and quiet. "Why are you holding my block?"

Sandra looked down at the wooden cube in her hand. "This? What is this, Ken?"

"Can I have it back?"

Sandra walked over to him, holding out the cube. "Did you carve this on here?" She asked, pointing to the crown over the rat.

Kenny took the cube from her without responding. He didn't look at it, just held it loosely in his hand, staring straight ahead.

"Why are you down here?" Sandra asked. "Did you hear something?"

Kenny pointed to the glass doors. "I just came down to look at the stars."

"Well you can do that another night, you need to go back to bed. Right now. And please don't wake your brother or sister."

Kenny looked up at her. "Tucker isn't in his bed."

"What?!" Sandra cried. Without waiting, she flew up the stairs and into the room Kenny shared with his brother. Tucker's bed was empty. Panic came to her in a hot rush that rolled through her stomach. She heard Kenny plodding up the stairs and she met him in the hallway.

"Where's your brother?" She asked frantically, taking him by the shoulders.

But before he could answer, Sandra saw that Jillian's door was now open a crack. She went to it and flung it open.

Tucker was kneeling beside his sleeping sister. He had a hand cupped to her ear and was whispering something to her. Despite this, Jillian remained fast asleep on her back.

"Tucker!" Sandra hissed. "What the hell are you doing!?"

Tucker turned and for a split second, she saw that his eyes were the color of tar, save for a small pinprick of white light at the centers. He blinked and they were back to normal, the transformation happening so fast Sandra almost couldn't believe she had seen it.

But she had. There was no mistaking it this time.

Tucker stood slowly, dressed only in his whitey tighties, and walked over to Sandra. He motioned her to come closer and then he whispered in her ear.

"It's cold, way up here."

Sandra took Tucker by the arm and pulled him out of the room, shutting the door to Jillian's room behind her. She grabbed Kenny in the hallway and dragged them both back to their room.

"I've had enough of this nonsense," she hissed, feeling an anger toward her kids for scaring her so badly. "Both of you get your behinds into bed RIGHT NOW and do not get up again. If you do, I'm going to tell you father and he is going to be extremely upset. Do you understand?!"

Wordlessly, they climbed into their beds and pulled the covers up over their heads where they lay motionless.

"Do you both understand me!?" Sandra said louder.

Very quietly, she heard Kenny whisper from under the blankets, almost to himself. "There's stars in here too."

Before she could respond, Mark came home. She heard his truck roar up the driveway and she flew down the stairs to greet him, her mind a tangled mess of confusion and fear. But Mark didn't come inside right away. Instead, she saw him run around the side of the house, phone in hand, toward the field out back. Sandra tracked his shadow past the windows, his heavy boots thudding across the yard.

She went to the sliding door and yanked it open, staring out at her husband, perplexed. He had his phone pointed toward the sky, like he was tracking something.

"Mark!" She called, her voice cracking.

He didn't even turn to look at her. He jabbed a finger toward the sky, his voice excited. "Did you see it!? Tell me you saw it!"

"See WHAT? Mark, the kids are acting-"

"The lights!" Mark babbled. "Didn't you see the lights!? I tried to record it on my phone, but I think I was too late, but holy cow, there were these lights that went across the-"

"MARK!"

He lowered his phone, finally turning to her, confusion painted across his face.

"What? What's wrong, hun?"

"Come inside. There's something wrong with the boys."

Even in the darkness, she saw his face go white.

"Are they ok? What happened?!"

Sandra held her hands up, calming him. "They're ok, for now. But they were walking around again and there was something wrong with Tucker's eyes and-"

"Sleep walking?" Mark interjected.

She nodded. "Yeah...well, no. I don't know. But I think I need to get them to a specialist tomorrow. Something isn't right. They were acting weird and mumbling nonsense and Tucker's eyes looked wrong-"

Mark reached her and gave her a hug. "Oh jeez, I'm sorry I wasn't here to help. I'm sure that was a handful to deal with on your own."

"No," Sandra insisted, pulling away. "You're not listening to me."

"I am," Mark soothed. "If they were sleep walking then I'm sure they were spouting all kinds of weird dream nonsense and their eyes looked all scary. They were asleep."

"They weren't though, I mean, they might have been but... heck, I don't know, but I need to get them in to see someone tomorrow. Tucker and Kenny both."

"Ok, we can do that," Mark said. He turned back to the star filled sky. "Man, I wish you had seen those lights though."

"Can we please go to bed?"

Mark took one last look out into the night and then nodded, smiling. "Of course, let's go. If the kids wake up again tonight, I'll handle them."

The next day passed without incident. Sandra called a couple specialists, but no one could see the boys until the following week. Frustrated, she booked the appointments anyway. She noticed that Kenny kept the small wooden block with him for most of the day, never letting it out of eyesight. At lunch, she asked if he could put it away and he had gotten extremely heated and after a short argument, she gave up and let him keep it on the table while he ate his sandwich. Tucker was the only other person he allowed to touch it, which caused Jillian to get very upset. Sandra vowed that when they all went to bed, she was going to take the stupid thing and throw it away. She didn't like how attached Kenny was to the thing, even though it appeared harmless.

Thankfully, Mark came home around dinner time and helped her get the kids to bed, spending a little more time with Jillian, reading her story after story until she finally allowed him to put her to sleep.

When they crawled into bed together, it was after ten and Sandra was wiped out. She had completely forgotten about the wooden cube and her mission to throw it away, her mind stretched thin by the worry of the day. She felt stressed out and exhausted and just wanted to close her eyes and go to sleep. She felt some comfort knowing that Mark was home to deal with any sleepwalking nonsense the kids might experience. She prayed the next time she opened her eyes, it'd be morning.

Instead, she woke to screaming at two am.

Both her and Mark rocketed out of bed, instantly alert.

"That's Jillian!" Sandra said, sprinting out of the room with Mark hot on her heels. Both of them skid to a halt when they saw that the kids weren't in their rooms, the doors flung wide open.

The screaming started again and Sandra realized that it was coming from outside. Together, Sandra and Mark bolted down the stairs and practically ripped open the sliding door that led to the field out back.

What they saw knocked them back in a blast of horror.

Tucker and Kenny had erected a wooden cross out of thick tree limbs, tied together with old rope. Hanging on the cross was Jillian, her tiny body was naked and bound to the erected cross. She was howling and screaming at her brothers to stop, tears running down her face in fear and confusion.

Tucker and Kenny ignored her. They were holding gas cans from the garage and were splashing her with it, dousing her chest and legs and soaking the cross.

"What are you DOING!?" Mark roared, running for them.

"Mommy!" Jillian screamed, shivering, limbs writhing in their constraints.

Kenny tossed the gas can aside and pulled a small box of matches out. Mark was still twenty yards away, bellowing at the boys to stop. Tucker turned to him, his face an unreadable mask.

His eyes were completely black as Kenny struck the match, bathing both boys' faces in matching expressions.

"The stars are here," Kenny said quietly.

He then tossed the match onto the gas-soaked cross and Sandra watched in mind bending terror as Jillian's skin sucked the flame to it, igniting her in a rush of fire. Both boys turned to Mark as he sprinted for them, lowering their shoulders suddenly and ramming into their father, catching him in the groin, spinning him to the ground with a thud.

Sandra raced to Jillian, her blood curdling screams echoing across the field as her daughter began to burn alive. With the boys focused on Mark, Sandra reached the blazing cross and slammed into it, knocking it back, but not down. The heat was unbearable and she could smell her little girl's flesh begin to cook and blacken.

"MARK HELP ME!" She screamed, slamming into the cross again. It tilted back further, the earth at the base uprooting the erected structure.

Tucker spun toward her, his black eyes dotted with tiny pricks of light at the center.

"Stop it!" He yelled, charging her. "They need to see the star!"

He grabbed Sandra by the breast and twisted it violently, shocking Sandra, a gasp of pain ripping up her throat. She tried to bat him away, Jillian's screams blasting down over her. Tucker brought his fist up into her crotch, his knuckles spiking agony up her body and down her legs.

Suddenly Mark was there, grabbing Tucker by the back of the neck. He threw him with a roar, sending him tumbling heavily across the ground and away from Sandra. He grabbed the burning cross with his bare hands, ignoring the pain, and began to push it over.

Jillian's head was on fire, her hair alight and filling the air with a horrible smell as she writhed and twisted. The ropes holding her in place began to fall away as they caught fire, and together, the cross and Jillian fell in a burning heap to the ground.

As they did, four white lights zipped overhead, bright and spherical, moving so quickly it appeared as if they winked into existence. It happened so suddenly that Sandra didn't fully understand what she was seeing. They hovered above the children, about a hundred feet overhead. They were huge, each one the size of a house, except shaped like luminescent moons, rays of pure white light shooting out of each of them.

"The rats are here, the rats are here!" Kenny and Tucker cried in unison, jumping up and down excitedly, their dark eyes glowing as the pin pricks at the center grew bigger and brighter.

Sandra and Mark were trying to pull Jillian off the cross, which was still burning, but Jillian's screams were growing more guttural as her parents desperately swatted at the flames that danced across her skin.

"Get her legs!" Mark screamed, squinting while the lights overhead shifted, the colossal orbs shifting and realigning.

Sandra bit back a scream as she ripped the blazing ropes off her daughters legs, her hands throbbing in pain as the fire licked them. Jillian's skin was almost completely black now and the smell was horrific. She had stopped thrashing, her hair completely burned away to leave a charred, bald crust that covered her skull.

"Jillian! Jillian baby we have you! We got you!" Sandra screamed, tears running down her face. Mark yanked her free and pulled her off the cross. He wrapped her in his arms and smothered the lingering fire against his body, calling her name, his voice hitching in panic.

Suddenly, the four orbs overhead stopped moving, painting the field in a still, quiet light. In unison, they emitted a low warble that echoed across the sky. It was low and insistent and Sandra felt it vibrate through her chest as it bellowed down at them.

Kenny and Tucker ran to stand directly beneath one of the lights, jumping and shouting excitedly.

"Get away from there!" Sandra howled, trying to stand, her hands red and pulsing in agony.

Without warning, a column of light shot down toward the boys from the orb, engulfing them in a totality that momentarily blinded Sandra. In a blink, the light vanished.

And so did the boys.

"No, NO!" Mark screamed, still holding Jillian. He looked frantically at Sandra who stared helplessly back.

Another long warble echoed out from the four orbs as they began to spin in a circle, rotating a hundred feet above them in perfect unison. Sandra stood, feeling sick, terrified, and completely out of her mind. She screamed for her kids, her voice hoarse and raw as she watched the lights continue to spin.

And then they were gone, zipping straight up into the sky at a horrifying speed until they looked like tiny stars before winking out of sight. Sandra collapsed onto the ground in a heap, covering her face, weeping, unable to comprehend what had just happened. It had all happened so fast and the finality of it all slammed into her like a freight train. Her boys, oh god, *her boys*.

Mark was screaming and Sandra, in a daze, looked over at him, her vision blurred.

"I think she's dead, Sandra!" He cried. "Oh god, I think she's dead!"

Sandra crawled over to him, feeling as if her mind was leaving her body, and looked down into her daughter's eyes. They were open and stared up at nothing, her blackened chest unmoving and still.

Sandra curled up on the ground and laid her head against her daughter's ruined body. She began to sob, her whole being in full rejection.

Jillian was dead.

And the boys had been taken.

Taken by the rats.

GUNJI

I was at the supermarket, standing in line to pay, when my phone rang. I fished my cell out of my pocket and answered, groaning internally when I saw the name on my screen.

"What do you want, Kyle?"

Kyle was my ex, an absolute shit bird and the unfortunate father of my five year old boy, Zach.

"Nice to hear from you too," Kyle said sarcastically.

"I'm at the grocery store, what do you need?"

"Damn, aren't you cheerful today."

I thought about hanging up, but gave him one more shot. "Last chance, Kyle."

"I'm just making sure you don't forget to pick up Zach from school."

I started to place my food on the conveyor belt. "Of course I'm not going to forget. Have I ever? Did you really feel the need to call and remind me?"

"I just know you have your hands full with your new boyfriend these days. I wanted to make sure you don't forget about our son."

"Jesus," I muttered, feeling my blood pressure rise. "Is that why you're really calling?"

"Just don't forget about him," Kyle said and then coughed heavily.

"I'm so thrilled to hear you've finally decided to take interest in our son's life," I responded darkly.

"You left me, Megan," Kyle spat. "You took him away from ME. All so you could hop on some fresh cock. Don't you ever forget that."

"Fuck you."

I hung up, tossing my hair over my shoulder. I jammed my phone back in my pocket and ground my teeth together. Kyle was a grade A piece of shit and he always did such a good job reminding me why I had left him. It made me sick to think he had gotten me pregnant. In my darkest moments, I silently wished he would get hit by a car and leave Zach and I alone forever. Things would be better that way.

I finished paying for my groceries and went out to the parking lot. As I tossed my bags into the passenger seat, I felt my phone ring again. Immediately, I felt my mood turn hot as I snatched the phone up again, ready to give Kyle some fire.

"Listen you ass-"

But it wasn't Kyle. Instead, a low female robotic voice spoke into my ear.

"Gunji has been activated."

I blinked. "What? Hello?"

"Gunji is 5.4 miles away. If you'd like to speak to a representative, please press 7."

After a brief pause, the line went dead.

"Ok then," I said dismissively, tossing my phone next to the groceries. I started the car and began traveling across town to Zach's school. I couldn't believe what Kyle had said. No. No, of course I could believe it. We had been together for two years before his drug habit had destroyed our sad little family. I left him six months ago and I was still fighting for full custody. Kyle wasn't making it easy. He never made anything easy. He was a moron and he thought I left because I had found someone else, which wasn't the case.

Meeting Jose had been a stroke of good fortune and I thanked the heavens every day for him. He was the complete opposite of Kyle. Hardworking, family oriented, he had his life in order and had loved Zach from the second they met. But all Kyle saw was some stupid form of betrayal.

"Please jump off a bridge today, Kyle," I growled as I crossed town, checking the clock. Zach would be getting out just as I arrived. Because I was a great mother and wouldn't forget about my own son. Especially not because there was someone new in my life. Never.

A few minutes later, I pulled up to Zach's school and waited as the line of cars inched forward, each parent waiting patiently for their child.

My phone rang again. I picked it up.

"This is Megan."

The robotic female voice filled my ear once again.

"Gunji is 0.3 miles away. If you'd like to speak to a representative, please press 7."

I ended the call, dismissing the spam once more. Somehow my number had made it onto a telemarketers list or something. Putting the strange call out of my mind, I waved to Zach as he trotted down the front steps of the school. As much as I loved the kid, I hated how much of his father I saw in his face. A high, pinched nose, the same wavy brown hair, those blue eyes that tilted down slightly.

But he wasn't Kyle, and I loved him to death.

"Hi Mom!" Zach greeted as I leaned back and pushed the back door open for him. He climbed in and threw his backpack down next to him.

"Hi Zach!" I beamed. "Did you have a good day at school?"

"I guess," Zach said, biting his lip. "I learned a joke today."

"Oh?"

"What has got two cheeks but can't chew?"

I smiled and rolled my eyes. "Whaaaat?"

"A BUTT!" He cackled.

"Well that's a very silly joke," I said. "Don't let your teacher hear you tell that one. Put your seatbelt on, kid."

Before he could though, something caught my attention. Screams. Screams coming from the front of the school. I whipped my head around and looked up the steps toward the glass doors that led inside. Kids and teachers alike were screaming and running away from the entrance in a frenzy. Their screams cut through my mind like it was taffy. Immediately, even as I was still processing what I was seeing, I went on full alert, every sense sharpening.

This couldn't be what I feared it was. My mind pulsed the same word over and over again in bright red neon.

Shooter. Shooter. Shooter.

A moment later, when I saw why everyone was running, my heart thudded dead in my chest.

Blood erupted against the glass panels, spraying in all directions from the inside. A moment after my brain registered this, children exploded through the glass, thrown at a force I couldn't comprehend. Their small bodies rocketed from the wall of glass like they were shot out of a cannon, landing ten or fifteen feet down the steps. Their bloody bodies left skid streaks on the concrete as they blasted out of the shattered glass, teeth, shoes, books, all flying like confetti.

Three, five, then ten kids all airborne, arcing through the air to land in a tumbling splat across the front of the school. Screams filled my head as I watched great gouts of blood stain the washed out concrete as the bodies continued to be expelled through the front of the school.

"Zach, keep your head down!" I yelled, panic roaring through my chest like a pillar of fire. I gunned the engine, the car jerking and clipping the SUV in front of me. I yanked the wheel and spun the car away, casting my eyes to the rearview mirror. As I did, a little girl thudded into the back window. I heard her bones crunch on impact and the glass cracked on impact, the fractures filling with blood as the dead kid slid off, her skull crushed.

What is HAPPENING!?

I grabbed my phone as I tore out of the parking lot, dialing 911 as I did so. When the operator picked up, I yelled until my voice was hoarse that there was an active shooter at my son's school.

But was there? I hadn't heard any gunshots, not a single one. Maybe I hadn't heard them. There had been so much screaming. But that didn't explain the children. They weren't dropping dead where they ran. They were being hurled through the air, through the front of the school, tossed like they were weightless. A gun wouldn't do that, would it? An explosion maybe?

I didn't pay any attention to the stoplights as I raced away from the school, my frantic mind not even registering them. I just needed to get Zach away from the school. Jesus, Zach!

I turned around and saw that he was crying, huddled in his seat. But he looked unharmed, just shaken.

"It's ok sweetie, we're ok! We're safe! We're going home! Do you want to talk to Jose? Do you want me to call Jose?"

Zach nodded and wiped his eyes. Jose was so good with Zach, I knew that just talking to him would calm my son down. I went to dial his number, but saw there was an incoming call already on the screen. I answered it.

"Yes, hello!?"

"Gunji is 1.2 miles away. If you'd like to speak to a representative, please press 7."

"Stop calling me!" I yelled into the phone, confused and disoriented. What the hell was this Gunji thing? Why were they calling me?

"Wait a second," I muttered, eyes trained on the road. What had that voice said? Gunji was just over a mile away? As in, back by the school?

"What the hell is going on here...?"

I pushed the thought aside and called Jose. He answered on the second ring.

"Hey Meg, what's going on, babe?"

"Jose, something horrible is happening at Zach's school. He's safe and I have him with me in the car. He's really scared right now and wants to talk to you. I'm going to pass the phone back to him, ok?"

It all came out in a breathless rush and I blessed him for not asking any of the million questions I'm sure he had. He heard that Zach was scared and wanted to talk to him and that was enough.

"Give him the phone," he said gently.

I reached back and handed Zach the cell. "Jose wants to say hi, baby. Do you still want to talk to him?"

Zach nodded, his eyes wet, and took the phone. "H'lo?"

I could hear Jose's muffled voice speaking to my son and blessed my wonderful boyfriend. I checked the rearview and could see Zach nodding, some of the fear leaving his face as he listened. When he had calmed down some, he handed the phone back to me. I took it and pressed it to my ear.

"Jose?"

"I'm here. What the hell happened? What's going on?"

"I don't know," I said, feeling the emotional weight of the trauma filling my throat. "I don't know, Jose, but there are dead kids. There's a lot of dead kids at the school, it might still be happening, I don't know, there was so much blood and screaming and -" I started to cry, hands shaking on the wheel as I raced through the middle of town toward the house.

"Are you ok? Are you hurt?"

I shook my head and wiped my eyes with the back of my hand. "No, we're ok. But Jesus, something terrible it going on at -"

I dropped the phone, jerking the wheel, eyes bulging as a car to my right soared into my lane, tumbling and spinning through the air like it had been launched off a ramp. It smashed violently into the car in front of me, the collision of metal and glass crunching and spraying across the road. I heard myself scream as I swerved to avoid the spinning, rolling cars as they plowed across my vision. I heard Zach scream and felt my neck whip back to hit the headrest.

Miraculously, I managed to avoid the wreckage as I righted the wheel and skirted around the smoking, crushed vehicles as they thudded to a halt. I felt my breath heave up my throat like it was fire, every nerve in my body trembling like it was touched by lightning.

"Holy shit," I gasped, heart thundering. "Zach!? You ok, Zach?!"

"I want to go hooooome!" He wailed, eyes streaming.

"We're going! We're almost there baby!"

What the hell had just happened? Where had that car come from? It had been flying like some great beast had just tossed it from a parking lot, directly into my lane. I was shaken to the core, felt the edges of reality twist and blur at the corners of my vision.

Just get home, just get yourself and Zach home.

I realized my phone was ringing at my feet, where I had dropped it. I blindly grabbed it and answered.

"Jesus, Jose!? You're never going to believe-"

"Gunji is 0.2 miles away. If you'd like to speak to a representative -"

"Stop calling me!" I screamed into the phone.

The robotic female phone paused for a moment, then repeated her message. Panting, I pulled my phone away and was about to hang up. But then, in a daze, I pushed 7.

There was a pause as I was connected with a representative.

The robotic voice spoke after a moment. "Please hold. All of our representatives are assisting other callers. You are 5th in the queue. We will return your call when the next representative becomes available. Goodbye."

"Useless SHIT!" I screamed, then immediately regretted the outburst. I heard Zach wail behind me and I turned to soothe him.

"I'm sorry, baby, we're almost home. Just a couple more minutes. You can watch as much TV as you want and we'll have McDonald's for dinner, how does that sound?"

Zach took a steadying breath and dried his eyes. "That sounds pretty good."

"Ok, hun, just keep your seatbelt on ok?"

"Ok. Did the cars crash?"

"They sure did, we need to be safe so keep your belt on, ok?"

"Ok, Mom."

What the hell is going on today? I thought, turning back to the road. I called Jose again.

"Megan? Are you ok?" Jose asked, worried now.

"Yeah, you're not going to believe what just happened. I'll tell you when I get home. Can you meet us there? I know you're working and-"

"I'm already on the way," he said.

"Thank you," I breathed, feeling my chest deflate a little. "I love you."

"I love you too. See you soon, Meg."

"Bye."

A couple minutes later, we turned onto our street. Our house was tucked away at the end of the road, a winding row of single story ranches that ended at a plot of woods. When I pulled into the driveway, I felt safe for the first time in what seemed like years. I shut the car off and unbuckled my seatbelt. I was about to get out when my phone rang again, for what felt like the millionth time today. I answered it. The robotic female voice filled my ear.

"Please hold. You are next in the queue."

Holding the phone to my ear, I exited the car and got Zach out. I picked him up and we walked toward the front door, his face buried in my shoulder.

A woman's voice, an actual person, chirped in my ear then. "Hello, thank you for holding. How may I-"

Beep beep beep.

Blinking, I pulled my cell away from my ear and looked at the screen. The battery was dead. I had forgotten to charge it last night.

"Goddamn it," I hissed, shoving it into my pocket.

We were home though. I could always call that number back once Zach was settled. For now, we were safe.

I keyed the front door open and went into the living room. I plopped Zach down on the couch and turned on the TV for him.

"You ok, Zach? Do you want a snack?"

He nodded, kicking off his shoes, his attention already pulled toward the TV. It was like the trauma we had just been through had never happened. Kids were unreal.

I left him on the couch and went to the bathroom. I shut the door and began to cry. The horror of what I had just been through crashed over me like waves on a beach. My shoulders shook and I let myself purge. When I was finished, I washed my face and went into the bedroom. I put my phone on the charger and grabbed a snack for Zach in the kitchen. I needed to know what had happened at the school, but with my phone dead, I had no way of looking it up. I still couldn't believe the carnage I had seen. I knew I wasn't going to forget those images anytime soon or the feeling of helplessness as I watched the children splatter onto the concrete.

I pushed the thoughts away, knowing they'd be waiting for me tonight. I went into the kitchen and heard the front door open.

"Megan!?"

"In here, Jose!"

My boyfriend swept into the living room, pulling me into his arms. His face looked pale and I buried myself in his chest.

"We're ok," I whispered. "We're safe."

"I cannot believe you went through that," Jose said, stroking my hair. He planted a kiss on top of my head and pulled away, studying my face.

"You sure you're ok?"

"No, I'm not, but that can wait," I said, shooting a look at Zach on the couch. Jose knelt down next to him.

"Hey buddy, you doing ok?"

"You're in the way of the cartoons!" Zach cried, leaning around Jose.

"I guess he's ok," Jose said, standing. "Jesus, what a nightmare."

"Did you hear anything on the news?"

"I checked Twitter. Looks like the police are still evacuating the school and searching for whoever did this."

"They haven't caught them yet?"

"No."

"Do they have a count yet...? Of how many...?"

"Eighteen kids so far."

I felt my skin go cold. I closed my eyes and said nothing. Those poor children. Those poor families. I couldn't even begin to imagine what they were going through right now. If I had been just a few minutes late...

"Hey, he's ok," Jose said, reading my face. "You're safe. He's safe."

"I know."

We both froze then, as something from the woods behind our house cried out. It sounded like a woman screaming, a piercing, warbling shriek that cut off abruptly.

"What was that?" Jose asked quietly.

I swallowed uncomfortably. "That sounded like a woman. From the woods." I started walking to the kitchen where our sliding glass door led out to the back deck. Jose followed me and together we stepped outside, listening.

There was nothing for a moment, and then a man's voice came from deep within the dark woods. It sounded like someone was yelling nonsense, the babble of words jumbling together.

"*Wolololo roo yeti mockbella!*"

"What the hell is happening today?" I shivered, stepping back into the house. "What is that!?"

The voice came again, deep, almost robotic sounding. "*Wolololo roo yeti mockbella!*"

"I'm calling the police," I said, pulling Jose back into the house.

"Good idea. I'll sit with Zach."

But before I could, the front door banged open and in walked Kyle. I jumped at the sound and then felt dread and anger fill me in equal parts as my ex entered the house.

"What the fuck are you doing here?!" I yelled, stomping down the hallway. "You can't just barge into my house Kyle!"

"You weren't answering your phone!" Kyle yelled. His face was flush and he looked ready to kill. "I heard about what happened at the school and I tried calling you!" He looked at Zach on the couch. When he saw him, he deflated a little. "Oh thank god. You're ok."

"My phone died," I said, storming to his side. "You still can't just plow your way in here, Kyle!"

"Cut me some slack you heartless bitch," Kyle snarled, turning to me.

Jose raised his hands. "Hey, none of that talk. Not now, not ever, you got it?"

Kyle waved a hand at him. "Oh sit down, hotshot. She'll be done with you soon enough and then you'll see."

"Dad?" Zach said, sliding from the couch. "Kids died at school today."

That seemed to cool the temperature in the room by about twenty degrees. Kyle took a deep breath and got down on one knee. "I know. I was so worried about you. I had to come here and make sure you were safe."

I closed my eyes and then opened them, forcing myself to calm. "I'm sorry you couldn't reach me. I'm sure that was scary, Kyle. But we're ok."

Jose reached out and touched my arm. "I'll stay here. You should go call the police."

Kyle stood, his face darkening. "Now hold on here, asshole, this is my kid and I have every right-"

"Not for you," Jose said. "We heard screams from the woods out back, right before you arrived."

"Screams? Like, human screams?"

"Yeah. We should all lock the doors until the police get here. With the incident at the school, we're not taking any risks here."

I went to the bedroom and powered up my phone. The battery was at 6%. That was enough. Before I dialed 911 I saw that I had a new voicemail. I made a mental note to check it later. As I pushed 9, my phone rang.

It was the same number that had been calling me all morning.

"Hello?"

"Gunji is fifty feet away. If you'd like to speak to a representative, please press 7."

I didn't move. In an instant, the massacre at the school flashed through my head, then the car that had been thrown into traffic. And now the screams and weird noises coming from the woods.

Before I could press 7, I heard Zach scream from the living room. I dropped the phone and bolted to him. He was huddled in Jose's arms, clearly shaken.

"What happened?!" I yelled.

Kyle pointed to the door leading out to the garage. "Something is out there."

"What do you mean? The garage is closed! There's nothing in th-"

My stomach plummeted as a woman's scream echoed in the garage. It was immediately followed by the hysterical laughter of a small child. A beat passed and then:

"Wolololo roo yeti mockbella!"

"Everyone, get upstairs," I said, pointing to the stairs. "Now!"

"Fuck that," Kyle said, stepping toward the garage door. "I'm not letting some psycho invade my kid's home." He shot a look at Jose. "Someone's gotta be the man here."

"Kyle, don't be stupid!" I said, reaching for him. He jerked his arm away and walked to the garage door. He yanked it open and stepped out of sight before I could stop him.

A split second later, he came rocketing back through the door, his body exploding into bloody pieces as if he had stepped on a landmine. Chunks of flesh and gore erupted through the open door and splattered wetly against the far wall. I saw fingers and hair, teeth and fractured bone rip past my face, spraying me in a wash of blood.

Zach screamed and Jose yelled, stepping back. Instinct took over and I grabbed Jose, who was still holding Zach and pulled them toward the back bedroom, heart crunching in my chest, thudding against my ribs so hard I thought they would break.

"Wolololo roo yeti mockbella!"

"Get into the bedroom!" I screamed, shoving Jose down the hall and into the bedroom, slamming and locking the door behind me.

My cell, discarded on the floor, was ringing.

I dove for it and answered.

"Gunji is fourteen feet away. If you'd like to speak-"

I pushed 7, my back to the door. Jose was in the corner of the room, clutching a weeping Zach to his chest. His eyes were confused and scared, pleading for me to give some explanation.

"Thank you for contacting a representative, my name is Mary, how can I assist you?"

"Hello?" I screamed into the phone. "Who is this?! What is going on!?"

The voice came from the other line, a human voice, not the robotic one I was used to hearing. "This is Mary. I'm going to have to ask you to please lower your voice so I can understand and assist you."

"What the fuck is Gunji!?" I yelled, eyes red. "Why is it here in my house!?"

A pause. Then, "If you'd like to recall Gunji, I'm going to need your seven digit passcode."

"I don't have a passcode you bitch!"

From outside the door, I heard heavy footsteps enter the house from the garage.

"Ma'am, I'm going to have to insist you lower your voice."

"It's going to kill us!" I shrieked.

The woman on the other end covered the microphone and said something I couldn't hear. It sounded like she was speaking to someone else on the other side.

"Hello?!"

The voice came back. "Ma'am do you have an account with us?"

"I don't even know who you are, lady! You've been calling me all fucking morning and now people are *dead*!"

The woman covered the microphone again and spoke to someone in a muffled voice. From down the hall, I heard children laughing and the sound of little feet running through the house. Then, it sounded like a woman was throwing up in the living room.

"Get out of my house!" I screamed.

"Wolololo roo yeti mockbella!"

This time, the voice was right outside the door.

"Megan, what is going on?!" Jose yelled, shaking.

The woman on the phone came back. "I'm so sorry, it seems there was a mix up. We ran a check on your phone number and it seems like there was an error on our end. I apologize for the inconvenience. The last four digits of your phone number are 9833 correct?"

The door shook at my back as something huge thudded into it, knocking me forward a couple steps. I could still hear the sound of children down the hall and the woman retching.

"Yes! Yes!" I screamed, tears filling my eyes.

"Ah, I see where the mistake is now," the woman said calmly. "Gunji was assigned to 9834, not 9833. We apologize for the mistake."

"Fucking do something then!"

Another blow rattled the door and I heard wood splinter. Zach was still screaming.

"Wolololo roo yeti mockbella!"

The voice was practically in my ear, a bellowing blast that sunk my heart into my guts.

The woman continued on calmly. "I'll reassign Gunji on our end. Please hold."

Another blow crunched into the door, knocking me forward again. I could see the splinters beginning to form at my back as whatever was on the other side continued to pound away in rage.

"Get him under the bed!" I yelled at Jose. "Get him under the bed and help me, Jose!"

But before Jose could move, the pounding stopped.

Everything beyond the door went dead silent.

The woman's voice returned to me. "We've gone ahead and reassigned Gunji. Again, from everyone here, we apologize for the inconvenience. Is there anything else I can do for you today?"

I held my breath, waiting. Silence continued to fill the house. It was as if nothing had been there at all. Slowly, Jose stepped toward me, Zach's face in his chest.

"Is it gone?" He asked, his voice trembling. "Did it leave?"

I swallowed hard and spoke into the phone. "Is it really gone? Did it leave?"

The woman answered in a maddeningly calm tone. "Yes, I have Gunji exiting the neighborhood now."

I leaned into the phone. "Lady...what the *fuck* is Gunji?"

Beep beep beep.

I looked down at my screen.

The phone was dead.

GORA

My boots squished up the hill, each step staining the treads in blood. I barely even registered it. The wind reeked of rotting flesh and copper, a warm tongue that blew my dark hair off my forehead. The red ocean that surrounded the island was loud today, red froth lapping across the black sand.

"Where are you, brother?" I muttered to myself, eyes scanning the expanse of the island as I crested the hill. I had traveled along the coast for hours, sure I would find him fishing monsters from the soupy sea or collecting their corpses from the beach. My search had been fruitless and the weather was turning. I needed to get back home.

I spotted a Gore Pole a couple hundred yards away, standing alone at the top of a distant rise. I started walking toward it, the flesh beneath my feet squelching. I gagged as another gust of wind smacked my face, bringing with it the foul stench that rose from the island. As I went, careful not to slip, I realized that my brother and I had been here for five years now. Five long years of watching the ocean, speaking to the Flags, waiting for the hell they warned was coming.

I reached the bottom of a hill and strode quickly through the long tufts of black hair that grew like grass. The pores they sprouted from looked like infected scabs in the pink skin that covered the island.

A land of flesh, bone, and gore. Five years we had lived among the stink, surrounded by the horrible sea that brought horrors crawling up the shore with each storm. As I made my way across the barren, fleshy landscape, I realized that I hadn't yet checked the tunnel today. I looked at the angry, darkening clouds that were forming on the horizon. I needed to get back to the house quickly and check it, to make sure the tunnel was still sealed before the storm came.

The island always bared its sharpest fangs during the storms.

I trotted the rest of the way to the Gore Pole, huffing and puffing as I climbed the hill it stood upon. When I reached the top, I craned my head back and stared up at the hundred foot pole, no thicker than my forearm. There were fifteen of these poles scattered across the island and to this day, I still didn't understand them fully. But they were useful.

I rapped my knuckles on the metal pole, the only thing on the island that wasn't made of skin or bone. I waited a moment and then knocked again. I looked at the sky, waiting.

"Come on you bastards, hurry up."

A moment later, I saw what I had beckoned. It was a sheet of flesh that blustered on the wind, two feet by three. It drifted and fluttered closer, dancing on the wind like a lost sheet of newspaper.

When it reached the top of the Gore Pole, it snapped onto it, fluttering like a flag at the height of it.

"Hey, down here," I called.

The veiny rectangle of flesh slid down the pole to my level. I found myself staring at the stretched face that filled the Flag. Its mouth had no teeth, its eye sockets were huge and empty, and its nose was cut off at the bridge, leaving two small black holes.

"Who are you?" The Flag asked in a gentle voice.

"My name is Renny. Can you help me out?" I had never spoken to the same one twice and had no idea where they came from or how many there were. They always came from the clouds and not once in five years had the clouds broken to see beyond. Perhaps there was a whole other world up there where the Flags lived.

The Flag fluttered gently in the breeze, its skin a spider web of veins. "What do you need?"

"I'm looking for my brother. There's a storm coming and I need to find him."

The Flag suddenly shot up the Gore Pole where it wavered for a few seconds before sliding back down, its dark sockets unblinking. "Yes, there's a bad one coming. Going to be bad. Bad bad. Why are you here?"

They always asked this. I didn't have time to get into it.

"Have you seen another that looks like me? Could you look?"

"You want me to help you?"

"Yes. It's important."

"Stupid. Stupid stupid. You shouldn't be on the island. It's bad. Bad bad."

"I know," I said, gritting my teeth. "But if my brother and I don't watch the tunnel, it could get a lot worse."

The Flag flicked itself on the pole, making a loud crack in the air. "Stupid stupid. Can't stop the storms when they want to go to the tunnel. Foolish foolish. Go back where you came from. I don't want to help you. You are ugly."

I forced myself to take a breath. The Flags were usually a pain in the ass.

"Look," I said, "could you please travel to the other Gore Poles and tell me if you see my brother? It won't take long and then I'll leave you alone."

"You are a bother. Bother bother. I don't want to help you. You are ugly."

On impulse, I reached out and grabbed the Flag, bunching its flat face in my fist like a wet towel. Its skin was cold and slimy.

"Say you'll help me or I'll rip you off this pole and use you to wipe my ass for the next decade."

The Flag's voice was muffled around my fist. "Fine fine. Only playing. I will look for the one who looks like you."

"And then come back and tell me what you see."

"Yes yes. Won't be long."

I let the Flag go and it snapped itself loudly again, as if to get the wrinkles out of its face. The Flag began to race up the Gore Pole again to take flight.

"You are still ugly," It called down to me once more before detaching itself to let the wind take it. The wind pushed the strange creature away from me toward the next Gore Pole, the Flags landing perches.

I anxiously tapped my foot, little puddles of blood splashing. I looked toward the red ocean and the wall of black clouds that continued to form on the horizon. Not good.

I winced as the wind gusted up toward me from the beach, particles of black sand hitting my cheeks like little needle points. I could see horrors, small ones, crawling out of the ocean. Black things with dozens of eyes and tentacles. I could hear their moans in the wind. I looked back to the sky. I wasn't worried about them. They'd die before they could crawl a hundred feet, just like they always did.

But the storm would bring bigger ones. Meaner ones. And I needed to get home and make sure the tunnel was still sealed before they inevitably reached it. After the last storm, I knew the tunnel didn't have much longer before it was split wide open. It was weak, battered, sliced and dying. The storms had been terrible the past month. This place was pushing back, sensing how close it was to breaking through. I knew my brother and I couldn't hold out much longer. It was a miracle we had made it this long. The tunnel didn't have time to heal anymore. The storms and horrors had been coming too frequently, too brutally.

And what happens when it ruptures?

I cast the thought aside as I saw the Flag returning.

"That was quick," I muttered as it blew to the Gore Pole and attached its flesh to the top. It quickly slid down to my level and looked annoyed.

"Found the other ugly creature that looks like you. Ugly ugly."

"Where?" I asked, taking a step forward.

"Two Gore Poles to the South. It was heading toward the structure by the marshes."

Two Gore Poles to the South. He was heading back home. That was good. What the hell had he been up to? If he hadn't been fishing for horror bait, especially with a storm coming, then I couldn't imagine what he had been doing.

"Ok, thank you," I said.

"Leave me alone next time," the Flag said with attitude.

"Thank you thank you," I called over my back.

The Flag sniffed and then shot up the pole, detaching itself to return to the clouds. I decided it was time to leave as well.

I began to trot toward home. I had a ways to go and the storm looked like a fast moving system. I prayed I'd make it back in time. As my filthy boots pounded the skin-covered earth, I estimated I'd make it back to our meager shelter in about an hour, if I kept up the pace. I prided myself on the shape I was in, my daily conditioning making for an effortless jaunt across the barren hills. The island was ten miles north to south and roughly half that east to west. During our first year here, my brother and I had painstakingly traversed our new home, measuring out the distance with a hundred foot length of string.

No trees or vegetation grew on the island. This place wasn't kind to anything that wished to grow and live. Instead, cold white bone jutted from the landscape, some of the formations rising hundreds of feet into the air along the northern edge. We called that part of the island the ribcage and we rarely traveled to it. The middle and southern edge of the island mostly consisted of rolling hills–pink, hairy, and rancid. Our house was built of bone fragments and dried skin that we had sliced from the ground and dried beneath a sun we never saw.

That was also where the tunnel was. The one and only exit off this rotting slab of meat.

But we dared not go back. Not if we didn't have to. Not after what my brother had done.

I picked up the pace as the wind began to chase me. Huffing, I shot a glance over my shoulder and saw the first blood red bolt of lighting fork out from the wall of black clouds at my back. Thunder boomed ominously a moment later, a deep rumbling snarl that echoed across the water.

This was going to be a bad one.

Thirty minutes into my run, I passed the Gore Pole the Flag had seen my brother from. There was no sign of him though. Frustrated, I pushed on, my socks wet with blood that seeped in from the battered soles of my boots.

The island always bled the worst before a storm.

Heart pounding, blood thumping in my ears, I went into an all out sprint as more thunder cracked the air. I knew the tunnel wasn't ready for a storm of this caliber. It had barely healed from the last one, a mere two weeks earlier. I mentally ran through what we had left in our cobbled supplies, trying to think of anything that could help sustain the tunnel.

I crested a hill twenty minutes later and saw our shelter, about a half mile in the distance. I also saw someone walking through the marsh that populated the acreage to the left of it. It was my brother. Thank god. Sweat staining my shirt, I pushed the final distance at a dead run, the sky filling with flashes of red lightning.

I reached the house the same time my brother did. He was holding two buckets filled with gunk from the marsh.

"Where have you been?!" I asked breathlessly, skidding to a halt in front of him.

My brother wiped sweat from his pale face, his long dark hair framing his worn, tired face. He was two years older than me, but he looked like he was pushing forty, not thirty-two.

"Massive storm coming," he said, nodding toward the border of black cloud at my back.

"Yeah, I noticed. What do you have there?"

My brother hefted the buckets. "Mud from the marsh. I figure we can mix it with the bone powder we made yesterday and smother the tunnel walls with it. Where it's still healing. It's not much, but maybe it'll offer some protection. We don't have many supplies left. We haven't had time."

"I know," I said, nodding. "Did you get any bait?"

"No."

"What the fuck were you doing all morning then?!"

My brother looked at the ground. "Doesn't matter."

I took a step toward him. "Were you talking to the Flags again?"

"We don't have time for this right now."

"Are you seriously still trying to find a way up there?" I asked, jamming a finger toward the clouds overhead.

"Renny. We need to see to the tunnel. We can argue about this later."

"Fuck me," I muttered angrily. "You could have at least brought back a couple dead horrors for the big bastards to eat."

"Hopefully there won't be any big ones today."

"Do you see the size of that storm?!" I scoffed. "We're going to get *pounded* here in about an hour."

My brother dropped the buckets, his anger rising. "Then cut the shit and help me! You want to stand there lecturing me or do you want to try and help me stop the fucking apocalypse?"

"Goddamn it," I growled, grabbing a bucket. My brother went inside for the bone powder while I hurried to the back of the house where the tunnel grew. As I rounded the house, my heart skipped a beat. The tunnel looked terrible.

It grew from the ground like a hose made from flesh. Its walls were covered in angry red veins and bruising, the wire cord stitching along its curved exterior still looked infected, despite our best efforts. The entrance to the tunnel was ten feet from top to bottom, but it was covered by puckered skin that retracted to the touch, revealing the long, thirty-foot throat that led into the ground.

Back to reality. Back to where everyone else was.

The tunnel was massive at the base, looking more like a funnel. If one of the bigger horrors wanted to, it could tear the tunnel out of the ground, leaving a hundred foot hole for them to pour through. So far, that hadn't happened. But the horrors were learning. Getting smarter each time they came, each time they found us. Usually we had bait to distract them, smaller, dead horrors that we collected from the beach. We impaled them on poles a quarter mile around the house and prayed the big ones would just eat their own and return to the depths. But we hadn't had time since the last storm to gather them. We had spent all our time fixing the tunnel, stitching it, covering it in mud and bone powder, which seemed to heal it.

The last attack had been the worst, but thankfully the storm had been short lived, passing over us and dragging the monsters back into the ocean as it went. But the damage had been done. They had sliced and battered and carved the tunnel into a critical state and when my brother and I had emerged from the house afterwards, we felt sick as we gazed upon it. Pus, blood, lacerations, tears--it was a small mercy the storm hadn't brought one of the big ones or it could have been the end of our feeble resistance.

"Here, mix this in with the mud from the marsh," my brother said, coming to my side, snapping my attention back to the present. More thunder boomed over the island and the wind nearly choked me in a rancid gust. I snatched the wooden bowl from my brother and dumped the white powder into the mud. I mixed it vigorously with my hands and then hurried over to the tunnel.

"Cover the stitching," I called. "At least we can hide where the exterior is weakest. It won't have time to absorb the mud and bone before the storm comes, but maybe we can at least keep the horrors from hitting the same place twice."

My brother began work on the opposite side of the long flesh tube and we worked in silence as the storm raged on the opposite side of the island. I could hear the distant waves pounding the sand on the southern shore, just a few hills from the house. It sounded like hammers striking rock, not water on sand.

I finished smearing the mud across some stitching and then moved down the length of the tunnel to the next patched wound. I went to work again, the hairs standing on the back of my neck as more red lightning lashed out to the north like a great whip punishing the land.

When my bucket was empty, I ran to the entrance of the tunnel which looked like a hollow, uncircumcised penis. My brother was already there, covering the puckered flesh with the rest of the mud.

"Do we have any more bone poles we can place?" I asked hurriedly.

He shook his head. "No. We have nothing. Everything was used up last time." He slammed his empty bucket down on the ground angrily. "*Goddamn* it. We needed more time. This isn't going to hold. We have no bait, no poles to armor the tunnel, the stitching is still healing—we are fucked, Renny, *fucked.*"

The air crackled with electricity as lighting cut a path through the sky, the storm wall breaching the northern shores of the island now.

"There has to be something else-" the words died in my throat as a monstrous roar shook the island, bellowed from the depths of the black clouds. It started as a low growl and then rose into an ear splitting screech that slammed into my skull like a hatchet. I covered my ears, wincing in pain, squeezing my eyes shut as the echoes of the call faded.

I blinked, slowly lowering my hands. My brother stared north, his face paling.

"Jesus Christ..." he whispered.

"What the hell was that?" I asked, eyes wide.

My brother turned to me, placing a hand on my shoulder. The rain had started, freezing ice that splattered across my face.

"We should get inside. They'll be here soon."

I looked at the approaching storm front. It looked like the northern part of the island had gone to night, the tar thick clouds spitting out angry bolts of red lightning followed by booming thunder that rattled my teeth. The wind threw the rain against us, picking up intensity in a matter of seconds.

"Look," I whispered hoarsely, pointing.

Even from this distance, we could see hundreds of smaller horrors being tossed out of the stormfront, expelled from the depths like vomit.

"The storm must have sucked them out of the ocean," my brother said, his voice shaking. "Jesus, I've never seen it this bad before."

Another deafening roar shook the island, a cataclysmic bellow that crescendoed into a screeching howl. And from the wall of night, I saw one titanic leg step out of the gale, a building-sized terror hundreds of feet high.

Before the rest of the horror emerged, I grabbed my brother by the shoulders and spun him to face me.

"This is it," I croaked. "Nothing is going to survive this one. We've known this was coming for weeks now and there isn't anything we can do to stop it." I pointed to the tunnel. "We have to get out of here. We have to go back home. We are going to die if we stick around."

My brother's face hardened. "Go home? You want us to go back?"

"Look at what's coming!"

"I am!" he roared, his eyes bulging. "I see it, Renny! And it'll all be right behind us if we go back! Leaving won't matter! They're *going* to make it through this time! I'd rather die here then watch what they do to everyone else!" He stepped toward me, his eyes bloodshot now. "Can you imagine how they'll rip through the world? Can you picture it? Kids, all of them, torn and ripped and eaten and-"

"I KNOW!" I screamed into his face. "But at least there we'll have a better chance to get somewhere safe! Have a shot at LIVING!"

"We'd only live long enough to watch everything be destroyed. And then they'd come for us. It would only be a matter of time. You've seen these things, you know how they are! Hell, hasn't five years surviving these horrors been enough to suck out any hope you have left?! We are the ONLY ones who have kept these fuckers at bay for as long as we have. It's a MIRACLE they haven't made it through yet!"

I grabbed my brother by the shirt. "I don't want to fucking die here!"

My brother pushed me away angrily. "We're dead no matter what. Either stay here with me or crawl back home. Go ahead and put yourself through that nightmare. You'll die miserable and alone. At least here we'd have each other."

"I should have never come here with you," I spat, panic ripping at my mind.

The rain had now soaked us, leaving me shivering and terrified. The crunch of thunder and booming footsteps of the colossal horrors nearly drowned out my voice.

"I'm going inside," my brother yelled against the gail. I could tell I had hurt him. He turned, but stopped, his face softening in the chaos. "Don't...please don't leave me here alone. This is the end and I'd rather die next to you, here, today. I don't want to spend the rest of my days running from the inevitable. I've done enough of that. It's what brought us here."

I balled my hands into fists, indecision clawing at me. I glanced at the storm, at the horrors as they rapidly drew closer. There were five of the titans now, each one so massive they disappeared into the blanket of cloud overhead, their enormous limbs striding closer with each passing moment. The smaller ones continued to spill out of the cloud wall, their screams and howls filling the sky.

I squeezed my eyes shut, fighting with myself. I was freezing. My head groaned. The noise of the approaching violence exploded through my skull.

I set my jaw, feeling my chest relax. Fuck it. Dead was dead.

"Let's go inside," I said, nearly blinded by the torrential rain.

My brother offered me a grim smile and we ran into our meager house, the dried skin flapping angrily against the bone spoked walls like a patchwork tent. We quickly went for the hole we had dug, pushing aside the bone benches and table we had carved. My brother heaved the slab that covered the hole to the side and we both dropped into the wet, stinking space. It was four feet deep so we had to sit in the scabbed flesh pit. It was our only solace against the storms and we had spent many days huddled here, waiting for the violence to pass.

My brother pulled the slab back over us, encasing the small pit in gloom. We exchanged a look and then our eyes rose to the low ceiling, waiting. The thunder continued to assault the skies and the booming footsteps of the colossal horrors made the ground shake beneath us. The sound of rain lashing the walls of our home was immense and the howl of wind rose to a scream.

We began to hear the house above us come apart as the island bowed to the power of the storm and approaching horrors. Filthy rainwater dribbled in from the cracks between the slab above us and something crashed and ripped away from the structure outside.

"This is it," my brother said softly, his eyes dim. "They're almost here."

The pit shuddered around us and I found that I was terrified. I didn't want to die, I so *badly* did not want to die here. The reality that this was the end, that my life was over, hit me in a wave of grief so strongly that I felt my chest heave. I looked at my hands and saw they were shaking. My throat felt tight and soon I was on the verge of tears as panic set in.

My brother reached out and took my hand, his face calm. "It's ok, Renny," he said gently as water continued to drip into the pit. "I got you. I got you. We're ok."

I found myself miserably craving his comfort as we heard the approaching hoard of horrors, big and small, crash over the house above. I huddled next to my brother, head down, eyes closed. The bone structures above us were torn from the ground and shattered as dozens of mutated, twisted feet thudded over the slab overhead, charging the tunnel.

A great, screeching roar blasted across the world, followed by the call of two others. Against my better judgment, I peeked through the crack in the slab. Passing directly overhead was one of the titan horrors, its looming mass so huge it disappeared into the blanket of cloud overhead. It strode toward the tunnel, its long, otherworldly legs passing over the pit, encasing us in momentary darkness.

And then we began to hear the horrors assault the tunnel. Their bellowing roars and screeching howls rose to a crescendo as excitement and hunger rippled through the ranks. I heard tearing and clawing as they beat their mangled bodies against the fragile tube of flesh, desperate to be rid of it, desperate to cross over, to go down, to reach the world that awaited on the other side.

And then, all at once, we heard a great tearing sound. It was as if the fabric of the universe were being torn in half, a great, gory, all consuming finality that left no doubt or question that the end was upon us.

The horrors let out a sky splitting roar of elation and I felt my heart sink into the pit of my stomach. My blood ran cold and I knew, after all these years, that my brother and I had failed.

"My god," I shivered, looking helplessly at my brother.

My brother hugged me and we waited to be found, exposed, and then gutted.

It never came. I don't know how long we sat there as the hordes of horrors passed over us. I don't know why they never hunted us, found us, ripped the flesh from our bones. Maybe we were never really a concern to them. Maybe they didn't care about us. Maybe the tunnel was all that mattered to them, and what awaited on the other side.

Lost in the despair of my own thoughts, I jumped when my brother shook me. I gasped and snapped my eyes open, unwilling to accept that we were alive. I blinked in the shadows, soaked and soggy to my core, and then turned to my brother.

"They're gone," he whispered, his lips blue with cold. He was shivering horribly. "They've all gone through."

I squeezed my eyes shut and forced my internal engines to start again. I peeked through the crack in the slab and only saw cloud cover. The rain was still coming down hard and I blinked against it.

"Help me," I croaked, bracing the slab of bone against my back. Together, my brother and I lifted it, shoving it to the side as we stood.

As I swept my eyes across the landscape, I felt myself go numb. The world was in ruin. The house had been destroyed, pieces of it littered across the ground in every direction. The skin-covered land had been churned and stomped into a great heaping wound, with bloody trails and seeping gashes marking a warpath across the island.

My brother suddenly gripped my arm, his voice hoarse. "The tunnel..."

I knew before I even turned my head. When I did, I felt as if I would vomit.

The tunnel had been uprooted and eviscerated, massive slabs of torn flesh cast and cut aside, leaving an enormous hole in the earth. A hole that marked the exit of every horror that had come. And now they had crossed over.

Back home.

"How are we still alive?" my brother shuddered, turning his face up to the rain. "Why didn't they kill us?"

"What's two when you can have billions?" I whispered, wiping trails of water off my face. Slowly, the two of us walked toward the hole. It was like sloshing through a medieval battlefield, each step a slog through gore and bloody bits of flesh.

When we reached the hole, I looked down into the gaping abyss of darkness. A pit of black greeted me and I was selfishly grateful I couldn't see or hear what was happening on the other side.

My body suddenly felt too heavy for my legs and I sat down hard next to the edge, rainwater streaming off the tip of my nose as my bloodshot eyes continued to gaze down into the maw.

At my back, my brother's voice trembled. "I'm so sorry, Renny."

I said nothing, mind stripping away into pieces.

"If I hadn't gotten into trouble, we wouldn't have had to run away to this place. This is all my fault. I shouldn't have dragged you into it."

His hand found my shoulder. "I would have been dead years ago if you hadn't helped me. If you hadn't come with me. If we hadn't found this place together." He paused for a moment, and then. "I love you, Renny. Thank you for not leaving me. Ever. You deserve so much better than this."

His words slid down my body like worms.

I raised my face to respond, but the words died in my throat. Shock rippled through me. I raised my hand and pointed to the sky for my brother to look.

Hundreds of Flags were drifting down from the sky, gently, slowly, as if being lowered to the earth in the arms of the wind.

They were all dead.

I covered my face with my hands and began to cry.

My brother sank to the ground next to me as the Flags fell around us.

Together, we waited to die, however it would come.

CACTUS

efore I even opened my eyes, I knew I was in deep shit.
Memories came flooding back like a current, slamming into
my mind like a locomotive. My body felt stiff and cold and I
could hear voices conversing around me. Slowly, I forced my eyes
open and looked around.

I was lying on my back in a small room. The walls and floor
were white tile and the cement ceiling overhead was lined with
one fluorescent strip of light. In front of me, burrowing into the
wall, was a hole, just big enough for someone to fit through. It
looked like some kind of tunnel, vanishing into darkness.

I looked down at myself, checking my aching body for injuries.
I was still in uniform, though my boot knife and rifle had been
taken away from me. I rolled my head on the cold floor and saw
there were three other people in the small room. I recognized two
of them. Yosef and Higgens, two troopers who had made the jump
with me. The third was an older man, dressed in a filthy uniform I
didn't recognize, but still looked military. A third party we didn't
know about, maybe? His eyes were wild and he stood in the corner
of the small room, watching the three of us like we were snakes.

"You ok, man?" Yosef asked, dropping to a knee by my side
when he saw I was awake. I sat up slowly, letting him help me.
Higgens came to my other side, a gentle hand on my arm.

"Easy, buddy. We're in trouble here."

I groaned, tenderly touching the lump on the back of my head where I had been struck unconscious.

"Where are we? What happened?" I asked, the white tile nearly blinding me.

Higgens sat me up against the wall, the dark hole directly in front of me. "I don't know where they took us. Seems like they were waiting for us on the farm though. We were supposed to rendezvous with the rest of the squad down there, but I didn't see anyone but you two."

"There was gunfire, about a mile away from where we landed," Yosef said quietly, eyeing the older man in the corner. "Don't know what that was all about. No one was supposed to know about our jump."

"I heard the gunfire too," Higgens said. "Right after I landed and cut my parachute. I think the bastards were spread out all through the valley, waiting for us. They were in the barn, clearly. Probably watched us jump from the C-47s, polishing their bayonets the whole time."

"Where's everyone else?" I asked, replaying the jump in my head. Twelve paratroopers had jumped and now I only saw three, including me.

"Probably dead," Higgens said gruffly. He was older than Yosef and I and had been in the military since his eighteenth birthday. Last I heard, he was coming up on his fortieth.

"Where the hell are we?" I asked, scanning the room again. There were no windows, so it was hard to tell how long we had been in here. It had been midnight when we jumped, but I had no clue how much time had passed since I had been knocked out.

"No idea," Yosef said. His dark eyes reflected fear and I felt for the guy. He was only twenty-one and this had been his first official mission. Not a good start to his military career.

"Who's that guy?" I asked next, jutting my chin towards the old man. "And who's side is he on? I don't recognize his uniform.

If he's in here with us, he's probably not with the fucking Aussies, I'm guessing."

Higgens shrugged. "He'll barely talk to us. I don't think everything's working properly upstairs, either. The few words he's spoken have been gibberish. Nonsensical."

"Great," I said, grunting as I stood. My head felt like the inside of a drum and I wobbled and caught myself against the wall before I went down.

"We only woke up a couple minutes before you," Yosef said, his eyes darting toward the hole in the wall. He bit his lip, eyes watery. "Do you think the Aussies are going to kill us?"

"Don't know, kid," Higgens said flatly. "They're not really known for showing compassion so I'm surprised we woke up alive after the ambush."

"What's this room?" I asked again, numbly. Yosef and Higgens had no response and so I turned to the old man in the corner. "Hey! Do you speak English? Can you understand what I'm saying?"

His huge gray eyes met mine and he nodded slightly.

"Where are we? How long ago did they bring us here?"

The man shook his head. "Don't matter. Dead soon."

I felt my heart drop into my stomach, but I pressed him further. "Who are you? What side are you fighting for?"

The man closed his eyes and pressed the heels of his palms into them. "Don't matter. Hole coming."

"Fucking looney," Higgens muttered. He turned and began inspecting the walls, testing them. As I watched him, I realized that there was no visible door. Just white tile all the way around with the hole in the one wall. Had we come through that? Dumped down some kind of shute into an underground cell?

I took a step toward the old man, raising my hands so he could see I meant no harm. "What's your name?"

The man didn't move, but surprised me with an answer. "Gunnert."

"Ok Gunnert," I said. "It seems we're all in the same predicament here so maybe we can help each other out. The three of us are American paratroopers. We were dropped into the Australian occupied territory of Brightbow last night at midnight. We were ambushed, knocked unconscious, and woke up here in this room with you." I pointed toward the hole in the wall. "Did we come through that hole? Is that how we got here?"

Gunnert suddenly stepped toward me and grabbed my shirt, pulling me in close. His breath was rank as he whispered urgently, eyes rolling.

"Stay away from hole! Hole alive! It took them all! Coming again!"

"Mental case," Higgens muttered behind me.

Yosef came to my side and gently removed Gunnert's hands from my uniform. "Easy, buddy. Easy. What do you mean? What is the hole? Were there other people in here with you before?"

Gunnert stepped away from us and raised his fingers. "Four! All gone! Hole is death!"

"Fantastic," Higgen's said, still prodding the walls. He paused at one spot and pressed again. "I think I found the door," he announced. "This spot gives a little. It's probably how they brought us here. You would think there would be a seam though." He leaned toward the wall until his nose almost touched it.

I turned in place, scanning our prison once again. It was rectangular and I paced it out, starting with my back pressed against the wall opposite the hole. Ten paces brought me to the hole. I walked to the far wall next and paced it out, the hole passing me on the left. Twenty paces.

I didn't know what I'd do with this new information but it made me feel slightly better to be doing something.

"How long have you been in this room?" Yosef asked Gunnert.

Gunnert retreated to his corner and stared at the floor. I noticed that he kept shooting fearful glances at the hole.

I went to it and squatted down. I couldn't feel any air on my face coming from the mouth of it. The interior was smooth, metallic, and completely seamless. I couldn't see further than five feet inside before darkness hid the rest.

"No!" Gunnert screamed suddenly. He ran to my side and frantically pulled me away from the hole. "Stay away! STAY AWAY!"

"Knock it off," Higgen's growled, pulling him off me. "Hysterics isn't going to solve anything so just take a deep breath and try to keep your goddamn ducks in a row. Got it?"

"No ducks," Gunnert strained, veins standing out along his neck. "No ducks!"

"Clearly," I said. I stepped away from the hole, brushing my hands on my pants. As I did so, the lights went out. Gunnert let out a little shriek and scurried back to his corner, getting as far away from the hole as he could.

"What's happening?" Yosef asked quietly. It was so dark in the room now that I couldn't even see his outline. Complete and utter black swallowed us whole, leaving an uneasy feeling twisting in my guts.

Before anyone could answer, a voice came from a hidden speaker somewhere in the room, a mechanical, automated male voice that cut through a wash of low static.

"*Seven. Twenty-two. Eleven. Yellow. Fifty-three. Pine. Amber. Sixty-one.*"

It went on like that for a couple minutes, the string of nonsense dolled out in the same monotone voice, the crackle of static popping around the words. Finally, after about two minutes, the voice stopped, leaving us in tar-black silence.

"The hell was that all about?" Higgens whispered.

The tension in his voice was felt by all of us. I placed a hand on the wall at my back to center myself, suddenly afraid that if I didn't I would fall into the darkness forever. Gunnert was still whimpering in his corner, his voice the only other sound in the room.

"Hey!" Yosef hissed. "Gunnert! What was that? What does it mean? What's happening?"

"Shhhh!" Gunnert responded. "No talking! No breathing! Shhhh!"

We decided to listen to him, the fear of the unknown clawing at my insides. I squatted down, hating my blindness, and waited. I heard Yosef and Higgens do the same, their boots scraping against the tile floor.

"It's coming," Gunnert cried, his voice just a wisp.

I felt my heart rate thump up a couple decibels and I vainly reached out to find Yosef's hand. He grabbed it almost immediately, our fingers brushing one another's and then locking together.

"What's coming?" Yosef whispered. I gripped his hand harder, urging him to be quiet. Higgens was a ghost in the dark, somewhere behind Yosef.

I knew the hole was directly in front of me and I scooted to the side, toward Yosef, away from the mouth of it. We waited, barely breathing, some inevitable apocalypse hanging over us. Seconds dragged into minutes, blood thundering in my ears.

"It's here," Gunnert said from the corner, his voice like a dream slithering through my subconscious.

What is? Where? Where is it?!

"It is looking right at you," Gunnert whispered hysterically.

I felt a stab of fear pierce my spine, pinning me to the wall. I couldn't see the hole, couldn't see anything, but the hairs on the back of my neck stood up and Yosef increased the pressure on my hand.

"Do. Not. Move." Gunnert hissed again.

A beat passed and then another, my head filling with so much pressure I thought my skull would combust. Sweat dripped into my eyes as they wildly roamed, searching for some unseen horror. I prayed silently, my breath stuffed back down into my throat, building like steam that would funnel out of me in a scream if I allowed it to escape.

Suddenly, the lights came back on.

I nearly did scream then, the sudden transition cutting through the unbearable tension like a hammer over glass. I blinked wildly, letting go of Yosef's hand. I stood, staring at the hole, all my focus sucked into it.

There was nothing there.

Higgen's finally let out a gasp of breath and I turned to see the neck of his uniform was stained dark with sweat.

"Fuck me," he muttered, his unshakable will teetering. "Let's not do that again."

"Are we ok?" Yosef asked shakily.

"For now, it seems," I said, running a hand over my sweating face. I turned to Gunnert who was unfolding from his corner.

"You want to tell us what the *fuck* is going on here?"

Gunnert just stared at the hole with wide eyes, his face slack.

"Enough," Higgen's growled. He marched over to the older man and grabbed him, shoving him hard against the wall.

"You've got about five seconds to explain what this place is before my knuckles purchase a one way ticket to Teeth Town. Now talk! TALK!" he yelled, shaking the man.

"Ok, let go!" Gunnert sputtered. "I talk! We safe for now, I talk!"

Higgen's let him go and Gunnert smoothed his uniform. "I am not your enemy. You Americans are always so angry. You want to know what is happening here, fine, I tell what I've seen."

The three of us settled in, waiting for the older man to continue. Gunnert took one quick look at the hole before he began, his voice low.

"I was part of covert operation. I was sent in with four others to spy on the American Australian Conflict. Gather intel. Observe. Even infiltrate if needed."

"Who backs you?" I asked.

"I am part of a Russian sect called Mother 4. We do not operate in the confines of Russian government. We are our own people. We are a new people with new ideas. The world..." He waved a hand. "It has become a messy place. Americans and Australians fighting endlessly, France and England destroying one another, the annihilation of Madagascar three years ago...I do not need to continue. You are soldiers. You understand this."

"Where does that leave you and Mother 4 in all of this?" Higgens asked.

Gunnert nodded understandingly. "We need allies. We are a small nation and need help in order to grow. We do not have a large military, but we are very good at finding out secrets." He pointed to each of us. "We have made ourselves strong by gathering much intel on our enemies and allies. Intel that might help you, the Americans." He shrugged then. "Or perhaps the Australians. Whoever values us more."

"A nation for sale," I muttered.

Gunnert shrugged again. "I am being honest, yes? I was part of a small team, one of seven such teams, that were dispersed to gather information on the Americans and Australians. But we were caught. How long ago, I do not know. But I do know that it wasn't the Americans who put us here."

"Aussie fucks," Higgens spat.

"Yes, it is as you say," Gunnert nodded. "They bring us to this terrible place, here, and leave us. How long ago, I do not know. Days? A week? When my team was put in here, they took our weapons but left us our packs so we could eat. Drink. Survive this room. Waiting for the hole to come for us."

"What is it, exactly?" Yosef asked, pointing.

Gunnert's eyes glazed over the hole in the wall and I saw the muscles in his face tense. "Death. It comes for us one at a time. Taking us when the voice comes. When the lights go out. And all we can do is wait until the next one goes. The last man with me, from my team, went mad after the other two were taken. Beat his head against the wall, clawed his eyes out. He could not stand the darkness. The fear."

"Yeah, but what is it?" I asked. "What's in there? Some kind of animal?"

"Gunnert shook his head. "No. It is no animal. Something else."

"Have you ever seen it?" Higgens asked.

"No, but I can sense it now. Feel when it comes, feel its eyes... if it even has eyes. Its presence fills me when it is close, like I am being sunk into cold water." Gunnert shivered. "We will all be dead soon."

Higgens stepped toward the hole, crouching down in front of it. "Why don't you just crawl through? Maybe there's a way out?"

Gunnert's face paled. "Are you mad? That would be like crawling into a grave. No. There is no escape from this room. I have searched every inch of this prison and we are trapped, like pebbles under cup."

"Maybe you Russians just don't have the balls to do what needs to be done," Higgens said, staring down the throat of the hole. "I for one ain't going to just sit here and wait for some poison gas or bogeyman to come kill me."

Gunnert shook his head. "One of my men tried this. He crawled into the hole."

"And?"

"He did not return."

"But that doesn't mean he died," Yosef said hopefully.

Gunnert sighed. "A few minutes after he went into the hole, the lights went out, just like they did a few minutes ago. The voice started. It said the numbers and words, but when it was finished, the static remained. Only it wasn't just static. We could hear our comrade as well."

"Screaming?" I asked, wincing.

"No. Not screaming," Gunnert said quietly. "He was crying. Crying like he had just lost everything he ever cared about. I have never heard a man cry like he did. Sobbing. The pain in his voice cut at me until I thought I would go crazy. He was hysterical. Begging." Gunnert looked at the floor. "They made us listen to him cry for hours."

"Jesus Christ," I whispered.

"So you understand now, you cannot go into hole," Gunnert said after a moment.

Higgens looked at Yosef and I. "You believe this crock of shit?"

Yosef looked at me. "I...I don't know."

I bit my lip, the hole filling my head. "Fuck if I know, Higgs. But we gotta try something. I'm not dying in the dark down here while the Aussie's fry our brains with some ass backwards psychological torture."

"But what about the thing in the hole?" Yosef said fearfully.

"What thing?" Higgens grunted. "Have you seen something I haven't? A monster? All we know is the lights went out, some voice came on and said some nonsense, and then nothing happened." He looked at me. "I think you're right about this place. I think this is some fucked up prison camp we've been dumped into by the Aussies to torture and break us mentally. It sounds like something they'd do, doesn't it? I mean shit, you remember two weeks ago when they released the Sand Tapes?"

I remembered all right. A group of Americans had been taken prisoner and been buried up to their neck in sand. Then their heads had been crushed by tank treads, an inch at a time.

"I'm not dying down here," Higgens stated again. "Who knows, maybe they're filming us somehow. Maybe we're the next set of tapes. Break us down, turn us mad, then show the world how they broke us. They're using fear tactics. Slow the recruitment process."

The more Higgens talked, the more I began to agree. This was war, not some hidden pocket of the world where the rules didn't apply. There was no monster in the hole. There was no bogeyman. There were just people who hated other people.

"Ok, I say we do it," I said.

Gunnert set his jaw. "Fools."

Higgens ignored him and crouched in front of the hole. "Do we have anything you can tie around me? In case I need to get pulled back?"

I looked at Yosef and then noticed Gunnert's pack in the corner. "You have anything in there we can use?" Gunnert tossed it to me wordlessly and I quickly rummaged through it, finding nothing useful. I shook my head at Higgens.

He took a deep breath. "Alright. Fuck it. If I make it out the other end, I'll come back for you once I make sure it's clear. If I exit with an Aussie gun to my head, well...I guess that'll be that.

But I can't just stand here and do nothing. I'm not dying here without trying."

I gripped his shoulder. "Good luck. If you suspect trouble, get your ass back here and we'll figure something else out, ok?" It was a lie that we all accepted silently.

"You got stones," Yosef said, coming to Higgen's side. "Be safe. I'll see you soon."

"Right," Higgens said. He looked at Gunnert who was stone faced, and then crawled into the hole. It was just big enough for him to shuffle through on his hands and knees. Yosef and I squatted by the opening and watched as he carefully crawled forward, slowly disappearing from sight as the darkness took him.

After a minute, I leaned into the hole. "You doing ok?"

"Nothing yet!" Higgens called back, his voice echoing. We could still faintly hear the sound of his boots scuffing the inside of the tunnel.

Yosef was sweating and he offered me a weak smile when he saw me watching him. Gunnert had retreated to his corner where he sat, looking lost.

Another couple of minutes passed and I could barely hear Higgens anymore. I cupped my hands and called again.

"Anything?!"

A beat passed and then Higgens answered, his voice sounding very far away. "Still ok! I think I see something though, it's-"

The words died inside the hole. Yosef and I exchanged a worried look and I leaned into the hole again.

"Higgens!? Hey, you ok!?"

We waited, blood pulsing in my ears. The seconds ticked by with no response. Silence emanated into the room from the tunnel, a totality that crawled up my spine and into my throat.

"Why isn't he answering?" Yosef whispered frantically.

"He's gone," Gunnert said softly from his spot on the floor.

"Shut up," I said, shooting him a venomous look. "You don't know that."

We waited by the hole for another couple minutes. I called Higgens name over and over again, the echo of my voice vanishing into the darkness without response. I could feel panic slowly take over and I fought it off violently.

"What do we do?" Yosef asked, his eyes bulging. "Do we go after him? Why did he just stop!? What did he see?!"

"Be quiet," I said gently. "We don't know what's happening. Maybe he found the exit. We just have to wait. Higgens is as hard as they come, if there's a way out of here, he'll find it."

I didn't believe a word of what I was saying, but I couldn't afford to have Yosef lose himself right now. I needed him.

Suddenly, the lights went out.

"Oh fuck," Yosef whimpered, grabbing my arm. I pulled him away from the hole quickly, putting our backs against the opposite wall. I felt the hair on the back of my neck stand up and fear slithered down into my guts like a cluster of worms.

"Easy," I whispered. "Easy. Just be still." I couldn't hear or see Gunnert to my right, but I imagined he was trying to make himself as small as possible.

A sharp crackle of static made me jump and then the voice from earlier began to prattle through some unseen speaker system.

"*Eighty-two. Seventeen. Sixty-four. Oxidize. Lunar. Fourteen. Twenty-nine.*"

The monotone voice continued for about a minute, repeating nonsensical words and meaningless numbers until the speakers went silent with no clue to their meaning. Yosef was breathing heavily in my ear and I could feel him shaking against my body.

We waited in the darkness, holding each other, waiting for some wraith or beast to claw at us, rip the flesh from our throats, enter our minds and drive us mad. In the total black, reason held no weight. I stared at the spot I knew the hole was, waited to see a pair of glowing eyes appear like flares before me, revealing the impossible and our inevitable death.

But instead of some predatory light, I began to hear something. Low and impossible far away at first. It grew in volume ever so slightly until I could just make it out. It was coming from the hole, deep, deep down the throat of it.

Crying. Horrible, violent weeping. The pain in each hitching sob was like a bullet to my chest, thudding into me with a dawning terror.

"Is that Higgens?" Yosef whispered in my ear, his voice cracking. "Jesus Christ, is that him?"

Before I could answer, the hidden speakers in the room flooded with Higgens' voice. We sat there, listening, dread filling us with each terrible, anguished sob. I had never heard another human being cry and weep the way he was. It was the most helpless, distraught thing I had ever heard, like a child in its innocence.

"We have to help him," Yosef cried. "We have to go get him!"

"Don't be stupid," I hissed, holding him. Every part of me wanted to do just that, though, as I continued to listen, each second sounding more desperate and broken, a man in complete ruin.

All at once, the crying stopped and the lights went back on. I blinked at the sudden flash of white as the fluorescent overhead popped back to life, momentarily blinding me. I rubbed my eyes and then stared urgently at the hole. It remained as it had been before, empty and silent. I looked around the room, assessing if anything had changed. I felt my heart crunch to a halt.

Gunnert was gone. His pack lay in the corner, but the man was nowhere to be seen. Yosef let out a mewling cry as he came to this realization as well, the two of us alone now in the white tiled room.

"Where is he!?" Yosef asked frantically, head whipping around. "Where did he go!?"

"I don't know," I said as evenly as I could. "Did you hear anything come out of the hole? Did you hear a door open or anything?"

"No! Jesus, he was right there just a few minutes ago!"

"People don't just vanish into thin air," I said, trying to force reason back into my screaming mind. "Someone must have taken him out of here when the lights went out."

"Or the thing in the hole got him," Yosef whispered fearfully.

"There's nothing in the *fucking* hole," I pressed, feeling anger at the younger man's fear. "They're messing with us, don't let them break you, Yosef."

Yosef wrapped his arms around himself and he reminded me of a child who had just seen something they shouldn't have.

"We're going to die in here," he whispered, staring at the hole.

"Knock it off!" I said, grabbing him, shaking him, his own infectious fear creeping into my voice. "Don't go there. We're not dying in here and I'm not leaving you, ok? *Nothing* is in there and if we stick together we can make it out of this. I need you to believe that. Please, don't go crazy on me, I need you."

Yosef's wild eyes met mine and he seemed to settle some. He took a stuttering breath and nodded. "Ok. Ok, yeah. We're going to get out of here."

I appreciated his taped-together courage and gave him a pat on the shoulder. "If the lights go out again, just hold onto me and I'll do the same. We won't let them separate us. If you go, I go."

"Ok. Thank you."

I gave him another pat on the shoulder and then walked across the tile floor and picked up Gunnert's pack again. I went through it once more, searching with fresh eyes for something, anything that could help us. I found a couple unopened MREs, an empty canteen, a tarp, a box of ammo that was also empty, and a pair of boots at the bottom. Frustrated, I went through the side pockets and felt my fingers wrap around a piece of paper. I pulled it out, smoothing it across my leg as I squinted down to see what it was.

It appeared to be the last bit of communication Gunnert and his men had received before their capture, a simple message printed in Russian which I quickly translated. It was one sentence.

The Australians have another hole.

I stared at the text, letting it wash over me, the implications rebounding in my head, thudding against the insides of my skull. They have another hole? Did the Russians have some kind of former knowledge about this place? Had they sent this message to

Gunnert assuming he'd know what it meant? And if that was true, did that give credence to what he had been warning us against? Were there more of these holes? These rooms?

"What did you find?" Yosef asked from behind me.

I quickly stuffed the note into my pocket. "Nothing useful."

I went and sat down next to Yosef, miserable, waiting for an answer or the end. Yosef took my hand in his and I let him. His warmth brought me little comfort. The note haunted me the longer I thought about it, torturing my imagination with possible meaning. Just what the hell was this place? I looked at the hole across from us and stifled a shiver. What if there actually was something in there?

I set my jaw and shut down. I wasn't going to start speculating on the impossible. There was nothing in there but fear.

The minutes stretched into hours, the two of us silent in the white washed room. I became impossibly thirsty and wished I had my canteen with me. Why had Gunnert been allowed to keep his but not Yosef and I? Was our tenure here going to be shorter? The thought brought back the fear and I closed my eyes, horribly tired.

"Please don't fall asleep," Yosef whispered next to me.

"I won't," I muttered. "Not a chance in hell."

Yosef squeezed my hand. "I'm glad I'm not alone down here."

"Me too." I exhaled heavily, the knots in my shoulders aching. "Never thought I'd be in a situation like this. Pretty fucked, isn't it?"

"This was my first real mission," Yosef said.

"I know. Bad luck, huh?"

"I thought I was going to make a difference. Help stop this useless war. Bring peace back to the world."

"That's what we all wanted," I said. "Except maybe Higgens. I think he just liked killing people."

"I don't want to talk about Higgens," Yosef said quietly. He shifted where he sat before continuing. "Do you have any family?"

"I had a wife and two kids," I said gently, mind drifting back to their memory. "They were killed two years ago during the Manhattan Bombings."

"I'm sorry."

"I wasn't even there," I whispered. "I was on deployment. I didn't know they had died until two weeks later." I ran my hand over my face, exhaustion bearing down on me. "Their bodies were found under forty tons of rubble, huddled together, crushed." I exhaled wearily. "I hate this fucking war, Yosef. It's taken too much. It's not worth it anymore. If we ever get out of here, I'm going to vanish, go up to the mountains, disappear where no one can find me."

"I have a house in the mountains," Yosef said distantly. "My wife and I built it last year in Wyoming. That's where she is now. Waiting for me to finish my tour."

"We'll get you back to her," I said, grateful to be talking again after the hours of uncertain silence. "You have any kids?"

"She was expecting when I was deployed. I'll have a son when I return. A boy. I always wanted a little boy."

"Congrats man," I said. "Did you guys pick out a name?"

Yosef offered me a small smile. "Yes, his name is-"

The lights went out.

I felt Yosef immediately reach for me and I grabbed onto him tightly in the sudden darkness. It was happening again, the black like ink in my eyes. My pulse quickened until I felt it thumping in my head as we waited, fear a knife in my gut.

"Don't let go," Yosef whispered, his voice shaking. "Please, please don't let go."

"I won't."

A crackle of static and then the automated voice began to recite a series of numbers and words, a meaningless string of non-sense. I focused my attention on the hole, trying to pick up any sound that might be coming from it, but it was impossible with the monotone voice droning on.

I felt my attention pulled to my left suddenly, something in the dark shifting, or moving. I didn't know if it was my paranoid imagination or if there really was something there, but I gripped Yosef harder, jaw clenched.

Suddenly the voice stopped, the static evaporating. At the exact same moment, I felt Yosef *lifted*. One moment he was clutching me in the total dark and then the next, he was gone. His hands weren't pulled from mine, he didn't scream as he was dragged away, his presence simply departed from the room in complete totality.

"Yosef!" I screamed, scrambling around, hands searching for him. "Yosef where are you?!" I scuttled on my hands and knees across the tile floor, panic rising in my chest like a mountain. For a split second, just a fraction of a moment, I thought I heard him whimper from the mouth of the hole before silence swarmed me once again.

"Yosef!" I yelled again, wincing as the crown of my head bounced off the far wall. I spun around, still blindly reaching out, knees scraping across the floor. My hands found the hole and I reached inside, hoping against hope that I'd grab his leg or arm, pulling him out and back into safety.

I screamed his name again, growing hysterical. I waited for the lights to come back on, but they never fluttered back to life. I pushed myself away from the hole, scrambling back against the wall, hugging my arms to myself. My chest heaved and I felt terror wrap its coils around my throat.

"Give him back!" I howled, hating how alone my voice sounded. I took a long, shaking breath and made myself calm down. My eyes rolled wildly in their sockets as I tried to force them to see in the total darkness.

And then the crying began. At first, I thought it was me, but then I realized it was coming from the hole, deep, deep down its long throat. I covered my ears, knowing it was Yosef, the gut wrenching pleas and sobs rising in volume. He sounded absolutely terrified, his anguished cries so full of heartbreak and distress that I thought I would go mad.

"Stop it," I whispered, spittle on my lips. "Stop it, stop it, please, please, *stop.*"

I don't know how long I sat there, in the dark, listening to Yosef weep from someplace far off. At some point his cries came from the speakers as well, intensifying his sorrow and fear. I didn't know what torture or mental stress he was being exposed to, what kind of terror he was undergoing, but his cracking voice worked itself deep into my mind where it burned and wriggled like a sparking wire.

And then I heard Gunnert's voice join his, both men howling like their minds were being pulled from their skulls. I didn't know what it meant, what kind of hell they were enduring. I didn't know where Gunnert had been in the space between his disappearance and I didn't know if I was relieved or terrified that he was still alive.

It went on for hours. I sat completely motionless, hands squished against my ears, jaw clenched, waiting for it to be over. The darkness was awful and it wasn't long before a terrible claustrophobia settled over me.

I slumped over on the floor, shutting my eyes, as the hours crawled forward. I was so horribly exhausted and tired, my head thundering, my eyes red rimmed and heavy. The thought of going to sleep was haunting, the horror of falling asleep to Yosef's droning wails too terrible to imagine.

At some point, hours, maybe even a day later, Yosef went silent. The speakers cut out and I was left alone in the black once more. It happened so suddenly that I jumped when his voice disappeared from the room. I blinked, heart pounding, and waited for something to happen. Waited for the lights to go back on. Waited for something to come get me. Waited for anything.

But nothing came. Nothing happened. I began to cry then, the hours and hours of Yosef's suffering breaking through my skull to expose the raw sorrow underneath. Closing my eyes, I cried until I fell into a feverish, shallow slumber.

Hours later, I awoke to a voice.

"Get up."

I rubbed my eyes in the darkness, scrambling to my feet. My head was still clogged with sleep and my thoughts came sluggishly. My throat was dry and I was agonizingly thirsty. I turned around, hands out, touching the walls.

"Who's there?" I called blindly.

A crackle of static came from the hidden speakers. "Enter the hole."

The voice was the same monotone, slightly robotic voice that recited the numbers from earlier. I ran my hands along the cool tile walls, hating the darkness.

"Let me out of here!" I demanded vainly, my throat feeling like it was stuffed with sand.

A moment passed and then the speakers chirped again. "Enter the hole. You have two minutes."

"Or what!?" I yelled. "You going to shoot me!? Well come on then, come kill me you fucking cowards! Show your face!"

Silence.

"You fucking animals," I growled, fear coming once again. "What is it you want!? What the hell is the point of all this? Where did you take Higgens and Yosef!? Where's Gunnert!?"

"Enter the hole," the voice repeated from the speakers. "You have ninety seconds."

"Fuck you!"

I could feel myself hyperventilating, indecision tearing at me. Why did they want me to go into the hole? Why didn't they just take me like they did the others? Was this the last stage of their psychological torture? Was this the finale for some tape they were filming to send back to the States?

"Sixty seconds."

"Goddamn it," I spat, sweat beading on my forehead. I wiped it away, finding the hole with groping hands. My fingers traced the smooth interior.

"Thirty seconds," the voice droned.

I balled my hands into fists. Fuck it. Either I died in the darkness or I went down the hole. At the end of the day, there wasn't any choice to make. I couldn't stand the thought of being killed without doing something, without taking action. I would rather risk whatever hell awaited down the hole then do nothing. I was going.

"Ten seconds."

"I hope you rot," I growled, terrified, as I climbed into the hole. Immediately, the speakers went dead.

"Is this what you wanted?" I whispered, slowly crawling forward. "Push me down this godless hole so you can film the end of your little snuff film? Well you aren't going to get shit from me. Not a peep."

I was babbling, knew I was babbling to keep the fear away, but I didn't care. I shimmied further in on my hands and knees, my back brushing the top of the tunnel. Sweat beaded on my nose and fell onto my hands as I pushed onward. I felt like I was going to throw up, every foot forward like a drum beat to my own inevitable doom. I knew that I was going to die at the end of this. I knew I had no chance of escape. But I was determined, fiercely so, to fight whatever came next until I was put down.

The minutes dragged on, the tunnel an unchanging maw of darkness. The only sound came from the shuffle of my hands and knees on the smooth, slightly rounded floor. My back began to ache from the cramped position and I horribly wondered if the tunnel didn't have an end. What if I was stuck in here, going forward on a prayer, until I collapsed from exhaustion and died of dehydration?

But then I heard something behind me. It was soft at first, but crept up in volume until the blood froze in my veins.

Something was speaking, a garble of words and numbers. It came and went, just touching the edges of my ears, just enough to confirm it was real. The voice went on for a couple seconds and then stopped abruptly. I crawled faster, the pit of my stomach gnawing holes in my gut. As I went, I realized that the metal tube was growing colder. It was a subtle change, but unmistakable, and I wondered passively what it could mean. Was I descending deeper into the earth? Would it continue to grow colder until it became unbearable to touch, freezing me in place forever in the hole?

I crawled faster, feeling the change of temperature on the palms of my hands. I heard another string of words muttered again from somewhere behind me, sending a choked surge of adrenaline through me. Who was back there? How had they gotten behind me? Did something follow me in from the tiled room, something that had been there the whole time?

I suddenly saw something ahead of me filled me with unexpected hope. Light. Just a slight pin prick.

"Please," I whispered, energy renewed. "Oh please, *please*..."

I scrambled faster, the tunnel growing colder with every passing second. I sensed something behind me in the passage, silent now, but growing closer. It overwhelmed me with terror, the light at the end of the tunnel widening, getting bigger, more real.

A low warble of noise erupted at my back, down the hole behind me. It spiked my heart rate, the sound shaking the walls of the passage like a moaning death rattle of some great machine. Sweat ran down my face, despite the temperature as I crawled ever closer toward the light. My knees thudded with pain I barely felt, my hands slapping at the metal beneath me.

The noise came again, closer this time, a churning, echoing eruption, the animalistic, machine screech almost indescribable in its nature.

"PLEASE!" I screamed, the light coming into focus, only a couple dozen feet away now. As I trained all my focus on the exit, I saw something new emerge from the edge of light.

It was a face. A human face peering down the tunnel at me. Uncaring who it was or what side of the war they aligned with, I closed the remaining distance, nearly knocking into the man as I tumbled out of the hole, falling hard on my shoulder, my head bouncing off the floor, stunning me momentarily.

"Close it!" A voice yelled. "For fuck's sake, close it!"

In a daze, I watched the man beside me push a great vault door on its hinge, swinging it closed in a crash of metal to seal the hole I had exited. Not two seconds later, something of great power slammed into the other side, rattling not just the vault door, but the walls as well, sending showers of dust and dirt raining down from the ceiling.

"Is he injured?" The voice said. "Did it get him?"

The man who had closed the vault door kneeled down next to me and flashed a pen light in my eyes, blinding me briefly.

"You with us?" He asked gently.

I squinted, my mind a cauldron of confusion. "Who...who are you? Where am I?" I croaked.

I was grabbed from behind and pulled to my feet, then spun around. A pair of firm hands grasped my shoulders and I found myself staring into the eyes of a weathered looking man, late into his fifties, dressed in uniform with his rifle slung over his shoulder.

"Are you ok? Do you know where you are? Do you know your name?"

Mind reeling, I stared blankly at him, my eyes running down his face to take in his uniform. I felt a relief sweep through me with such a current I thought I would drown in it.

"You're Americans?" I nearly sobbed.

The man nodded and I saw there were three other soldiers with him. "We're getting you out of this hell hole. Can you walk?"

I nodded, eyes brimming with tears, more grateful than I had been my entire life.

"Good," the officer said, slapping my shoulder. He turned to the other three that were with him. "We won't be able to take the other two with us, not now. Grab their tags and let's torch this place."

"What about the Russian?"

"Piss on him for all I care."

Head finally clearing, I looked around, taking in the small room I found myself in. I felt the air leave my lungs as the details came into focus.

On the far wall of the small, dimly lit room, was a long metal desk with five dead Aussies sitting slumped in their chairs. Blood from gunshot wounds dripped down a row of computer screens displaying lines and lines of code that blinked green against a black screen. They scrolled endlessly, some unknown data stream still transmitting or receiving information from an unknown data cache. Next to the computers was a machine that was slowly spitting out a long, continuous coil of paper. Printed on the paper, as it dutifully operated, were hundreds and hundreds of numbers and words. Seemingly without reason, one out of every thousand was printed in red, standing out from the rest. At a glance, I saw some of the words that had been spoken over the speakers in my tile cell.

As the soldiers dumped cans of gas onto the computers and dead Aussies, I turned around and felt my legs turn to jelly. Sitting against the opposite wall, slumped dead in their chairs, were Yosef, Higgens, and Gunnert. They were bound, their lifeless eyes staring at nothing. Hanging from the ceiling, directly in front of them, were microphones. The corpses looked unharmed, as if no physical torture had been applied.

"Jesus Christ," I whispered, unable to tear my eyes away from them. "What the hell did they do to them?"

The officer hurried up next to me, taking my arm. "What almost happened to you if I hadn't gotten your ass out of the passage. Sorry I had to scare you like that, we don't know how many other stations are monitoring this hole. We had to make the Aussies think this station hadn't been compromised if they were listening."

"You?" I said, turning to him. "You were the one who spoke to me at the end there?"

He nodded.

I looked back at the bodies sitting before the microphones. "They made me listen to them. Made me listen to them die."

"I know," the officer said. "I wish we had gotten our intel sooner. Maybe we could have gotten them out as well."

"What did they do to them?"

The soldier guided me toward a stairwell leading up and out of the room as the remaining Americans tossed their empty gas cans on the floor.

"We don't know exactly," the officer said hurriedly. "But there's been multiple reports from various locations about these fucking holes being discovered and experimented with. This is the fourth one we know about."

"What is it?" I asked, staring at the vault door, remembering the terrible power that had plowed into it.

"We still don't understand them," the officer said as the men around him readied a Molotov cocktail. "But there's something inside of them. Something that can be activated. It changes a person, infects them, breaks them, alters them in some way if they pass through it while it's alive. We don't know if it's a machine or some terrible act of nature. But the Aussies have been experimenting with them, using POWs to learn more about what they do. Your friends over there were just some of the poor souls that have been exposed to the holes. I don't think the Aussies have any goddamn idea what they're playing with, but we found another room similar to the one you were kept in. This was about six months ago in Eastern France. Six French soldiers had been put in a room just like you were. All of them went through the hole. The Aussies recorded the whole thing, used the results to fuck with the remaining survivors who hadn't gone through yet, much like they did with you I'm sure. They were learning, experimenting, and torturing all at once. I heard they sent the French government the tapes."

"Christ…" I muttered, turning back to stare at Higgens and Yosef.

"Fire out, Chief," one of the soldiers said, all of us pushing up the stairs.

"Purge it," the officer commanded.

The Molotov went crashing into the wall of computers and immediately, everything went up in flames, the heat an intense wave that shoved us up the stairs.

Out of the room. Back into the world of the living. Back to the open sky.

Away from the hole.

Away from whatever was inside it.

FIRST DAY BEST DAY

I smoothed my tie and checked my notepad for the hundredth time. I knew I had everything in order, but I couldn't stop the flutter of butterflies in my stomach. I ran a hand across my forehead and licked my lips, cursing myself for being so nervous. It was just an interview, there was nothing to be nervous about. They were just feeling me out.

You need this.

I squeezed the bridge of my nose and took a deep breath.

What happens if they don't want you?

I shook the thoughts away and concentrated on the empty chair across the table. The fluorescents hummed overhead, casting stark light across the off-white walls. I ran a damp hand across the front of my suit and forced myself to relax. I had spoken to my potential employer twice via Zoom before they invited me to the in person interview. I had advanced past two of the three tiers and clearly they were interested in hiring me. This was more a formality.

Surely.

The door opened at my back and I jumped in my seat. I turned quickly and plastered a smile to my face.

"Sorry to keep you waiting, Russel."

A man came around the table and sat in the empty seat across from me. He was about fifty and had short gray hair, frameless round glasses, and a soft, open look about him. His suit was a crisp blue and in his hands he carried a file that he neatly set down on the table between us.

"Dave, I'm assuming?" I asked, offering my hand. The man shook it with a smile and a nod.

"That's me. I've heard a lot of good things about you from my team."

I chuckled nervously. "Everyone I've met so far has been amazing. I'm glad I have the opportunity to speak with you in person about the position. I really think I'd excel-"

The man, Dave, raised a hand with a small smile. "Russel, you don't have to make your pitch to me. That's what I have my team for. If they tell me you're qualified, then I believe them. I'm here to meet the man behind the resume. I want to get to know Russel the *human being*."

I felt myself relax slightly. "Sure, great, I'm an open book, please, what would you like to know?"

Dave tapped the folder in front of him, which remained closed. "You married, Russel?"

I shook my head. "No, never could find someone who could tolerate my snoring." I laughed weakly.

Dave tapped the folder again. "Russel. I need honest answers, please. I appreciate that you have a sense of humor, but I really want you to think before you respond. I'm looking for what's in your heart."

I shifted uncomfortably in my seat, caught off guard. "Ok yeah, no problem, you got it."

Dave paused and then found his smile again. "So Russel. Why aren't you married?"

I let a moment pass and considered my response. I needed to nail this. This guy didn't want bullshit.

Finally I sighed and felt myself decompress. I spread my hands. "I mean look at me Dave. No woman wants to be with me. I'm not attractive, I don't have much money, I'm currently unemployed, and I'm a social nuke. Not exactly a catch, am I?"

Dave rubbed his fingers across the folder. "That's a very honest answer. I appreciate that. I really do. But there are plenty of women out there who would be happy with you. You listed off your negative qualities, but what about your positives?"

I shrugged, in slight shock at how this whole thing was playing out. "I don't know. When given an opportunity, I always try to excel to the best of my abilities. I'm a hard worker and loyal-"

Dave raised a hand once again. "Russel, you're doing it again. You're talking to me like I'm your resume."

"Sorry, sorry. I guess I just wasn't expecting this line of questioning."

"Does it make you uncomfortable?"

"A little, yeah. But I'm game. Ask away."

Dave leaned back in his chair, studying me over his glasses. "Russel, do you think you haven't found a partner because you don't value women?"

I blinked. "What...?"

"Do you view women as human beings with dreams, ambitions, opinions, who can provide meaningful contributions?"

"Of course I do," I balked. "Dave--yes, of course I do."

Dave flipped open the folder finally, adjusting his glasses as he poured over the first page. "Is that why all the pornography you watch is some form of sexual abuse towards women?"

I coughed, feeling dizzy. I leaned forward into the overhead light. "Excuse me?"

Dave tapped the page. "You watch a lot of very hardcore pornography. I'm trying to understand why. I told you, I'm trying to understand Russel the *person*."

"I...I don't watch that kind of porn-"

"Horny daughter gets raped by daddy's friend," Dave said, poring down the list. "Naughty blonde cums while being beaten. Squirting sisters give blowjob while cut. Milf gets anally fucked by broken coke bottle, BBW gets flogged while trampled." Dave looked up. "Should I go on?"

I felt like I was going to pass out. The room swam and I struggled to keep my composure. I felt my forehead break out in a sweat as I fought to speak.

Dave leaned forward. "Russel? You ok?"

"I...I don't know what that is," I said, pointing toward the folder, my voice weak.

Dave sighed. "Come on, Russ. You know this is your porn search history. Sounds like you're very specific. I'm assuming you found some videos in the past you were hunting down. We only checked the past three months of your search history." Dave looked up at me. "It appears you masturbate a lot."

I finally found my voice, my face flush. "What is all this? Why are you humiliating me? Obviously you're not interested in giving me the job, so why not just tell me over the phone instead of having me come all the way down here?"

Dave furrowed his brows. "What makes you think you're out of the running?"

I let out a bark of a laugh. "Are you serious?"

Dave shrugged. "Everyone masturbates, Russel. I just wanted to know how honest you would be with me. Honesty and trust is a massive part of this position. We need complete transparency. No secrets, no lies, nothing hidden. I need to be able to trust you and you need to be able to trust me. Do you understand?"

I nodded dumbly, feeling like I was in the twilight zone.

"Good. So I'll ask you again. Do you feel like you hold an equal respect for women that you do for men?"

My throat felt like sandpaper. "No. No I don't."

"Thank you for being honest," Dave said gently, pulling out a pen to mark something on the page.

"Yeah, no problem," I croaked, feeling completely exposed and ashamed.

Dave clicked his pen and then flipped to the next page. He paused and looked up at me, planting a smile on his lips.

"You're doing great Russel. Relax. I know this is somewhat unorthodox, but I'm sure you can understand. Considering."

I nodded.

"Good. Great. Shall we continue then?"

"Yeah, ok."

Dave glanced down at the folder again. "Can you tell me why you think you'd excel in this position? And I don't want your work history or cover letter babble. I want you to dig deep and tell me from the heart."

I studied Dave from across the table, feeling every pressure point in my body. I looked hard into his blue eyes and took a second to gather my thoughts.

I took a deep breath and jumped into the deep end. "Because it's something I've obsessed about ever since I was a little kid. Hell, for as long as I can remember. I've tested myself time and time again and have never failed or quit a project once I started. I've done a ton of freelance work and I know I can handle the workload, both mentally and morally. Obviously you won't see that on a resume or cover letter, because this is a passion that goes beyond words on a piece of paper. I've made this part of my identity, part of my daily life, and I know that I can deliver for you and your clients. There is not a doubt in my mind. I was born different and I've accepted that and I've realized that I'm one of the best at what I do. I'm assuming you saw the videos I sent in, the attention to detail, the techniques in my editorial process. I notice the little things, realize that those things are what makes a product stand out, and I try to subtly bring those details to life while accenting the entire production."

I leaned back in my chair, exhaling heavily. There it was. I felt like a deflated balloon, but it felt good to get it all out. I knew my worth and it was time to stop dancing around.

Dave's face was unreadable as he listened. When I was finished, he steepled his fingers. "You're very good at what you do, this is true. Your video editing is better than most I've seen in this

field. That isn't up for debate and it's what drew us to you, initially."
Dave leaned forward across the table then, his face in shadow.

"But let me be clear. This is the big leagues. What you've done is high school ball compared to what our organization handles. It requires a degree of professionalism that will test even you. Our product is at the top of our industry and we need an editor who has an appreciation and respect for the work our team does. You are the wax on the Ferrari. Do you understand?"

"Absolutely," I said, feeling a little more balanced now. "And I know that I've never gotten to work at the level you operate on, but it doesn't intimidate me. I know I can handle it."

"You almost walked away when I asked you about your pornography preference," Dave chided gently.

"Yeah, I know, but I was just caught off guard," I said quickly. "I wasn't expecting you to ask about that."

"You seemed ashamed."

"Just exposed."

"That's fair."

"What porn do you watch?" I asked suddenly.

"Hentai, mostly," Dave said without missing a beat.

I raised my eyebrows. "I wouldn't have guessed, all things considering."

Dave folded his arms. "I'm just being honest. I told you that I need your trust as much as you need mine. In order for this business to work, we need to be open. Once you start here, we are bound. You, me, the whole team. We understand this. Do you?"

"I do," I said, then paused. "Wait, you said once I start here? Does that mean I'm hired?"

Dave teased me with a grin. "I would say we are trending in that direction. But there's one more thing."

"Ask me anything," I said eagerly.

Dave then thumbed a button beneath the table I hadn't seen before. We waited in silence then, my heart thudding in my chest. After a moment, the door at my back opened once more and two people walked in. One was a man about my age and the other was a little boy about five years old. The man held a leash in his hand, collared around the child's throat. They walked to the side of the table where they stood, awaiting instruction.

The boy was crying.

"I'll take him," Dave said to the man, reaching out to take the leash.

The man handed the kid off and then exited the room wordlessly. Dave turned to me.

"This is Michael. We've worked with him for three years now, if you can believe it." He reached out and patted Michael's cheek. "Time flies, doesn't it, sport?"

The boy, Michael, wiped tears off his cheeks, his long brown hair framing his young face. He looked at the floor, his skin pale, his eyes bloodshot.

"What is this?" I asked quietly.

"Consider it a tour," Dave said, shaking the leash loosely. "What we film here is extremely illegal, obviously, and so our offer letter is a little more...final."

"What do you mean?" I asked, shifting, feeling my heart thud heavily against my ribs.

Dave frowned. "You seem nervous. Certainly you're not uncomfortable with this content are you? We've hacked your history and I know you've watched plenty of our videos. What seems to be the problem?"

I tried not to look at the boy. "I don't know. It's just different when it's..."

Dave smiled. "Real?"

"Yeah, I guess."

"Does it deter you?"

I shook my head. "No. Again, I'm just surprised."

"A bit of a voyeur aren't you?" Dave chuckled. "I guess that comes with your profession, doesn't it?"

"I'm not there when the filming takes place," I said quietly, listening to the boy at my side continue to cry. "Even when I watch your videos, it's different than being in the room. I'm a video editor. I clean up the past."

"Indeed you do," Dave said. "And I'd like to extend a formal offer to you, if you'll accept. My team already reviewed with you the starting salary, how many videos you'll be editing a week, all the specifics. We have an extremely strict release schedule so I expect you to adhere to that. Our clients do not like to wait when they *want*. You understand?"

"Yes, of course."

"Good. That's very good Russel."

The boy, Michael, rubbed his nose with the back of his hand, still whimpering.

Dave reached into his suit jacket and pulled out a revolver. He pushed it slowly across the table to me.

"I want you to shoot Michael in the head."

I felt the breath leave my body. "You...what?"

Dave pointed to the pistol. "Pick up the gun and shoot this child in the head."

The blood drained from my face. "Jesus Christ...are you serious?"

"Very."

I looked at Dave and then at the boy, before looking back at Dave. "This isn't...this isn't what I do. I'm not an executioner. That's not what I came here to offer. You have a talented team here, I've seen almost every snuff film you've ever released, you don't need me to do this."

Dave gripped the leash tighter. "This is your offer letter. All I need you to do--" he made a gun with his fingers and then shot it at the boy, "--is sign."

I felt slightly sick. "You're dead serious aren't you?"

"You said you were born different. You've watched hundreds of hours of snuff. Death doesn't disturb you, it excites you. That's why we chose you. That's why we had you apply. That's why we want you editing our videos. This is a contract that cannot be broken and that's what's expected of all of our employees. I know this is different from watching it in secret, behind a screen, but like I said before–this is the big leagues. You're going to be paid a lot of money and have a lot of access to content that could get us all executed. We need your commitment. I need to know you want this as badly as you're telling me you do."

Dave jerked the leash and the boy, Michael stumbled forward and banged his head on the table. He cried out and clutched his forehead, shrinking into himself.

"This product," Dave said. "Is all used up. He's useless to us now. Spent. Worthless. So pick up that gun and sign on the dotted line." Dave jammed a finger at the kid's head. "Right here."

Slowly, I picked up the revolver. It felt heavy in my hand. I looked up at the boy. It was true, I had watched hours and hours of torture, murder, rape, the most inhuman acts ever committed, but it had been at my house. Alone. Without an audience. And if I ever felt the slightest modicum of guilt, I told myself that the films had already been shot. The people I viewed had already been murdered. They were dead. It was history I was witnessing.

But this child was still breathing and very much alive.

You've wanted this job for so long. Just do it. It'll be over in three seconds and then you can have the life, the money, the status you've craved your entire life.

I pulled the hammer on the revolver back and the cylinder cycled.

Dave watched me intently, his blue eyes buzzing behind his glasses. The boy had his hands over his face and was openly weeping, terrified.

"Please don't kill me," he begged, his voice cracking. "I don't want t-"

I raised the revolver and shot him.

There was a loud *pop!* and the back of the boy's head exploded in gore, his skull and brains splattering against the wall. His body crumpled to the ground and blood pumped from the ruined orifice.

"Jesus Christ," I whispered, still holding the smoking gun. My hand shook. "Holy shit..."

Blood thundered in my ears and it sounded like I was caught beneath a river. Slowly, Dave stood across from me. A smile split his face. He stretched out his hand toward me.

"Welcome aboard, Russel."

PARTY PARTY PARTY!

I felt like I was going to vomit. The greasy burger and fries churned in my stomach. I took a sip of water, the straw loudly pulling the last of the liquid through it like a dehydrated vein. I pushed my tray away, aware that Mark was saying something across the booth from me, but I felt so sick that I kind of just tuned him out. I didn't like him anyway and his perfect teeth flashed between his lips like little marble tombstones.

Yuna's arm brushed mine and I could tell she wanted to leave. Her slightly sweet perfume filled the space in front of me and I felt my eyes water as I ingested it.

You're going to throw up.

"Dude, are you listening to me?"

I looked up at Mark who was staring at me expectantly. His wavy brown hair swayed across his forehead, his wide gray eyes appraising me from a handsome face. The fluorescents overhead reflected in his eyes and I wanted to reach across the booth and smack him for no reason at all.

"Sorry, what?" I mumbled, still feeling the fast food crawl up my throat.

"Kev is throwing a party tomorrow night, are you and Yu going to come?"

I felt Yuna shift in her seat next to me and I knew Mark didn't really want me to go. He just wanted Yuna. In every sense of the word. He was probably praying I wouldn't wanna come. To piss him off, I gave him a slim smile.

"Absolutely."

No part of me wanted to go, but the slight recline in Mark's posture made my response worth whatever stupid shit happened at Kev's party. I knew Yuna would want to go. She would have a lot of friends going and wouldn't want to miss out. Her and Mark were best buds and since the day I met him, I knew he wanted it to be more. He hounded her every chance he got and it made my blood boil.

Yuna and I had been seeing each other for a couple months now. Nothing too serious, but I was curious to see where it was going. Plus I had never been with an Asian girl before and I felt a shameful kind of pride the first time we fucked.

"Is everyone going?" Yuna asked. What she meant was, will I know anyone there?

"Yeah, the whole crew," Mark said, regaining some of his composure now that he was talking to her, not me.

Mark was a fuckin' douchebag and had one of those faces you just wanted to grind under your boot, but I refrained from doing so because I knew he was part of Yuna's "Crew".

Yuna touched my hand. "You sure you want to come? It's ok if you don't."

"Yeah, don't feel any pressure," Mark said. I imagined my fist plowing through his fucking tic tac teeth.

"I'll come," I assured. "Can't wait."

The food and the fluorescents continued to pound me and I felt a headache coming on, a follow up punch to the nausea. It was Friday night and I was sitting in a shitty fast food joint with a dude I hated and a girl I kinda wanted to keep fucking. I was suddenly overwhelmed with a deep seeded depression and I covered my eyes with my hands and wondered where it had all gone wrong. I was twenty-four years old and should have had my life pointed toward something meaningful. Instead, I was here and felt like I was seconds away from puking my guts up in a melancholic puddle.

"You ok?" Yuna asked gently. I felt her hand caress my back.

"You want to go?" I asked.

"Yeah, let's."

I stood, wobbled a little, head really starting to pound, and grabbed my tray.

"Bye Mark, see you tomorrow," Yuna said with a smile.

I didn't say goodbye, the thought so depressing I couldn't even fathom how bad the words would taste if I said them. I followed Yuna to the trash can, dumped my garbage, and pushed out into the night.

The parking lot was mostly empty as we walked to Yuna's car. Mine had been stolen a couple weeks ago and I had little hope the cops would ever find it. They didn't care. They had barely paid attention when I called them.

The air stank of fried exhaust and the tar beneath my boots was wet even though it hadn't rained. A warm breeze lifted dark hair off my eyes and I brushed a hand through it, knowing I needed a shower, but couldn't seem to find the energy lately. There was a liquor store on the other side of the parking lot and I told Yuna I would be right back. I trotted to the storefront without waiting for a response, unable to cope with her inevitable protest. I grabbed a forty of malt beer and spilled some change and crumbled bills onto the counter, ignoring the judgemental look from the cashier. I felt like I didn't deserve the look and had a sudden urge to smash the bottle over the young woman's head, but somehow resisted, despite the thunder now crashing between my ears.

I walked back out into the parking lot, twisting the cap off as I did so. I walked to the passenger door and plopped into the car where Yuna waited with a disapproving frown.

"Really, Rodney?"

I drank half of the malt beer in one pull, knowing it was stupid, knowing it wouldn't help the hurricane in my guts, but didn't care. I felt so sick and miserable that I just wanted to fade it out a little.

With a huff, Yuna started the car and we began to crawl back to her apartment. I rolled the window down, letting the warm night air in, and I began to feel a little better. I finished the bottle with a couple more valiant gulps and let the glass bottle clink at my feet, wiping my lips.

The city was lit by a full moon, though its light was swallowed up in the swath of store lights, street lights, and all the other kinds of lights. I began to count how many different kinds of lights I saw as we drove, waiting for the cheap beer to hit my system. After a few minutes, I began to feel even more sick, despite the breeze on my face.

"I don't feel good."

"I wonder why?" Yuna mocked, grim faced.

"Sorry," I muttered.

"You were rude to Mark back there."

I felt my stomach lurch and I burped, tasting stomach bile. "So?"

"So?" Yuna said. "He's my friend. You have to be nice to my friends."

"He just wants to fuck you," I mumbled, starting out at all the passing lights. There were so many.

"*Excuse* me?" Yuna asked, clearly offended.

"Sorry."

"Is that what you think about all my male friends?"

I squeezed my eyes shut, just wanting to lay down. "No."

"What's your problem tonight?" She asked, half to herself.

"I just don't feel good."

"Can I trust you to behave at Kev's party tomorrow night?"

I suddenly felt a white hot bolt of anger hit me squarely in the chest. I sat up a little, swallowing the bile back down.

"Are you serious right now?"

"I just don't *do* guys who try to control who my friends are."

"I'm not trying to control anything, you fucking idiot."

Wide eyed, she turned to stare at me.

"Watch the road," I said, regretting my outburst. And then, humbly. "Sorry."

"Don't talk to me like that. Ever."

"I know. I'm sorry. I really just feel sick."

"So you pound a forty and talk shit about my friends?"

"I just said he wanted to fuck you. Mark seems like a -"

-a rich, so-handsome-he's-ugly, snake who thinks with his cock

"He seems like a decent guy," I finished, trying to hide my knuckle-white fists.

"He is," Yuna said. "He's been there for me through a lot of shit, ok? So be nice to him and stop acting so insecure. It's unattractive."

In my head, I turned into a werewolf and tore the door off, howling beneath the moon as I sprinted toward Mark with a blood lust that could not be tamed.

Instead, I turned back to the open window. "Sorry again. I shouldn't have cursed at you. We good?"

Yuna seemed to eat another lecture, instead deciding she had won. "Yes. Of course we are." She reached over and rubbed my thigh. "Sorry you don't feel good, hun. We're almost to my place."

Was she better than I deserved or did I deserve better than I thought? It was too much of a headache to think about and so I pushed the conversation out the window and rubbed my temples. My head felt like it was going to be torn in half, each heartbeat like a hammer. I felt slightly buzzed from the beer, but the greasy fast food absorbed most of the benefits. In that moment, I just wanted to vomit and start over.

We reached Yuna's apartment and she parked. As we headed up to the fifth floor where she lived, I reflected on the first time I had climbed these stairs, not that long ago. I had met her at work, she being a customer, and had hit it off. She had apparently found my usual dour mood to be funny and slightly charming. I had met most of her friends in the weeks between and had started to entangle our lives. We went to the movies, hung out in my car talking (before it had been stolen), fucked like animals, and had cautiously grown closer. I didn't know much about her, but I knew she had gone to college in Florida and had moved back up to the city where her friends had all settled after she graduated. She was a class above me and it was something I think we both knew, but she gracefully never brought it up. Though I could feel the disconnect whenever we hung out with her rich, fast talking, up their own ass, perfectly manicured, immaculately trimmed friends. They were not the type of people I grew up with and it was a world I was disinterested in. I put up with it and spent time with them though because she wanted to, felt it was important for us, and I vainly hoped that one day I would feel like I fit in, if our relationship lasted.

We entered her apartment, which always smelled like laundry detergent for some reason, and I went right to the bedroom. I kicked off my boots and collapsed onto her bed, hoping the world would stop crashing over me in big ugly waves. After a few minutes, I felt Yuna tap my shoulder.

"How about you take a shower before bed, Rodney?"

I *would rather drown in a Taco Bell toilet.*

"Good idea," I said, knowing I stank.

I heaved myself up and went to the bathroom, shutting the door behind me. I turned on the water and stared into the mirror as the shower heated.

I looked like a mess. I needed to shave, my blue eyes had dark bags beneath them, my black hair needed a trim, and my skin was pale.

Why is she with you?

I tore my clothes off and stepped into the shower.

Maybe she just wants to fuck someone different than who's on her usual roulette wheel.

I let the water wash over me, clearing my head some. I grabbed her soaps and lathered up, washing my hair and scrubbing my balls. As I did so, eyes shut as the suds dripped over my face, I realized that I had no future.

I worked a dead end job at a department store, barely finished high school, didn't have a car (anymore), and most of the kids I grew up with were either in jail or dead. It was a modern miracle I wasn't either. I had a deadbeat older brother who I barely talked to and two dead parents. Should that be something to celebrate? Should I feel good about my life because I was simply breathing free air and not dead? Another wave of depression hit me like a locomotive and I leaned against the shower wall and started to cry. It came out half hearted and I felt pathetic as soon as I started so I scrubbed my face and finished up.

I exited the bathroom with a towel wrapped around my waist, and saw that Yuna was lying naked on her stomach, her perfectly toned body arching across the bed sheets. Her dark hair spilled across her nude back and shoulders as she cocked her head at me.

"Eat my ass?" she asked coyly.

I felt a rush of blood shoot into my cock as I pulled the towel off me and climbed onto the bed. I buried my face in her ass and began to lick and slurp greedily, feeling validated for the first time all week. Yuna moaned and pressed herself harder into my face as my tongue worked into her, blinded by her impossibly perfect body. As I licked her ass, I reached under her and tweaked her nipples, hard. She let out a gasp as I teased them, feeling so horny I thought my dick would contact NASA and blast off at any second.

Yuna pulled her ass off my face and spun me around onto my back. Breathing heavily, she climbed onto my face and ground her pussy into my lips. I began to lap like a dog, as I stared up at her, her body twisting and writhing as my tongue slid along her clit. She grabbed my hair and began to moan louder, thighs shaking violently as I brought her closer to climax. Before she came, though, she pulled herself off my face and plunged her wet pussy over my cock. I gasped as she rode me, hands massaging her perfect, tiny tits, and felt a rush shoot through my squelching dick. I groaned as I came, knowing I had shot my load too fast.

"No, no, no," Yuna moaned.

I pulled her off me and threw her onto her back, sliding down between her legs. I began to lick her pussy until she came.

With the taste of my own semen coating my tongue, I knew I had at least been useful today.

I spent the next day at work, mindlessly working the register. I spent the hours thinking about last night, thinking about the way Yuna felt, looked, tasted. I was frustratingly horny and during my lunch break I went into the bathroom and masturbated. When I clocked out, I checked my phone and saw I had no new notifications. I texted Yuna to see what time she was picking me up for Kev's big stupid fucking party tonight, but didn't hear back from her as I took the bus home.

Kicking off my boots, I sprawled out on my couch, noting for the hundredth time how filthy my little apartment was. Five hundred square feet I could barely afford to call my own, sitting high up on the seventh floor of a building that should have been demolished fifty years ago.

I turned on the tv, but it put me in a melancholic state so I turned it off and stared up at the ceiling as the setting sun filtered in through the yellowing blinds. I was hungry but the kitchen seemed a world away and so I let my stomach rumble, waiting until the need was unbearable.

My phone rang and I snatched it off my lap, hoping it was Yuna. To my surprise, I saw it was my older brother, Jake.

When's the last time we talked? A month? A year?

"Hey."

His familiar raspy voice responded in my ear, sounding both familiar and foreign. "Hey Rodney. What's up?"

"You tell me."

An awkward pause, as if we were both acknowledging that this call was out of the ordinary.

He cleared his throat. "Just seeing how you're doing."

"I'm fine."

"Cool, cool. What are you up to?"

"Nothing. I just got off work."

"Nice."

I felt exhausted all of a sudden and I wanted nothing more than to end the call and forget it had ever happened.

"Can you come over to my place? I'm still across town at the same place."

I closed my eyes, feeling another headache coming on. "Why? What happened?"

A long pause, then. "I'm in some trouble. I just need a small favor."

"Jesus, Jake," I muttered, running a hand down my face.

"I'm not going to jail or anything," he said hurriedly.

"I'll be sure to throw you a party for that."

"Don't be a dick, Rodney," he said.

"What do you need? My car got stolen so if I came I'd have to take the bus."

Silence.

"Which would be a huge pain in the ass," I finished. Outside, a police siren blared.

"Please Rodney?" Jake asked and I heard an edge of desperation enter his voice.

"I have a party I'm supposed to go to in a couple hours."

"This won't take long."

"Goddamn it," I exhaled. "Fine. I'll be there soon."

"Thanks man I-"

I hung up. No part of me wanted to go, but I felt some kind of weird obligation to hear him out. I wouldn't ever consider Jake a friend, just a brother, which made it worse, which is why I felt like I had to go hear him out. He was the only family I had, whatever that meant, and I couldn't ignore our rusting, degrading familiar bond.

I shot Yuna a text, asking if she could pick me up from my brother's place for the party. She finally texted me back and said she would.

Groaning, still hungry, I pulled my boots back on and left.

When I reached Jake's building, the sun was just a smudge of orange paint grease, the last rays of light winking between the skyline. I trudged up to Jake's apartment, wondering what he had gotten into. I knew he must be desperate if he had called me for help. We didn't talk much and never asked one another for help. Ever since our parents died, first my father, then my mother a year later, neither of us had maintained much of a connection.

I knocked on Jake's door, apartment 403, the numbers a sad stain on the wooden door. Jake opened it immediately and I saw that he had lost weight since we last saw each other. His pale skin was taut against sunken cheekbones and his eyes had a somewhat lost look to them. His dark hair was buzzed tight against his scalp and he scrubbed a hand over it as he stepped aside to let me in.

"Hey man, thanks. It's uh, good to see you," he said uncomfortably.

"You look like crap," I said, stepping inside. His place was weirdly clean and I didn't know if it was because he barely owned any furniture or if he was a good housekeeper.

"You want something to eat?" Jake asked, ignoring my comment.

"I'm starving, yeah."

He shuffled to the fridge, glad to have a task, and pulled out a plastic ziploc full of pizza. He removed a couple pieces and then handed them to me on a paper plate. I looked down at the cold food, annoyed he hadn't even bothered to heat it, but dutifully took a bite regardless.

"So what's going on? What's the emergency?" I asked, plopping down on his futon, mouth full of old cheese and hard crust.

Jake took a seat in a chair opposite me, eyes roaming aimlessly around the room. "It's always something isn't it?" he stated.

"I don't know what that means, Jake."

He chuckled and it seemed to hurt. "It's just been a rough couple months."

"I wouldn't know," I said, putting the plate down next to me. I couldn't stomach any more.

"Come on man."

I sighed, letting my guard down some. It took too much energy to be a smartass. "What happened? What kind of trouble are you in?"

Jake bit his bottom lip and stared down at his lap. "I know how this must feel. Me calling you out of the blue because I need help."

I waved a hand dismissively. "Ah."

"I mean it," he said, his eyes rising to meet mine. "I'm sorry I've been such a shitty brother. I just can't seem to get out of my own way sometimes. I've been meaning to call you. See how you're doing. Just seems like something always got in the way."

I didn't like his odd humility. This wasn't like him and it scared me. Just how much trouble was he in?

"It's a two way street," I offered, feeling uncomfortable. "It's not all on you. We've never had that kind of relationship. I don't have any expectations."

"Thanks," Jake said. "Seriously, Rodney. I've felt so damn heavy lately. Just can't seem to crawl out from under it. I keep going further and further down, hoping things get better and I keep making more of a mess."

"What kind of mess?"

Jake stood and began to pace. "I owe someone money. Couple thousand dollars."

"If you're going to ask me for that kind of cash-" I started

"No, no, I wouldn't ask you for that."

"Ok, so why am I here?"

Jake stood by the window, looking out. "I did something really shitty, man."

"Ok...?"

Jake turned to face me looking like a lost lamb. "You know how your car got stolen?"

I stared at him, blank faced. "How...how do you know about that?" I stood, pieces connecting. "What a second. Dude. Don't tell me YOU stole my car?!"

Jake flinched. "I was just borrowing it. I needed it for collateral until I got the money together. Once I paid my debt, I was going to return it. I swear, Rodney, I mean it."

I shook my head. "Fuck you. I cannot believe this."

Jake took a step toward me. "Please don't be pissed. My back was up against the wall. Rodney, they were threatening me."

"So you STOLE my car!?"

"I'm going to get it back! I promise!"

"Yeah, you can wipe my ass with that promise, *bro*."

Jake sat back down on his chair looking miserable. He put his face in his hands. "I can fix this."

"How!?"

"You know Mark, right?"

I frowned. "Mark? The rich dickhead who wants to fuck my girlfriend? Yeah, I know that toilet brush. How the hell do YOU know him?!"

He shrugged. "I don't, really. I was at a bar the other day and he was there with his friends. They were loud, hard to ignore. They were also pretty drunk and were talking loudly about how there were too many..." he paused and then looked up. "How there were too many spics at the bar and he was worried about getting jumped on the way out. I think he was just drunk and running his mouth, but I approached him and offered to sell him a gun."

I just shook my head, waiting for him to continue. I couldn't believe how small the world felt.

"I still have Dad's old pistol and I offered to sell it to him for a thousand bucks. I didn't think he'd go for it, but he was more than willing. The more we talked the more we realized we had a connection. You. He couldn't believe I was your older brother. Small world, right?"

"I fucking hate that guy," I said in a low voice. "He is literal human waste wrapped up in expensive name brand toilet paper."

"I don't care," Jake pressed. "I don't care what kind of person he is. I just need to sell him the gun and I need to do it tonight. I have to pay these people the money I owe them tomorrow morning."

"So?"

Jake went to the kitchen and opened a drawer. He pulled out a pistol and laid it on the counter.

"You're going to a party tonight, right? The same one Mark's going to?"

I snorted. "Hold on. You want me to sell him the gun for you? Are you serious?"

"If you do, I can get your car back for you in the morning. I'd do it myself, but I have to go talk to these people. In person. They insisted. I don't have a choice. They are supremely unhappy with me and I need to buy a little time."

I stared at the gun, hating my brother. All the sympathy I felt for him earlier was gone, burned away beneath a furnace of anger. Everything he had said to me earlier turned to rot, all the weepy eyed apologetics, and I deleted them from my memory with a snarl.

"Rodney, please. Both of our problems go away if you do this. We can go back to square one. You'll get your car back and I'll have the rest of the money I need to pay these fuckers what I owe them."

I slowly walked over to the counter and picked up the pistol. I stared down at it. Everyone was using me. I was just a gear someone needed for their own machine. I felt my body contort and twist, bones breaking and realigning to fit someone else's blueprint.

"I don't want to talk to you after this," I said in a low whisper. "I can't *believe* the balls you have, doing this to me. There's nothing left between us once I get the money from Mark."

"I'm sorry, Rodney. I mean it. I don't want to be this guy."

I walked out the door without another word.

"What's the matter?" Yuna asked as she drove us to the party.

The gun dug into my lower back and I squirmed, my waistband keeping it in place. "Nothing," I muttered.

"Why were you at your brother's place? I thought you said you guys don't talk," Yuna asked, the car swimming with her perfume.

"We don't," I said.

Yuna rolled her eyes and seemed to be irritated. "You're not going to embarrass me tonight are you? This is the first time Kev's invited me to one of his parties and I don't want to make a bad impression."

"Is that what I am?" I asked absently. "A bad impression?"

"I don't like it when you're moody."

"I'm always fucking moody."

"Just try to have fun, ok?" Yuna said, frustrated. "Mark will be there, you can hang with him if you feel out of your element."

"I'd rather hang *myself.*"

"What?"

"I said I'll behave," I pivoted. "Don't worry, I won't embarrass you. God knows I wouldn't want to make you look bad in front of Mark and Kev."

"Thank you," Yuna said, clearly missing my sarcasm. Her voice perked up then. "Come on, Rodney, this will be a blast!" She rubbed my leg and smiled. "There's going to be a ton of people there, Kev's house has a huge pool out back, and he even hired a DJ!"

D*J*, I thought. *Dumb Jock. Hurray.*

Yuna chatted with me the rest of the way and I listened half heartedly. The conversation with my brother had turned my mood black and our inevitable arrival at the party only darkened the sun further. I felt frustrated and restless, craving both isolation and a crowd at the same time. I wanted to be left alone but needed someone to make me feel better. My mood met at these crossroads where everything collided, leaving a ruined mess that burned me up on the inside.

When we pulled up to Kev's house, a massive architectural wonder that sat atop a long winding road, I felt my stomach twist.

Cars were parked along the road and I could hear the thump of music as Yuna fitted her car into a space.

After we parked, we walked up the hill toward the house, Yuna still chatting away. The huge bay windows blinked and faded with neon light and shadows darkened the spaces in between. I felt like I was walking onto a movie set with every piece meticulously placed for maximum impact. This was a Party with a capital P.

We were greeted at the door by a clean cut frat dude with a jawline that would make a ruler blush. He was wearing a touch of makeup, just enough foundation to make his skin look eerily perfect, and the updraft of dyed blonde hair rising from his forehead was immaculately fluffed. He looked at Yuna with glassy eyes and then smiled, his perfect white teeth emerging from behind pouty lips that had been shined with gloss.

"Yuna!" He cried, embracing her in a hug. "Oh my god, I'm so happy you're here! Mark told me you were coming and I was ecstatic! Come on in!" He looked at me and his perfect features wilted a little.

"You must be Rodney," he said, one hand still resting on the small of Yuna's back.

"That's me," I stated flatly.

"Well I'm Kev," he said, turning his attention back to Yuna. "That's short for Kevin." He giggled and I knew this was going to be a long night. Yuna gave him another hug and then they all went inside, swallowed up by thumping music and loud conversation.

"Give me strength, Lord," I mumbled, following them in. I felt like I was an extra on a movie set as I waded into the crowd of people. Everyone was laughing or talking, red cup in hand, barely shooting me a passing glance as I followed Yuna and Kev inside, slowly growing further and further away from them.

The house was just as impressive on the inside as it was on the outside. Marble floors in the entranceway, a sweeping wooden staircase painted white, a high hanging chandelier that was currently dark, and rooms pushing out in all directions filled with people and music. As I took this all in, Yuna and Kevin vanished into the party. I wandered aimlessly for a bit and then found myself in the kitchen. Everyone was dressed in fuck-me-clothes, every shirt comically tight, every dress and halter top exposing perfectly tanned skin, hard bodies, and my head was filled with a hundred different collogues and perfumes. I started to feel a little nauseous from it all.

I grabbed a bottle of tequila from the counter, splashed a healthy pour into a red cup, and dropped a couple ice cubes in it. I drank it all in one swig and then poured another. I pushed my way out of the kitchen, electronic music crashing like thunder throughout the house. I almost laughed as I wormed my way into an expansive living room that held three massive couches, a modern marble fireplace, and a glass wall that looked out into the pool area.

"This shit can't be for real," I said, feeling the tequila warm my stomach. Everything was just so hilariously cliche, every person, every track that played over the loudspeakers, even the red cups clutched tightly by everyone I passed.

This just isn't your world, I thought as I made my way toward a couch. *This is normal for them. Hell, your life would probably look like a cliche to them if things were switched.*

I suddenly felt extremely depressed. The light machines, the music, the loud conversation, everything pressing in around me, compressing my atoms down to one singular pinpoint that didn't belong here. Everything about the party felt manufactured, carefully assembled from an expensive kit, and I wondered if we were all just enacting different scripts that were handed out to us at birth. It seemed like all these people were fighting to look the part they had been cast in, to look like they belonged here, in the moment, leaning into the scripts they had been given. Why, though? What was all this accomplishing?

They're just living in the moment, I thought gloomily. *Maybe you should find a moment to live in.*

I realized I was sitting on the couch, cup almost empty, as the party raged around me. The gun in my waistband dug into the small of my back and I blinked, snapping out of my introspective moping, and snorted.

You're a moody fucking idiot, you know that?

I drained the last of my tequila, ice cubes crashing into my nose.

"Let me top you off, my friend."

I turned to see Kevin plop down next to me on the couch, shoving a girl out of the way. Bottle in hand, he refilled my cup, grinning at me the whole time.

"You like the place?" He asked.

Why are you talking to me?

"Very impressive," I said truthfully.

"How'd you and Yuna meet?" He asked. At this proximity, his lip gloss practically blinded me.

I took a slow sip of tequila before answering. "She came into the store I work at. I guess you could say we hit it off." I took another sip. "How'd you meet her?"

"Through Mark."

"Where is she now, by the way?"

Kev smiled again. "With Mark."

At the mention of Mark's name, I became aware of the gun I was hiding beneath my shirt.

"Can I ask you something?" Kev asked, shifting, practically bouncing next to me. His breath smelled of liquor and his eyes were having a hard time staying locked on mine.

"It's your party," I said, "ask away."

"Are you having an out of body experience?"

I laughed, despite myself. "What's that supposed to mean?"

He scooted closer until our thighs were touching. "Don't take this the wrong way, but you look like a little lost goldfish that just flopped up onto land for the first time."

"I guess you could say this isn't the pond I usually swim in, if that's what you're asking."

He nodded thoughtfully, eyes still dancing. "People like you don't usually come to my parties, is all I mean."

"What do you mean, people like me?" I asked.

"I don't mean to be rude," he said, throwing his hands up. "But you look like the type of person who thinks the Olive Garden is fine dining. And you frown a lot. You look like you got a hook in your mouth and you don't know how to get it out."

"I'm not known to be especially cheery," I said, getting annoyed. "It's just really loud in here and everything looks very expensive. What are Mark and Yuna doing?"

He ignored my question. "If Yuna hadn't brought you, I wouldn't have let you set foot into my house."

I clenched my jaw. "For someone trying not to be rude, I'd say you're doing a pretty poor job of it."

Kev cocked his head apologetically. "I speak what's on my mind."

"You don't have to do that, you know. It's called manners. Maybe if you spent less time slapping foundation all over your face you'd have time to look up the definition."

"Oh, you're spicy," Kevin said laughing.

"I have a gun in my waistband right now."

"What'd you say?" He asked, leaning closer.

"I said where's Yuna?"

"Oh, who can say," he said, leaning back on the couch now.

"Just what do you get out of all this?" I asked, waving a hand at the crowd.

"What do I get?" Kev asked, cocking an eyebrow. "What do you mean? Have you never been to a party before? I get to have a good time, enjoy my friends, forget about life for a little while and just live one minute at a time. We have music, food, drinks, everyone here is happy and having a good time. Isn't that what life's all about? Enjoying the benefits of your labor?"

"I highly doubt your work ethic got you all this," I muttered.

"Hey, I heard that!" he laughed. "You really are a sour patch kid, aren't you? Jesus, what a *grouch*. Do you think you're better than everyone here, is that it? Do you think all my friends are diluted idiots who don't know how good they got it? Do you hate them because they're pretty and rich? Don't give me that look, your disdain for them is painted all over your scowling face." He patted my leg. "You hate them. That's ok. But I think it's because they have something you don't, something past all the expensive clothes and dental work. Can you guess what it is?" He fanned his hands out. "Look at them all. They're smiling. Happy. Grateful to be here. They're having fun. You see? I think you should give yourself permission to have some fun too, wouldn't you say?" His thigh pressed tighter against mine.

"You have my permission to leave me alone," I said.

"You interest me though," He protested. "I find your discomfort endearing. You clearly don't come from money, I have no idea how you managed to score a honey like Yuna, and you have a really huffy outlook on life it seems. Why does all this scare you so much?" He asked, looking around the room.

"You think I'm scared? Dude, I could shoot every single person in the room right now."

Kevin laughed again. "What a weird thing to say."

I gave him a sarcastic smile. "I say what's on my mind."

"Maybe I need more friends like you," Kev chuckled. "Everyone I know plays it so safe. Happy and safe."

"I thought you wouldn't let people like me step foot in your house."

"Oh, we could clean you up."

I finished my tequila and Kevin poured more into my cup from the bottle. "Drink up, goldfish. We'll have you swimming by the end of the night."

"Where's Yuna?" I asked again. I realized that I was getting very drunk, but didn't care. I stood, staring down at Kev and repeated my question.

"Where is she?"

Dejectedly, Kevin waved a hand across the living room. "Bedroom, three doors down the hall on the left. I'll be waiting for you when you get back."

"Don't wait too long," I said, storming across the room. I shoved people aside, stumbling slightly as the tequila filled my senses. I was grateful to be away from Kev's prying conversation, his insistent touch. I felt like he had been trying to crawl inside my head, mouth open in a shocked smile at what he found. He didn't know a damn thing about me or why I was the way I was. I didn't want any of this. Filling a house with people and pumping up the music would never be a reason to put a smile on my face. It felt like everyone was enjoying themselves at arms length, afraid to get anywhere near an introspective thought. I didn't need distance. I didn't need crowds of people.

I reached the bedroom door, heart thumping. The liquor in my system was working overtime and the couple bites of bad pizza I had eaten at my brother's did nothing to dilute its conquest.

I tried to open the door but found it locked.

My heart rate spiked immediately and I began to pound on it.

"Yuna? Yuna open the damn door!"

I felt like I was being shoved further and further away from everything, pushed out, blacked out, an arm extending, shoving me away from the chaotic scene. I hammered my fist against the door again, anger exploding up my throat.

"Yuna open the fucking door!"

Suddenly the door jerked open and Mark stood before me, a lopsided grin slanting across his mouth.

"Sorry man," he said casually, "didn't realize it was locked."

"Get out of my way," I growled, shoving past him. Yuna was sitting on the bed, fully clothed, one leg crossed over the other. Her face was red and she looked pissed.

"What is your problem?!" She spat, clearly embarrassed at my behavior.

"What were you two doing in here?" I demanded, planting myself in front of her. Mark came to my side and put a hand on my shoulder.

"Chill man, we were just hanging out."

I slapped his hand away. "Don't touch me. I'm not an idiot, I know you've been dying to sniff her pussy for ages now."

Yuna's jaw dropped. "Rodney, what the fuck!? What is wrong with you?"

"Oh shut up," I snarled. "Please don't patronize me, I'm not blind and I know what a locked door means."

Mark gripped my shoulder then. "Hey, don't talk to her like that. I don't care who you think you are, you treat her with some respect, do you understand me?"

Between the ocean of tequila churning in my guts and the rage burning through my skull, I felt myself lose it in cataclysmic fashion.

I balled my hand into a fist and plowed it through his front teeth, knocking him to the floor.

Yuna jumped up, eyes bulging. "Rodney, stop it! Are you insane?!"

I shoved her back onto the bed, "Shut the fuck up and sit down." I stepped over Mark and pulled the gun out, pointing it at his face.

"Get up."

Yuna let out a little shriek at the sight of the gun and all the blood drained from Mark's face. A trickle of blood oozed from a split lip and he raised his hands.

"Whoa, dude, whoa whoa whoa."

"Yeah, whoa," I said. "Now get up."

He stood, backing away from the gun.

I advanced on him. "Tell me the truth and do not bullshit me. Tell me if you were planning on fucking Yuna tonight."

"Chill man, I don't-"

I stepped into him, shoving the barrel of the gun into his cheek. "The truth. Now."

"Yes!" He stammered. "Yes, I wanted to, ok! I'm sorry, it wasn't personal!"

I felt a spike of rage spear up my spine, an uncontrolled fire that blazed through me. I was so tired of feeling small, feeling like everyone was in on the joke except me. I was so tired of feeling out of place, unappreciated, ignored, and pushed aside. I didn't know why I was surrounded by people who looked down on me, a convenience when needed instead of a necessity that was valued.

I was so fucking *done* with all of this.

My voice grated over my teeth. "How about I fuck you instead, huh Mark?"

"H-huh?" Mark babbled.

I pointed the gun at Yuna suddenly. "Lock the door."

"Rodney!"

"Lock the fucking door, Yuna, or I will put a bullet in his eyesocket."

Yuna, now crying, scrambled off the bed and locked the door, retreating back to the bed when she was finished. She pulled her knees up to her chest, her voice a pleading mew.

"Rodney, I wasn't going to have sex with him, I swear, we were just talking!"

I turned back to Mark. "Take off your clothes."

"W-what? Why!?" He cried.

"Cause I'm going to *fuck* you. That's what you wanted right? Now take off your clothes. All of them."

Shaking, Mark stumbled out of his clothes, staring wide eyed at the gun the entire time. He stood in front of me, hands covering his groin, naked as the day he was born.

"Climb onto the bed," I said, waving the gun. "Hands and knees, ass out." I felt like I was going to vomit, the room swaying, bile tickling the back of my throat.

"Please man," Mark begged.

"I'm not going to ask again," I said, shoving the gun into his face.

Slowly, he did as he was told, the bed creaking as he climbed up. Yuna backed away from him until she sat against the headboard, hands covering her mouth.

"Stop man, please, I'm begging you," Mark cried from his hands and knees, turning his head to look back at me.

The sight of him disgusted me.

"Bark," I ordered. "Bark like a dog. Look at Yuna and bark."

Mark, shaking, just closed his eyes, whispering for me to stop. I shoved the gun barrel against his asshole, hard.

"BARK!"

He jumped, legs quivering, and began to bark like a dog between sobs. Yuna was crying, but I barely paid her any attention. I twisted the gun harder into Mark's asshole, bringing forth a desperate, howling bout of barking as Mark squirmed in terror.

"Where's your money?" I asked, keeping the gun in place.

Mark stopped, spittle leaking from his lips. He turned back to me. "W-what?"

"The money for this gun, where is it?"

"I-I don't-"

"The MONEY!" I yelled. "My brother Jake said you wanted to buy this gun so where's the cash, idiot!?"

"In my pants pocket!" Mark cried.

"Don't move a muscle," I instructed, backing up. I bent down, still pointing the gun at Mark, and scooped up his discarded pants. I found the money in his front pocket, a tight roll of bills wrapped in a rubber band.

"Yuna," I said, my voice a low drawl.

She looked up at me from behind her hands. I could see terror and anger, disgust and fear. She hated me in that moment but dared not voice it. She had never seen me like this. No one had.

"Tell Mark he's repulsive."

She clenched her jaw, eyes flaring, but I raised the gun and the look vanished. She glanced at Mark, still naked and on all fours.

"You're repulsive."

It came out weak and without conviction but it was the best I could ask for, given the circumstances.

I walked back behind Mark and flipped the gun over in my hand, gripping it by the barrel.

"I'm going to leave now. You can have Yuna. I don't think she was really all that into me anyway. Catch you on the flip side, asshole."

And then I brought the gun up, like a hammer, and smashed his balls with the butt end. He screamed and went rolling off the bed, howling as tears rolled down his face. Yuna screamed and scrambled to the floor next to him, eyes huge.

I walked to the door and unlocked it, throwing it open. I turned back before I left the room, eyes dark.

"By the way, the gun isn't loaded."

I tossed it onto the floor and left.

I hurried through the crowd of people, every one of them oblivious to what had just gone down in the next room. The world swam and I stumbled, feeling sick, my stomach a knot of bile and pain. I was so angry and disgusted that I thought I'd erupt, popping like a puke filled balloon. Faces blurred in front of me and I pushed them aside, stumbling for the front door. Music thundered around me and multicolored lights flashed like neon bombs going off. Someone was calling my name over the noise, but it was just background as I lunged for the front door, boots clacking across the marble floors.

I grabbed the handle and yanked it open. As I did so, a hand caught my shoulder and spun me around. I found myself staring face to face with Kevin.

"What's going on?" He asked, suspicious. "Why are you leaving already? Where's Mark and Yuna? Did you find them?"

"Sure did," I slurred, fighting against the sudden pain in my head, the tickle of vomit in my throat. Darkness bled into the corners of my vision as I tried to focus on Kev's face.

"Why are you leaving then? What happened?"

I grabbed him by the shirt and pulled him in close, my breath tickling his glossed lips. "I'm sorry I fucked up your party."

And then I was gone, out the door and down the driveway, disappearing into the night.

Yuna had driven and so I ran on foot, unsure if Mark was coming after me or not. I didn't know if he was that type of person, but I didn't want to risk waiting around. I ran for almost an hour, twisting and winding down streets, getting lost in the process. Eventually, I came to an intersection and decided to call my brother Jake. I wanted to give him the money, get my car back, and be done with this whole mess.

What the fuck did you do back there?

I pulled out my phone and dialed Jake. My stomach rolled and I felt the tequila protest against the miles I had gone. My face was coated in sweat and my shirt was stained down the back. I gagged once as I put the phone to my ear, begging my body to hold it together. Flashes of what I had done to Mark blasted through my mind and I squeezed my eyes shut, repulsed, disgusted, and terrified.

Jake's phone rang twice before he picked up.

"Yes?"

"Jake," I said weakly, out of breath. "Hey, I have your money, but I need a ride. Please. I'll drop a pin. You have to come get me, please."

"Is this Rodney?"

I stood up straight. The voice at the other end wasn't Jake, I realized.

"Who is this?" I asked.

The voice continued, a monotone drawl that brought the pain in my head to the forefront. "I'm afraid your brother had an accident tonight. The man didn't understand timelines, it seems. Glad you have the money though. Leave it in your brother's apartment. Tonight. I'll send one of my guys to get it."

"What did you do to him?" I whispered, voice rattling. My stomach was in my throat and I felt my hand shaking as I pressed the phone into my ear.

"We gave him every chance. He owed us pennies compared to some other shit I'm dealing with, but if you can't set an example, an expectation, then you're never going to collect with the big boys. You understand, don't you? Shit though, I am sorry about your brother, kid. Ain't easy losing a family member." He paused as I sank to my knees on the street, unable to believe what I was hearing.

"Just be sure to leave the money in his apartment," the voice repeated and then hung up.

I felt tears find my eyes, the pain in my head spinning like a blender. Gone. Jake was gone. Done. I would never speak to him again. The only family I had left, however tenuous, was no more.

I was truly and completely alone.

My phone beeped and I saw I had a text from Yuna.

Crying, I opened it.

"You're a fucking sicko, I called the cops and told them what happened. I gave them everything I had on you. You're done, I hope you rot in jail."

I let my phone clatter to the street. Cars passed by, honking, as I curled into a ball on the sidewalk. I had no future. I had no family. I was totally and completely alone.

None of the cars that passed stopped to offer me help.

WORM

I felt myself slide through the rebirth tube as my body completed the final evolution that had been forced upon it. I slithered through the exit mouth, slime coating my face. I felt the impulse to wipe my eyes, but my arms had been molded to my body, elongated to stretch down my sides in a mass of flesh.

I squished into the mud, face first, as the tube spit me out. I wriggled helplessly, eyes burning, my legs now boneless and stretched, my feet conjoined to end in a knotted nub.

I was a worm now. I had managed to avoid it for so long, but it had been an inevitability. Only a few thousand humans remained in their original form and they would soon meet a similar fate. Capture. Containment. And then rebirth.

I opened my mouth and gasped in the filthy air. The world around me was a squelching bellow of ironworks and repurposed flesh. My head filled with the stench of smoke and rust and as I raised my eyes to the cloud covered sky, I knew this new form would lead to madness.

I wriggled in the mud, inching my way forward, away from the retracting tube that had just birthed me. All around me were other people, reformed by our new gods. They wriggled in the mud, weeping, screaming, or immobile in shocked paralysis. Hundreds of brown pods lined the barren landscape, each one the size of a skyscraper. Thousands of tentacle-like tubes extended from the pods, burping out new worms for the world.

I watched as the ground crawled with people, the worms, the expansive plains seemingly alive as the reformed creations struggled to learn their new locomotion. Tears filled my eyes as I looked down at my naked body, now just a tube of muscle and skin, my appendages smoothed, molded, and creaseless. I was a torpedo of flesh with a head, a wriggling, pathetic reincarnation.

Tears filled my eyes and my guts filled with dread. How long had it been since I had been captured? How many days or weeks had I been in the pod, floating in that pink jelly, my mind in stasis? And where would I go now? What purpose would I fulfill?

I knew the answer and it chilled me to ice. In the months since the arrival, I had fled and hid as the world around me changed. As our new conquerors stripped the landscape of rock and wood, of house and concrete. They had terraformed the earth into a churning ruin of mud and dirt where the captured humans were belched back out after their rebirth. And there they slithered, wandering aimlessly, helplessly, until they were collected for a higher purpose.

A world of worms.

I inched forward again, desperate to be away from the pod I had been confined in for so long. Other worm people squelched around me as they were discharged from their tubes, their bodies falling with a wet thunk. A great haze of eye watering stink filled my head and I vomited. I grit my teeth as I tried to stand, prop myself up with my arms, my phantom limbs useless reformed blobs of flesh. I could feel them, glued in place by my own melted skin, and the sensation tore at my mind.

My cheek dragged in the mud as I coiled my body up and then pushed out, advancing my form another foot. I repeated the exercise but soon found myself out of breath. Gasping, I turned my head in the mud, panting, to stare out at the world.

Titanic iron towers littered the landscape around the looming birth pods. Huge pistons pounded the earth from the center of these towers, continuing to alter the landscape, filling it with water, tilling the soil, churning and churning and churning like an alien heartbeat. I felt the vibration across my body, in my skull, along my jaw. I counted seven towers, but there were thousands of them across the world, each with a singular purpose, the pistons rising into the heavens, beyond the wall of cloud as one, only to come thundering down in unison, over and over again.

Stretched between the towers were long coils of corded wire as thick as subway cars, stretching for miles between the machine-like constructs. Hanging from the coils were our oppressors, each one hundreds of feet in length. They hung upside down from their perch, their forms monstrous to behold, their eyes ever watching us.

They appeared to be half machine, but there was an undeniable intelligence that lay within the creatures. The economy that they had built and repurposed spoke to a systematic logic that was self aware rather than automated or animalistic.

They hung from the cords by some kind of clear jelly that covered their entire form. The layer of jelly or goo moved almost of its own accord, slithering and forming appendages when needed. The ones hanging from the cords had purposed this jelly into a tail that coiled and secured them to their perch.

Beneath the layer of clear goo was a mash of machine and flesh. They did not have legs, for the jelly that covered them formed a means of propulsion if needed. Their bodies were bulky and brown, their skin like patchwork sheet metal that had been left to rust for decades. Each one had a colossal engine growing out of their back with a propeller that could carry them through the air if needed. They had no arms either, but there was a head, a giant block of flesh the color of bruised muscle. They had a mouth, but it was dwarfed in size. The puckered hole emitted sound, some form of language that was expelled in a series of low blasts, like foghorns across a darkened sea.

They had four eyes embedded in their hairless heads. They protruded from the sickening flesh like boils, convex, unblinking orbs the color of dying embers. Two of the four eyes sat above the puckered mouth, one on top of the other, vertically. The other two were on the sides of their head where the ears should have been. The burnt orange irises rolled and spun seemingly without intention, a chaotic, constant film reel of their surroundings.

"Help me!"

My attention was pulled back to the mud fields as the call for help reached me. I looked to my left and saw a fellow worm man, fighting to wriggle his way over to me. His eyes were wild and filled with horror, a panic as he fought his way through the thick sludge.

"Please, help me!" He screamed again, inching closer. Thousands of other new worm people echoed his cry across the barren land, drowned out by the thunder of the automated metal towers. Churning. Churning.

I ignored the worm man. What was I supposed to do? I was fighting my own eclipsing panic and could offer no aid. We were all doomed. I knew what happened once we were repurposed. It was only a matter of time.

Instead of answering the call for help, I pushed my way forward through the mud, away from the man. Other worm people squirmed around me, breathless, terrified, trying to make sense of their new forms.

I needed a goal, something to set my mind to. Something to keep me centered and whole. I looked ahead and saw a small rise about a hundred feet ahead of me. I focused on it, scooting my way forward, one painful foot at a time. I filled my head with a singular mission. Get to the rise and see what lies beyond.

As I pushed my way forward, body coated in mud, a roar of engines shook the sky above. I cocked my head and saw forty or fifty of the massive machine creatures whirring by, their unblinking eyes rolling in their sockets. The wind from their expansive propellers blasted down on the worms, spraying us with mud. I squeezed my eyes shut and clamped my mouth shut against it. The machine creatures, which the surviving humans had taken to calling Helies due to their helicopter-like propulsion, soared past me overhead, down the line of freshly birthed worm people. I knew what they were doing, knew what would come next. When I had still been human, I had seen this process dozens of times over, hidden away, knowing that one day my turn in the mud would come.

I was halfway to the rise now, the skyline that sat above it nothing more than a dull gray smear. I squirmed forward, panting, and began to hear the Helies communicating to one another in their puckered, horn like language. They were coordinating. Relaying information. They were calling out for our death.

"Please..." I sputtered weakly, feeling my stomach roll in fear. "Please god let me die..." I choked on a wad of mud that pushed its way past my lips and I hacked miserably, face stained, trying to breath again.

Another cluster of Helies whirred overhead in the opposite direction now, their enormous frames patched together with sickly skin, their protruding engines snarling. More horns following, short, hooting calls as coordinates were sent for pick up.

I was almost to the rise now and I felt a feverous need come over me. I had to see what was over the hill before I was taken. I needed some glimmer of hope or a finality of my end. I put everything into what lay over the hill, acceptance or resistance, depending on what I saw. It was a fruitless need, a pitiful scale that balanced my mental state, but it was there nonetheless.

I looked behind me and saw other worms were now following me, trailing behind my mutated form like a diseased tail. I didn't know what they expected or why. Perhaps they thought I had a plan.

It didn't matter. A new sound overcame us. A crunching, thumping wave of mechanical growls, an announcement of new engines, much bigger than the Helies. I looked toward the rise ahead of me, terrified, and saw a massive ship stretching across the world, cresting the skyline. It was the shape of a torpedo, but aimless in its design, at least to the human eye. Massive coils of wire encased the ship, some hanging loosely like severed power lines, drooping to the earth where they dragged through the mud.

As its shadowless form burrowed through the clouds overhead, I watched as a massive net was dropped from its belly. It thudded to the ground ahead of me and the other worms where it was dragged by wires across the earth towards us. A collective scream rose all around me as it drew closer and then began to scoop us up.

I was helpless. I wriggled wordlessly as the edges of the net came for me and then I was rolled up into the hard weaving where I tumbled and bumped into other worms, all of us in a full throated panic.

The ship above us turned, a bellowing creak of ancient machinery, and proceeded down the line of newly birthed worm people, collecting them into the great net. Hundreds, thousands of us. I was soon compressed beneath the weight of them, my vision going dark as wet, thrashing bodies threatened to suffocate me, the stink bringing bile up my throat. I wanted to vomit again, but I didn't have the breath beneath the weight of my fellow worms.

With a great heave, I felt us begin to ascend back up toward the ship. I felt the pressure on my lungs ease a little and I gasped, a howling panic, a chorus of a thousand voices slamming into my head. I turned, squirming, trying to see anything beyond the mass of bodies, trying to get a glimpse of the hill I had been so desperate to reach, to see what lay beyond it.

I was denied this last attempt and I felt the weight begin to crush me again. I knew I was crying, everyone was, and I hated that my last moments would be ones of fear and desperation.

At some point we reached the ship and the net started to fold in on itself, forming a colossal sphere of flesh. The pressure on my chest and head increased and I felt as if I would be blinded by the pain, but at the last second, my slick, useless form slipped between the worms around me and I saw light and then the wire mesh was digging into my face. I had ended up on the exterior of bodies and I wept in relief as I heard thousands of worm people crushed and compacted around me as the net closed completely. We hung there like a wriggling, dripping mass of fish that had just been scooped out of the ocean.

It was ironic, I knew, to think of ourselves in such a way. In truth, we were the literal worms. The bait that our oppressors had created. We were the lure, the hook, and bobber all in one. During my days in hiding, before I had been forced into my new form, I had seen these nets, these ships, dozens of times. Fishing boats of the sky, trolling for bait before being shot out into the atmosphere, past the cloud layer.

I didn't know what our captors were fishing for, out there beyond the stars, what they were hunting, but I had seen this process enough times to put the morbid pieces together. I had decided that it must be the stink our new form emitted that constituted our evolution. A pungent, horrific odor that bled through every worm's pores after they were rehabilitated into bait.

What great titans were our captors hoping to hook? What planet sized leviathan lay beyond the borders of known space? What cosmic terror swam between the solar systems, awaiting our charred corpses?

I felt us move again, darkness slowly dusking around me. I craned my neck, desperate to look out into the world one last time, pitiful sobs rising in my throat as I strained to see what lay over the covetous hill so far down below me.

The net was being fitted into a deep space capsule, two half spheres coming together around the balled worms, entombing us. The metallic sphere was pocked with holes, to allow our stench to escape, luring whatever moon eater awaited beyond the stars.

I heard a deafening crash as the two halves of the capsule enclosed around us, locking with a great hiss. The bodies around me wriggled furiously, the ones not crushed, and I felt stinking blood and fluids drip into my eyes. I blinked, blinded momentarily, eyes burning in agony as I fought to clear them. Gasping, feeling like there was fire on my face, I cleared my vision just enough to see out of one of the capsule's portholes. I felt a stinking wind of my face as I took in my last seconds. The capsule's engines primed around us, a shaking, violent sensation that threatened to knock my teeth loose.

We were about to be launched.

Crying, I twisted, thrashed, fought with every ounce of strength I had left to see the outside world. To see what lay behind the rise so far below.

"Please..." I spat, tears and blood and puss streaking down my cheeks. "Please..."

A moment before we were launched, our bodies cooked as we passed through the atmosphere, I caught a final look at the outside world. I saw what lay beyond the rise, the destination of my feverish mission.

There was only mud.

SNOW BURN

I'm an old man. Well, at least I feel old. I'm fifty-eight and I can feel every year etched into my bones. It's not easy getting old and it's even harder when you do it alone. My wife passed away twelve years ago, but I'm not here to talk about that. I do miss her though. Every single day.

I live in northern Maine. I've lived in my house for over thirty years now and have raised all three children here. Two boys and a little girl. They've all moved on and out of state, but we still talk and visit. I miss them too. The house sits on a plot of land spanning some two hundred and thirty-seven acres and it's all mine. Twice now I've had an offer placed on the land and the house, but I always decline. I don't have much need for the big dollars flashed in front of my face. I like the land. I like the quiet. I like knowing that I'm surrounded by trees and animals and mountains. It's more valuable to me than any amount of money. This house and this land is my home and I treasure it dearly.

Which is why I've chosen to recap the events of the past couple weeks. Someone has to know what's been going on here. It's not right and I'm going to use this account as a centerpiece when I go public about what's been happening on my property.

You see, a couple weeks ago, the U.S. military began bombing the woods behind my house.

I sat in my chair, watching the snowfall outside, nursing a fresh cup of coffee. I had been splitting wood all morning and I ached. The wood stove to my right crackled and popped as a couple fresh logs burned. I needed to take a shower, but the coffee came first. Out my front window I could see my long, winding driveway begin to pile with snow. I would need to crank out the snowblower later, but I would wait until the clouds had emptied themselves first.

As I sipped my coffee, I heard something I had never heard before. It was a plane. Not just a private plane, one of those little runway skippers, but a full blown sky screamer. And it sounded low, low enough to rattle the windows. I hoisted myself out of my chair and went to my back door. When I opened it, letting in a gust of frigid air, I spotted it. It flew east to west across my property, about a half mile from where I stood. It was huge, a massive gray beast that roared only a couple hundred feet above the treetops.

As it flew, it dumped a trail of something red in its wake, like it was dousing the land in some kind of liquid. I watched the red rain fall, a curtain that filled the horizon, falling into the woods. My woods.

"The hell is going on here...?" I growled, knuckles white on my coffee mug. I looked at the plane again and to my surprise, I saw that it was a military aircraft. It continued its journey, still dumping red in its exhaust, coating the trees and land. I silently watched it until it had completely emptied its tanks, the red liquid vanishing in the snow choked sky. Then, the aircraft ascended quickly and disappeared into the clouds, headed south now.

Dumbfounded and pretty ticked off, I went to my computer and looked up the nearest military base. I didn't know what the hell was going on, but something had just been dumped on my property and I had no warning or explanation. After a quick search, I saw there was an aircraft base in Bangor, which was hours south of me. I tried to call them, but couldn't get through. I wasn't terribly surprised. Still fuming, and extremely confused, I went back to my chair to think. I finished my coffee and didn't come to any conclusion or plan of action. It was infuriating. I took pride in my ownership here. On some days, I almost felt like the gatekeeper to the land I owned, protecting it from loggers and construction.

I ended up calling my oldest son and he was just as confused, if not annoyingly curious, about the whole thing. He said to keep trying the air force base in Bangor. He then asked me something I hadn't thought of.

"You think the stuff they dumped is poisonous?"

I blinked, holding my cell against my ear. "What do you mean?"

"Do you think it's safe for you to stay there? What if the wind blows the fumes over to the house?"

"I hadn't considered that."

My son continued. "Well I'm sure whatever they dumped wasn't strawberry juice, Dad. Maybe you should get out of there until you get some answers. How far away was the plane from the house?"

"I dunno, under a mile I'd say. Wind's blowing away from the house right now too, so I don't think I need to worry."

"Have you heard anything on the news about this?"

"I don't watch the news."

"Maybe you should. I'll see what I can find out about this as well. For now, it'd make me feel a whole lot better if you drove down to Mass and stayed with Anna for a couple days."

"Your sister has better things to do than babysit her father," I said. "Besides, I'm not leaving the house. Not when my land has been trespassed on."

"It's the United States Military, Dad, not a couple meth heads with guns."

"Even so," I rebutted stubbornly. "I'll keep you posted, ok?"

"Please do. Love you, Dad."

"Love you too. Talk soon."

I refilled my mug and went to the back room where the big paneled windows looked out at the woods. I plopped myself down in my recliner and waited. For what, I don't know. I could still see a slight pink tinge in the sky, where the plane had dropped its load.

I wasn't sure what to expect, but three hours later, another plane came. I went outside as I heard it approach, the snow really coming down now. I craned my neck and spotted the aircraft coming in from the east again. It looked like this plane was even bigger than the last and as it roared overhead, I saw that it too, was military. I watched it pass over the house and then bank left, soaring over the same spot the previous plane had ejected its load. A moment later, it began to dump red liquid over my land. I felt my blood pressure rise as the land and trees were soaked in its wake. Just what on earth was going on?

I went back inside and tried calling the base in Bangor again, but never reached anyone. Frustrated, I began to pace my living room, listening to the plane slowly depart back south. This was my land. My property. I didn't care if it was the United States Military, I just wanted an explanation and then maybe, an apology.

As if.

I went back to my computer and spent the next couple hours trying to find anything online that would explain what was happening. I searched local news sites, called a few newspapers, hell, I even checked social media. I didn't find anything and when I closed my laptop, I was no closer to figuring out what was going on.

With the snow still falling and dusk in full swing, I made myself dinner. As I sat down to eat, I heard a car come down the driveway. Curious, I went to the door and saw that it was a Hummer, a military one, its huge tires making short work of the snow.

"Now we're getting somewhere," I muttered, crossing my arms in the open doorway as I watched two men in full uniform exit the Hummer.

"Evening," the lead one greeted. He was about my age and accompanied by a younger gentleman who looked as stone faced as his comrade.

"You folks coming to explain why the hell you got planes dumping loads of shit over my land?" I asked as they stomped their snow caked boots up the front porch.

The one my age stuck his hand out. "I'm Colonel Bridges. I apologize for not getting to you sooner, the snow slowed us down."

I looked over his shoulder at the Hummer, cocking an eyebrow. "Yeah, I bet." I looked at the second gentleman in uniform. "And who are you?"

"He's with me," the Colonel said stiffly.

"Right," I said, feeling myself getting angry. I didn't know why. This was what I had been waiting for. Some answers. Someone who could tell me what was going on.

"You mind if we come in?" Colonel Bridges asked.

"I'd rather you tell me why you're here so we can all get on with our evening."

Straight lines formed on the Colonel's face, but he continued on in an even tone. "Unfortunately, we're going to have to ask you to vacate the premises. Temporarily."

I snorted. "Is that so? Any why's that?"

"I'm afraid it's not safe."

"Because of the shit you're dumping on my land?" I asked sharply. "You do realize that this is all MY property." I waved my arms around for emphasis. "And I wasn't notified that the fuckin' U.S. military was going to be conducting flybys today, pissing whatever the hell that stuff is, across MY land."

"Please don't be difficult, sir," Colonel Bridges said. "Like I said, we were delayed because of the snow. It's very important though, that you remove yourself from the premises for a short time. We'd be happy to escort you to a family member or a hotel. Whichever you prefer."

"I bet," I said, crossing my arms. "But you have to tell me what is going on back there." I jerked a thumb over my shoulder. "What are you all doing on my land?"

"That's classified, sir. Now please, pack a bag."

I ran a hand over my face. "You can't do this. You know that, right?"

"We can," Colonel Bridges said unapologetically. "Please, it's for your own safety."

"You keep saying that!" I yelled suddenly. "Can you at least tell me what you're doing back there?!"

The younger man stepped forward then, his voice low and quiet. "Something bad is happening back there, sir. We're ushering in ground troops as we speak. It's not safe for you to remain here, not when you're this close to-"

"That's enough," Colonel Bridges barked, shooting a hard look at the younger man. He took a beat to compose himself then turned back to me. "Would you like to drive yourself?"

I pushed back my frustration and forced myself to take a breath. I clearly wasn't going to get any answers from these two and I certainly wasn't going to leave my house, unsure if I would ever return to it. Not without knowing why.

"Fine," I lied. "Yes, I would like to drive myself. You can come back in a couple hours if you'd like to make sure I'm gone, but I wouldn't waste your time. I have a daughter in Massachusetts that I'll go visit. I'm sure she'll be thrilled to see me."

Colonel Bridges nodded. "Thank you for your cooperation. I'll send a car back here in an hour to make sure you've gotten out safely. I'll be in contact when it's safe to return to your house."

"I'm sure you will," I said. "Now please, I have some packing to do."

Colonel Bridges and the other man turned to go. "Thank you again. Stay safe."

And then they were gone. I had no doubt they'd be back in an hour, which gave me a very short amount of time to hide my truck, turn out the lights, and pretend like I had left. I had no idea if they'd come *inside* to make sure I was really gone, but I was willing to risk it. Even so, I had to make it look like I had truly vacated. If they saw that my truck was gone and the lights were off, reason would dictate they'd turn around and leave. I slipped into my winter boots and bundled up, tossing on my heavy coat, gloves, and hat. I knew of a spot just down the road where I could hide my truck, in the woods, and with the snow falling so heavily, my tracks would be covered.

You're being stupid, a voice chirped as I gathered my things. *You have no idea what's going on and you might actually be in danger. What if that red mist is poison?*

"They weren't wearing gas masks," I responded to the empty room. I put out the fire and shut off all the lights. I checked my watch and saw it had been forty minutes already since they left.

Throwing my pack over my shoulder, I grabbed my keys and went outside, climbing into my truck with a grunt. I guided the truck down the driveway, the snow still coming down in big, fluffy waves. I turned on the headlights as the last of the light bruised the treetops, swathes of purple and black clouding the sky.

When I reached the main road, I turned left out of my driveway and drove a quarter mile down the street. There was an old fishing spot I had used a couple times, years ago, with a pull off for parking. I navigated the truck into the small opening between the trees, tires bouncing across the rock and dirt. I parked and shut off the lights, listening to the freezing creek gurgle outside.

Exhaling, I exited the truck and pocketed the keys. My breath billowed out in huge, cold clouds as I zipped my coat up.

Get back on the road and go see your daughter. You're acting like a fool.

Ignoring my better judgment, I clicked on my flashlight and began the hike back toward my land. Back to where the planes had flown. I had only gone a couple steps when I heard cars on the road behind me. I glanced over my shoulder, through the wall of trees, and saw a line of military Hummers barrel down the road, their engines roaring. When their tail lights disappeared, I took a moment and then pressed on.

You have no idea what you're walking into.

I let the sound of the falling snow fill my head as I crunched through the silent forest. I took my time, and was careful with my footing. I set a course so I would loop around and not come straight at the spot I thought the planes had been targeting. It took me the better part of an hour before I began to hear noise in the trees ahead of me. The sounds were still fairly far off, but I estimated I was getting close to where the red mist had been dumped. I sniffed the frigid air, but I didn't notice any kind of chemical trace.

As if you'd know.

I clicked my flashlight off and pressed forward, headed toward the distant commotion. I thought I heard shouting and doors being slammed shut. What had that young military kid said? That they were issuing in ground troops? Was that what the line of Hummers had been?

I pressed forward, careful now. As I grew closer to the sounds, I began to see light filter through the trees, blinding white light like someone had erected industrial lamps in the woods. After a few more minutes of slinking between the trees, I heard shouting, the voices clear now. Someone was barking orders. I pressed my back against a tree, heart thumping and then slid my way between the shadows, trying to hear what was being said. After a couple breathless moments, I saw soldiers in full gear holding guns. I guessed there were around fifty of them, all of them rushing toward a centralized location where the lights were pointing.

The voice giving orders cut through the trees once more.

"Take your positions and wait for my order!"

I was about twenty yards away now and couldn't see what the soldiers were congregating around. I let out a long, quiet breath, then pressed closer. Finally, at ten yards, I stopped behind a tree, not daring to get any closer. I peeked out and what I saw sucked the oxygen from my lungs.

It was a hole. A colossal, dark hole that spanned at least thirty feet across. The soldiers were lining the lip of the gaping abyss, guns trained down into the black as snow fell across the opening in the trees above.

"FIRE!"

I jumped back, heart sputtering, as fifty guns reported all at once. I slammed my gloves over my ears as full automatic fire exploded through the silence. Every single one of the soldiers was shooting down into the hole at a target I couldn't see, empty shells expelling into the snow.

"Cease fire!"

The gunfire stopped and I peeked around the tree once more. An officer strode to the lip of the massive hole and peered down. He struck a flare and sent it spinning down into the throat of the pit. Whatever he saw seemed to satisfy him because he stepped back and thumbed the radio on his shoulder.

"This is Riggs–Hole 4 has been suppressed. What's the status of the other three?"

I blinked where I stood. Hole 4? There were *four* of these back here? How? What were they and where had they come from?

A voice on the radio squawked back. "Hole 1 and 2 have no sightings yet. About to commence extermination on Hole 3."

The officer looked up at the men around the hole. "Keep your weapons ready. If you see anything moving down there, shoot it, don't wait for my signal."

The soldiers didn't move, statue-like, their shadows long from the light above. They looked ready to kill the second something, anything so much as twitched.

"Movement!" One of the men suddenly yelled. Immediately, the gunfire started again as more men sighted something happening in the hole. I covered my ears, but continued to watch from my spot. The soldiers were clearly aiming at something specific, the muzzles of their guns making micro adjustments with each burst of fire.

"Flares! FLARES!" someone screamed. A second later three flares went down into the hole, washing the clearing in a haunting red light. The men continued to shoot down into the darkness, fresh clips replacing the spent ones. Whatever was down there was not going down easy.

The officer in charge jerked a desperate finger toward three men, his voice a hoarse yell. "Cease fire and get the M9s! NOW!"

The three men immediately shouldered their guns and ran to the Hummers. A second later, they were back, taking a three-point triangular position around the hole.

"Torch them!" the office yelled.

Three flamethrowers heated the air as great gouts of fire were shot into the hole. The men with the guns never stopped shooting as the flames filled the darkness, joining the onslaught.

It was then that I heard something that chilled me to the core.

I heard screaming. Dozens and dozens of people screaming from the hole.

Get out of here, you need to get out of here right NOW!

This time, I listened. But before I could leave, I heard the officer yelling into his radio again, his voice on the brink of panic.

"Hole 4 is compromised, requesting immediate air support at the marked location! All troops evacuate! BOMB THE TARGET AREAS!"

With gunfire and anguished howls filling the night sky, I turned and fled. I ran as fast as I could back toward my house, pushing and stumbling through the woods. My chest felt hot and my head thundered. It felt like I was fleeing a warzone, the echo of automatic weapons and human pain pushing me faster and faster through the woods.

Far off to my left, I heard more gunfire erupt in the night, a peppering of desperate echoes that marked the location of another hole.

I knew I was way in over my head and as I ran. I wished fervently that I had listened to reason earlier and had just gone to see my daughter. I knew that if I was caught now, if I stumbled across more soldiers, that I might be shot on sight. They didn't know who I was, what I was doing here, but from the screams in the pits, I knew they were slaughtering *people*.

Gasping for air, legs burning, I breached the treeline and stumbled into the field that backed my house. Huffing, I jogged through the snow, ignoring the fire in my calves. At my back, I heard more gunfire, now coming from all directions. And screaming. Painful, agonized screaming.

I reached my house right before I collapsed, thumping into the back door and yanking it open. I went sprawling across the floor in an exhausted heap, gasping for air. The room spun and I felt as if I might pass out. Blindly, I kicked the door shut, muting the sound of gunfire outside. I lay in the darkness for a few minutes, mind reeling. It was nearly impossible to process what I had just seen, what I had witnessed happening right in my own backyard.

I pulled myself to my feet, noting how cold the house felt now that the wood stove was out. I needed to get out of here, the desire for answers fading like the warmth. This wasn't about knowing what was happening, it was about getting out before something worse happened. I needed to get back to my truck and high tail it south as fast as I could. The answers I needed would come later.

Suddenly, I heard the roar of a plane overhead. I stood paralyzed by the front door as it passed over the house, shaking the windows. It sounded huge and angry, like a dragon hunting for prey.

A few heartbeats later, the bombs came. The sound of them was enormous and I put a hand to the wall to steady myself, the ground shaking as the payload was dispensed into the woods. The night glowed as huge columns of fire shot up into the sky, the sound of rolling thunder booming and echoing as each bomb found its target.

And as soon as it started, it was over. A decisive, focused strike that took only seconds once the targets had been identified.

Had they known this was a possibility? I thought as the snarl of the plane began to fade once again. *Is that why they dropped the red mist? Were they painting their targets?*

I realized I didn't care about the answers anymore. I raced into the bedroom and grabbed a few of my things, my chest tight with nerves. When I felt ready, I went to leave, but before I could, my backdoor crashed open.

I spun, terrified, stomach lurching, and found myself staring face to face with a naked man covered in dirt. He was shivering violently, his eyes huge, wild, and scared. His dark hair covered even darker eyes and his normally brown skin looked like it was turning blue in the cold.

"Who are you?!" I yelled, shock hitting me full in the face. I didn't know what else to ask.

He advanced on me, falling to his knees and began to cry, begging me for something in a language I didn't understand. I backed up as he crawled over to me, his nudity and desperation shaking all reason from my mind.

"Whoa, whoa, stop!" I said, backing up. "Stop, please!"

He continued to babble in his own language, his knees scraping across the hardwood floor. He held his hands out to me, tears carving through the grime on his face.

"I don't understand you, I'm sorry," I said as my back hit the wall. "But I'm not going to hurt you, I promise. Where did you come from? Who are you?"

He halted his advance on me, teeth chattering, and closed his mouth. He looked up at me with watery eyes and spread his hands wider. In that moment, he looked heart wrenchingly pathetic and I felt some of the fear leave me.

He opened his mouth and uttered a single word in broken English.

"Please."

I took a step toward him, cautiously. "Can you understand me? Do you speak any English?"

He just stared at me, shivering, eyes lost to shock.

"Ok, ok, that's alright," I said. I grabbed a blanket that was draped over the couch and tossed it to him. "Put that on, I don't want you freezing to death in my house."

He wrapped it around his shoulders and then sat back, staring off at nothing. He seemed lost, his mind hardly there.

I pointed to the woods out back. "Did...did you come from the woods?"

He didn't move. Didn't even look at me.

"Did you come out of...of one of those holes?"

He muttered something, his voice shaking, but I couldn't understand any of it.

I pulled my hat off and handed it to him. "Here, take this. Put it on. You look like you're about to die."

He took the hat, slowly, and pulled it over his dark head. He was crying quietly now, still muttering in his own language.

"Fuck me, what the hell am I supposed to do here?" I whispered to myself. After a moment, I knelt down in front of the filthy man and looked him in the eye.

"I'm not going to hurt you," I said gently. "I know you have no idea what I'm saying, but you're safe here. Can you tell me where you came from? Are there soldiers chasing you?"

He can't understand you, stupid.

I looked out the back window and saw the woods on fire, great columns of smoke rising from the bombed out trees. I half expected to see a platoon of soldiers sprinting across the field toward the house, guns raised.

"Can you stand?" I asked, touching his shoulder. I pointed toward the door. "We need to go. I can drive you wherever you want, but we need to go."

The man looked at the door and then shook his head, words tumbling from his lips. He looked wildly around the house, still talking. I shushed him gently and gripped his arms gently.

"We have to go." I pointed to the door again and then at myself. "Me, I will take you somewhere safe, but I'm worried about the soldiers coming back. I don't think either of us are supposed to be here right now."

What if he's infected with something? I thought suddenly. *What if they were stopping some kind of disease from spreading?*

I looked at the man again. *By murdering them?*

It didn't make sense. The holes, the slaughter, the bombing. I felt as if my skull would split in two. What were the holes? Why were there people in them?

Suddenly the man stood up, the blanket falling from his shoulders.

"Hey, easy pal," I said, standing with him.

He went to the book shelf by the woodstove and pulled something off of it. He desperately flipped through the pages, as if searching for something.

"What are you doing?" I asked, coming to his side. I looked at the book he had pulled off the shelf.

It was my wife's old Bible.

He turned to me then and pointed to a page, to a single word. His eyes burned with clarity.

I looked down at the word.

H*ell*.

"I don't understand," I said, "What does this mean to you?"

He jabbed the word over and over again and then pointed to the smoking woods.

"It was hell back there, I know," I said.

He shook his head and then pointed back to the word. Hell. He took the Bible in one hand and began to motion with his hands. He stuck his pointer and middle fingers up and wiggled them like a little person. Slowly, he began to pull his hand up, wiggling his two fingers.

"Wait a second," I said, disbelief washing over me. "Hold on now..."

The man pointed to Hell again and then wiggled his fingers, like he was trying to convey an action.

I stared at him, our eyes locking, and I saw the madness and fear that filled him.

"Are you saying," I said, "that you...climbed out of Hell? That the holes are..." I shook my head, unable to believe him. Whatever trauma this man had been through had left him insane. He had to be.

The man pointed to the word again and I nodded.

"Hell," I whispered.

He nodded and then pointed to the woods.

"Jesus," I whispered. "How can I believe that?"

I stooped down and picked up the blanket, covering him with it once again. I realized that it didn't matter if I believed his story or if I understood exactly what he was trying to communicate. Our current situation was the same it had been moments ago.

"Ok," I said reassuringly, "Ok, hell, yes, I understand. Hell."

He nodded vigorously and began to cry again, tears running down his face. I touched his arm gently, guiding him to the door.

"You're safe now. Safe. Come with me. We need to leave. I'll make sure no one finds you, ok? No one deserves to be gunned down and burned. I don't care where you're from."

The man let me guide him outside and together we headed toward my truck, away from the blaze and violence at our backs.

It's been two weeks since that night. I took the man to a hotel and we've been there ever since. I've been staying with him. He doesn't talk much and even when he does, I can't understand him. His mind isn't right. I can see the trauma in his eyes every time he looks at me. I feel responsible for him. In his current state, he seems so helpless. So lost. So I'm going to stay here with him until he recovers some and then we can figure out the rest later.

I don't believe his story, but that look in his eyes...I find myself starting to wonder. What were those holes? Where did they lead? Who were the people trying to escape them?

I don't know the answer and I don't know if I ever will. But I discovered something about the man that I couldn't explain and it frightens me.

He doesn't eat. And he doesn't sleep. For two weeks now, he hasn't done either and he seems to suffer no effect from the absence. He hasn't gotten any thinner and displays no signs of hunger. When I go to sleep at night, he remains in a chair by the window, looking out. When I wake, he hasn't moved, his eyes still darting across the parking lot.

I know it sounds crazy...but it's almost like he's dead.

PUMPJACK

Log 1

It's been three days since everything changed. The shock hasn't worn off, but enough time has passed that I can document some of this. Thankfully I still have my pack and my journal, where I have filled pages and pages of my hiking expeditions. None like this though.

I was in northern Maine, trekking through the part of the Appalachian Trail known as the 100 Mile Wilderness. It's the most remote part of the A.T. and I hadn't seen anyone for days. I had planned on doing the hike in four days, but packed enough food and water for six. I was on my second day of the hike when I stumbled across something I never expected to see during my trek. It was an oil deposit. Off to the right of the trail, I happened to see the sun hit the massive pool, the light reflecting eerily off the surface. Naturally, I investigated. The pool was in a clearing about fifty feet in diameter. Surrounded by towering conifers, the oil looked like an invasion or corruption of beauty.

I knelt by the edge of the pool, perplexed and curious. Foolish. I know that now. I dipped the tip of my hiking pole into the oil, half convinced it would turn out to be a stagnating mud pit or pond.

As soon as my pole touched the surface, I was sucked in. Sucked *down* into the oil. It was as if some invisible hand reached up and grabbed me, jerking me into the pool. I thought my life was over. I just kept going down, the air held captive in my lungs. I thought I would drown.

But instead, I ended up here. Where I am now, writing this.

How do I even begin to explain what I've seen or what I'm looking at now, as I write this?

I'm not alone either. Two other men and a woman are here with me. I find some comfort in their presence, despite their various mental states. We're all afraid. Unsure. Though harm hasn't come to us yet, I fear the days ahead.

Log 2

After I was pulled into the oil, I awoke (though I don't think I had lost consciousness) in a ruined city. I don't know which. But it was rotting, corroding. The street signs were in a language I didn't recognize. I saw signs of past life though. Rusting cars. Storefronts. A single shoe lying in the street. Something terrible had happened here, a long, long time ago. The buildings surrounding me were in a state of ruin, as if a bomb had detonated a decade ago and left only the ghosts of commerce in its wake.

The two men and the woman I mentioned in my last log were there with me when I awoke. Naturally, we panicked. Our entire world had just been stripped from us and in a moment, we were here in an unknown city that appeared as if it had been through a war many years past.

It took us a while to collect ourselves. I'll spare you the frantic, useless questions we asked one another. None of us had answers. What we discovered though, was something in common. The oil. Each one of them had been exposed to some misplaced pool of it. The woman, Kay, had gone down into her basement to change the laundry only to find half her floor had turned into a swamp. Daniel, a young man of about twenty-five with ridiculous blue hair, had been in a bar when he discovered one of the toilets was bubbling over with the stuff. It overflowed and touched him. Curtis, a man my age of about fifty, had been splitting wood at his home in Utah. As his axe split the last log, an eruption of oil burst from it, coating him. Transporting him. *Moving* him.

Once we discovered this odd, common thread, we revealed what date it had been on the day we each discovered the oil. To our shock, they were wildly different. The gap between the four of us was extensive. Kay, Curtis, me, and Daniel. That was the order of discovery. An entire month divided the time Kay discovered her flooded basement and when Daniel went into the bar bathroom, with Curtis and myself between those dates. But for all of us, only a moment had passed. We were in one place in one instant, and then the next we were here. How was that possible? Were we all held in some kind of timeless limbo until Daniel entered the bathroom? Was there something special about the four of us? We discussed this for hours in a ruined building, huddling together, trying to piece this puzzle together. Kay was a public defender, Curtis owned a tractor parts company. Daniel worked at a gas station. I ran an AR department for a moving company. Nothing about us stood out. Despite the discovery of the oil, we really didn't have much in common.

As we discussed our history in frightful whispers, I found myself beginning to withdraw from the conversation. Whatever had happened to us, wherever we were, we weren't going to talk our way into the truth.

Night came. I shared some food and water from my pack with the group. I didn't even think about rationing at the time. After we ate, we decided to sleep and then set out in the morning to see if we could find answers. Or anyone else besides us.

As I slumped over and closed my eyes, we heard them for the first time.

The pumpjacks.

Log 3

We left the city in the morning. All of us had slept poorly, due to the noise. That distant, haunting sound that echoed through the night. None of us knew what it was at the time. Not until we left the city and saw them.

The pumpjacks. We had walked for a couple hours through the empty streets, rather aimlessly, until we found ourselves free of the towering iron ruins. Stretching before us was a great plain, an expanse of dirt and dead trees that rolled all the way to the horizon. We all stood there for a while in silence, the city ending abruptly at our backs.

Littered across the expansive stretch of land before us were hundreds of pumpjacks. And they were huge, their great, rusting steel frames towering dozens of feet into the air. I had seen pictures of them before and knew what their function was. To pump oil to the surface when there wasn't enough natural pressure. When activated, they would bob on their axis, the craned heads lifting and rising as the machinery worked.

None of us knew what to do. There appeared to be nothing out there except the pumps. Daniel wanted to turn around, his blue hair soaked in sweat. Kay agreed. Curtis and I weren't so sure. We argued. Yelled a little. Eventually, we decided to stay put, right on the edge of the city to see if the night brought any signs of life. Light, maybe. A campfire. Something that would give us hope. There was a little gas station with blown out windows facing the great plain and the jacks. We holed up there, hunting for food and water. We found nothing so I shared more of my own from my pack. It was then that I began to worry about sustainability.

And so I sit here, having caught you up on the events so far. I don't know what tomorrow will bring, but I will continue to journal. It gives me comfort.

Log 4

It's night now. As soon as the sun set, the pumpjacks started. We can't see them, there's no moon or stars lighting the sky, but we can hear them. At first it was only one or two, but after a few minutes, they all started. It sounds horrific. Like the night is moaning at us in huge, rusty gasps. Daniel is terrified. He started rambling and screaming at us about an hour ago. Kay talked some sense into him. I tried not to pay much attention to his panic attack. Didn't want to feed into it. We are all scared. Those damn pumps surround the million questions we have with an audible dread. Nothing about this place is normal.

For the love of God, where are we?

Log 5

Dawn didn't bring us any comfort. Kay and Curtis were up all night. Daniel slept, though he muttered a lot in his sleep. We didn't see any lights. No campfires. No flashlights. I think we are all beginning to understand just how alone we are. And how alien this place is. We didn't notice the differences at first, when we were in the city. Now that our view is no longer obstructed and our attention isn't on the pumpjacks (which mercifully quieted after dawn), we saw something that chilled us. Kay noticed it first. She was looking up into the sky, the sun a hazy blur cresting the horizon.

Almost completely hidden behind a wall of orange haze, was a sight I will never forget. It was a planet. A planet that looked horrifyingly like Earth. We could only see a sliver of it, but there was no denying the similarities.

We looked at one another. Daniel was the only one who spoke. Then he started going hysterical. Curtis grabbed him and dragged him back into the ruined gas station that had become our shelter.

I stayed outside with Kay, staring up at the mirrored Earth. I could hear Curtis yelling at Daniel and then trying to calm him down. Kay and I said nothing, though I saw dread filling her eyes.

I don't know where this is. What horrible land we've been pulled into. We can only wait and hope we discover the answers.

Log 6

It's night. We're huddled together along the back wall of the gas station by the empty coolers. *Something* is outside. We can hear it…them…stalking the parameter of our shelter. The pumpjacks are back on, booming and moaning. They're making it hard to track the path of whatever is out there. It sounds like there's dozens of them. Walking, scurrying. I keep thinking I see shadows pass by the broken windows. Whatever they are, they're not human and they know we're in here.

Log 7

We made it through the night. Whatever was outside left us alone. For now. We ate the last of the food from my pack this morning. I talked to Kay and the two of us are going to go scavenge for supplies in the city today. Curtis agreed to stay with Daniel who's too afraid to step foot outside.

The haze is bad today. The planet above us is completely washed out by it. I can barely see the first of the pumpjacks out there in the wilderness. Maybe it's for the best. It'll hide Kay and I on our expedition from whatever stalked us last night.

I noticed something else this morning as I investigated the area around the gas station, where we heard the mysterious predators. Oil. Little puddles of oil.

Log 8

Kay and I spent the day in the city. We didn't speak much, afraid our voices would attract something we'd rather not confront. I spent a lot of time today in my head, thinking. It's been days since we all arrived here and we've barely uncovered any hint of what this place might be. That planet in the sky, the one that looks shockingly like Earth...I can't get the image out of my head. It sounds insane, but I'm starting to believe that wherever we are, it's not home. Not how we know it. The city, the destruction, the pumpjacks, the complete isolation...everything is starting to point to a revelation that I'd rather not confront. But we're all thinking it and I'm starting to lose faith that this situation we find ourselves in will ever revert. Wherever this is, whatever mirror world or timeline or crazy science fiction we've been exposed to, I think this place, this world, will be our grave.

Kay and I did find some supplies today, though. Shockingly. A couple bottles of water and some packaged goods. We haven't eaten any of it yet, it may have turned years ago, but I'm going to try to stay as optimistic as I can. Once that's gone, there will be nothing left.

When we returned to the gas station, right around dusk, Curtis met us outside. Daniel was sleeping by the register. I could tell something was wrong because Curtis looked ghostly. He spoke to us in a low voice. He told us that he had left Daniel at some point during the day and gone out into the wasteland, toward the pumpjacks. He confessed he had become stir crazy and Daniel was driving him mad. And so he had gone to investigate the nearest pumpjack. The towering construct revealed no secrets, but that wasn't the point of Curtis's tale. He said when he reached the jack, he saw something on the horizon, through the haze, below the smudge of orange sun.

He said he saw moons. Or he thought they were moons. He described them as orbs of white, lining the distant sky. They were faint, but unmistakable. He counted nine of them. He leaned in close then, his breath hot and sour. He told Kay and I that they had been moving.

Log 9

We're in trouble. Something is co

Log 10

Daniel is weeping by the broken coolers. It's dawn now and I didn't expect to make it through the night. I cannot even begin to describe the dread and shock I feel right now. The night was a horror unto itself. I am convinced now that we will all die here.

Kay and Curtis are dead.

I'm going to try to transcribe exactly what happened. If my hands stop shaking. I feel so dizzy. Emptied. This may be the last day I'm alive.

Last night, at full dark, the pumpjacks started once again. Thundering their iron hammers like a war drum. We were all inside the gas station, eating. Waiting. All too aware that whatever came the night before might show up again. And goddamn it, they did. They did. But not at first. First was the light.

About two hours after nightfall, Curtis noticed that the sky outside was brightening. We all went to the door and looked out into the wasteland. Cutting through the curtain of black, were nine huge white orbs, hundreds of feet in diameter, with ribbons of pure light emanating from their mass like glowing fabric.

The orbs of light hovered over nine separate, towering creatures. They were colossal in size, dwarfing the landscape before them. From what we could see, they looked to be composed completely of metal. They looked like stick men, their limbs and bodies nothing more than bundles of steel, seemingly held together by cords of thick, fiber cable. Their heads, featureless, bloomed upward and appeared to be mammoth funnels, widening from the neck up. Each creature or being held what had to be thousands of gallons of slopping oil inside the funnels, rivulets dripping down the length of their bodies, illuminated by a single, enormous orb of white light that floated just above the surface of the oil.

Daniel sank to the ground, whimpering as we watched these titanous creatures lumber toward us in great, booming strides. They passed through the miles of dusty land in a matter of minutes, their size making short work of the distance. The creaking pumpjacks beneath them seemed more like a chorus now, announcing a doom that was so otherworldly we couldn't comprehend just what we were seeing.

The nine moon shaped orbs cast light across our faces and I saw absolute terror in my companion's faces. I felt my bladder go at some point, my body in disbelief. The hulking monsters eventually crossed the distance to us and stopped, about three hundred feet from the gas station. Their size made it feel as if they were right on top of us, my head craning, eyes bulging as I took in their immense height. The clank of their metal bodies echoed down to us, nine in total. I could hear oil from their great funneled heads dripping down their bodies to hit the dry land like black rain.

At their feet, something scurried toward us, dozens of things. It was hard to tell at first what we were looking at, the shadows from the hovering moon creatures casting slices of moving darkness. As they got closer, the four of us took a step back, then scrambled, and fled back into the gas station.

The skittering things crawled toward us on all fours. They looked like piles of junk with sharp metal poking in all directions, their legs their only discernible appendages. They rose about three feet from the ground, each one dragging some kind of black hose behind them like a tail.

The four of us crashed into the far corner of the gas station, by the coolers, cries of terror following us. The junkyard creatures swarmed us almost instantly, clattering and clanking, crowding us as they pressed closer.

Curtis kicked one. Kay booted another. That was all it took. Immediately, the creatures jabbed at them with their jutting metal legs, stabbing Curtis in the thigh, piercing it. Kay took a piece of rebar in the side. Blood poured from the punctures and we all screamed, trying to hold onto one another as Curtis and Kay were dragged back, away from us, outside. The swarm of machines followed, their prey seemingly hooked. Daniel and I watched in utter shock, trails of wet blood staining the floor. Curtis battered at the moving junk pile that had stabbed him, but to no avail. Kay was panting, gasping, her wound much more severe.

I inched forward, Daniel at my back, watching as the machines pulled their captives back under the light of the moon gods. I saw that there were thousands of small creatures now, an ocean of them. They circled Curtis and Kay, moving in excited, erratic patterns. The metal titans remained immoble, as if content to just watch the madness below. Great slops of oil continued to fall from their funnel-heads, splattering the smaller creatures below. Each time this happened, the creatures chittered, the sound like metal pincers clicking together at a high velocity. The longer I watched, the more I realized that the oil was sending them into a frenzy.

Daniel tried to pull me back inside, his face wet, but I shook him off. My heart galloped and I couldn't take my eyes away from the chaos. Curtis was still screaming. They had him on his back, pinned in place by a lance of metal through his thigh.

Eight or nine of the machines swarmed him and I saw their rubber hose tails begin to rise and flicker. Then, all at once, they jammed them into Curtis's mouth. Only three or four could fit and I saw his eyes bulge as they were forced down his throat. He gagged, heaved, then threw up wetly, all the while making horrible *ugh huuughh!* sounds.

Then the creatures began to pump oil into Curtis's stomach, down through the hoses, spilling, spraying as others fought for a chance to participate. I stepped back now, one hand covering my mouth. Curtis gagged and vomited more, his body rejecting the poison. But the creatures continued and I saw Curtis begin to swell, his skin darkening. I don't know how long it took for him to drown, but by the time he stopped thrashing, his bloated body was almost unrecognizable. The hoses were removed and the creatures skittered back, creating a space around the now dead man.

They appeared confused, poking and prodding the corpse when it didn't move. The one that had speared Curtis in his thigh paused and tapped him on the chest.

Kay was screaming at them, her face ghostly white from the blood loss. In an instant, all the creatures seemed to forget about Curtis and turned their attention to Kay.

She was pinned to the ground, as Curtis had been, the horde clanking excitedly again. But instead of filling her with oil, they tried something different, as if straining to understand who or what we were.

They began to cut her. Little cuts at first, lines of blood two or three inches deep. Their sharp, jutting limbs traveled through her flesh like a knife through warmed dough. After a couple awful moments of this, watching as her blood dripped down her lacerated body, they became more aggressive.

They began to dissect her. First a finger, then a foot, then long incisions that exposed bone and organs. Kay screamed like I've never heard someone scream. She sounded like an animal. Once the creatures opened her belly and saw her guts, they began to shred those too, stabbing and slicing, ripping and pulling. Mercifully, Kay died shortly after that, but the creatures didn't stop until she was an unrecognizable pile of bleeding gore. She had gone from human to a torn deposit of uncooked hamburger meat.

It was my turn to vomit then, eyes bloodshot. I wiped my mouth and then finally retreated into the back of the gas station to wait my turn. I knew it would come.

But it didn't.

Shortly after they were done with Kay, the creatures and the tower-sized entities left, retreating back into the horizon through the plains of moaning pumpjacks.

Log 11

I can't see them when the sun is out. Those giant creatures. But I know they're out there, hidden in the haze, just behind the horizon. They'll be back. I am sure of it. They've poked at us and they'll return with new curiosities.

I didn't sleep. Daniel is lying next to me as I write. His eyes are open, but he seems catatonic. His mind has retreated, fled, left him. I don't know how to help him. I don't know how to help us. I keep replaying what happened last night, over and over. The way Kay died. The way they pumped Curtis full of oil. I'm sitting away from the gas station's broken windows so I don't have to look at their ruined bodies. I can smell them though, starting to cook under the hot sun. The smell is indescribable.

I cried some earlier. Haven't done that in years.

Maybe later I'll go out, go back into the city. Find someplace quiet to die. Away from the moon head titans and their slopping, dripping funnels full of oil. And the little ones with their sharp, clacking limbs.

I thi

Log 12

Daniel is gone. He just popped up screaming, eyes huge, right in the middle of my last log. Scared the hell out of me. He crashed into the empty racks next to us, stumbled again, then bolted out into the wasteland. I called to him, screamed his name. No use. I watched the dust trail he kicked up and the spot of blue hair slowly vanish into the haze, disappearing among the hundreds of quiet pumpjacks. As I was about to turn back, I heard him begin to scream again. His voice was so thin. It didn't sound like it had when he woke up. Now, he sounded like he was in agony.

Something found him out there.

Log 13

It's dusk. The sun is setting, the haze is clearing. Those goddamn pumpjacks are going to come alive again soon. I can see a faint white glow on the horizon as the sky darkens. I wonder if they'll come back tonight. I don't want to stick around and find out. Which leads me to what I discovered just a little while ago.

After Daniel left, I couldn't sit still. I began to wander, feeling hopelessly alone. And as I wandered, I found something. Something I think those lumbering monsters left behind.

It was a pool of oil, wide and dark, the surface a murky, rotting rainbow that caught the light and belched it back out. It was about half a mile from the gas station. I surmised that it had spilled from the heads of those creatures. I stood at the edge of it, eyes going from the surface of the pool up toward the faintly visible mirror Earth that hung in the sky.

Where the hell am I?

It was a thought that beat against my skull like a ball point hammer. Was the distant planet really Earth? Was this pool, COULD this pool be a way back? Was it madness to think such things? No. Everything was madness here.

I went back to the gas station, indecision pulling me in two separate directions. There was a nagging pull to the pool, as if I knew it would take me somewhere. I can't explain it. Even now I feel myself drawn to it. My gut assures me that it is a door. I think of the planet that looks so much like Earth hovering just above it. Were the creatures giving me a way out? Had they played with us enough and decided to open a portal back to where we had come from?

I'm going back to the pool. It's almost full dark now and I can see the glowing moon heads of the nine titans out there in the wasteland. They're so distant though that their light doesn't reach me. Are they watching me? Do they want me to do this?

Ah. The pumpjacks have begun. I cannot stand to listen to this anymore. I'm going.

Log 14

I'm here. I'm at the oil pool. I'm going in.

Lg 01

S.U.N.

L8

S.U.N.

00000.0

S.U.N.

L0g 339219

Hpw long 832 day

Lo 372719

ROT .M.E.

Log X

Don't know long. Been palace. Trying hard remember how I write. Blood again. Teeth gag. Cities in sky raping me.

citieies in sky raping me

Log X2

Writing keep me sane. I've learned how again. Will run out pages. Until then I write. Keeping my mind my own. So hot. Bright. Counting days. Stopped after years. Will not let me die. Fingers falling off again. Use. Teeth. Write. I AM ME. Can heare the WILLYS again. Coming.

Cut. Rot. Put me back together.

Am. not. Home.

GENERATIONAL RAGE

The dim lights of the bar bore into my skull like fluorescent drills. I squeezed my eyes shut, counted to three, and then drained the rest of my lukewarm beer. My head swam as I ordered another, bourbon this time. The dull chatter of patrons droned around me, a scattering of locals and regulars. I looked over my shoulder at the door to the street outside. Olivia was late. I turned back to the bar as my bourbon was set down in front of me. I sipped it, tongue burning.

I felt awful. Mentally, physically, emotionally drained, all my energy sucked down the toilet. I ran a hand over my face, feeling my fingers drag lines through sweat and grease. I needed a shower. My clothes stank and I could smell my armpits.

As I pondered these things, a woman of about thirty slid onto the stool next to me. She had short blond hair, puppy brown eyes, and her lips glistened with freshly applied gloss.

"Hey Olivia," I muttered, turning back to my drink. "Didn't even see you come in."

Her hand found my back. "How're you holding up?"

I grunted in reply and took another sip.

Olivia put her purse down on the bar and ordered a glass of wine before her hand found my back again.

"Bad day today, huh?"

I said nothing, the dark bags beneath my eyes saying more than I could ever vocalize.

Olivia shook her head. "Stupid question, I'm sorry. I never know what to say when this day comes back around."

"How about, 'sorry your brother killed himself'?"

Olivia compressed her lips, her shoulders slumping. "Two years ago now, yeah?"

I nodded, memories of my younger brother flooding back. He had been the best kid you could ever hope to know. Kind, generous, would give you the shirt off his back. Everyone who knew him, loved him. Olivia had grown up with us, on the same street, and she knew this as well as anyone.

"Dan was the best," Olivia said. "He wouldn't want today to be such a sad occasion."

"That's what you said last year."

"Well, I still think it's true."

I glanced at her. "He put a bullet through his skull. It wasn't a happy ending for him."

Olivia winced. I knew I was being too hard on her, but my chest was killing me. Each memory of my brother opening it up further.

I took another sip of bourbon, conjuring Dan's face. Buzzed brown hair, blue eyes, skinny, short, but he had a hell of a smile. One of those smiles that could punch the shit right out of a bad day. He had been twenty-five when he ended his own life. It had come as a shock to most. Not me, though. I knew. I knew what we had been through. I knew what he carried with him.

Olivia rubbed my back again. "Tell me something about him."

"What do you mean?"

"Tell me something about Dan you haven't shared with me before."

I paused. I appreciated what she was doing and I forced my aimless anger and bitterness away for a moment as I reflected. Dan. Danny. Growing up, we were inseparable. We spent as much time as we could outside the house, in the woods, creating our own little worlds. We fought occasionally, but it was minor squabbles. We knew we needed each other. Neither of us let it get out of control. We had always been kind to one another. He had been so damn innocent. So undeserving of everything we went through.

"I remember once," I started in a low voice, clearing my throat. "I remember the first time we watched an R rated movie together."

"Oh man," Olivia smiled.

I nodded, letting the memory fill me. "Dad was out of town. Mom was passed out in the bedroom, but it was still early. We knew Mom wouldn't wake up until morning and so we went into her purse and took her credit card. We ordered pizza and when it came, we parked ourselves in front of the TV. Blade was on. We had both been dying to see it."

"How old were you?" Olivia asked as her wine finally came.

"I was probably thirteen. The movie ended up being a little too violent for Dan though. I could tell the blood and gore were getting to him. I asked if he wanted to watch something else, but he was too stubborn to admit defeat. That night, he slept in bed with me." I felt my eyes begin to mist. "I should have turned it off. It really freaked him out. I could have at least spared him that."

Olivia played with her wine glass. "You were there for him afterwards. You always were."

I shook my head. "I can't count how many times I failed him."

"You were both kids," Olivia said. "Hell, everyone on the street knew what was going on, but they didn't do anything about it."

"I was there, though. I watched it happen so many times."

Olivia shifted uncomfortably. This wasn't something I ever elaborated on and I knew she would be horrified if I shared even half of the truth, so I closed my mouth.

"Loved that fuckin' kid," I said, wiping my eyes. "He didn't need to go like that." I felt my hands ball into fists. "He hid it so well from everyone. Everything that cunt did to us."

"You both hid it," Olivia said quietly. "

I was silent for a while. I never mentioned it to Olivia, but on these days, this anniversary especially, I felt a longing for my father. The older I got, the more pieces of his face, his voice, his cologne, I lost. I knew one day he would just be a name. I had no pictures of him, didn't know where he was buried, nothing. It was as if he had vanished.

Because of her.

I couldn't imagine the pain, finding out your wife had been unfaithful for years. He had given everything to her. Heartbreak destroyed him. I had been a fresh fourteen when he left. My mother told me three months later that he had gotten drunk somewhere in California and had driven his car off a cliff. She said it had been intentional, but I think she said that just to hurt me and Dan. I think grief had killed him.

That's when things got really bad. Those were the years that loaded the gun Dan shot himself with.

Olivia took a gulp of wine before asking, "You haven't heard from her, have you?"

The question surprised me. "Mom?"

A cautious nod.

I paused, staring at my hands. "No. She probably drank herself to death years ago."

Olivia said nothing. I glanced at her and I could tell she regretted asking. I felt bad for her.

"You know," I said, "Dan had a huge crush on you when we were kids."

Olivia smiled. "I know."

"Really?"

"Of course. He was young, though. I was into older boys. He was so damn sweet though. Did I ever tell you he wrote me a letter and put it in my mailbox? He was probably only like seven when he did this."

"What? I didn't know that."

Olivia chuckled. "He didn't sign his name, but I knew it was him. Sure as hell wasn't you." She elbowed me playfully.

"What'd the letter say?"

Olivia sighed. "It was the cutest thing. All it said was 'you are very pretty. If you want to borrow my toys, that would be ok.'"

I smiled. "The balls on that guy."

"My parents thought it was adorable," Olivia went on. "I never told him I got the letter though." She paused. "I should have thanked him."

"Did you talk to him much before he left us?" I asked, knowing the answer already, knowing we had talked about Dan a ton in the two years since his departure. It felt good though, to relieve our memories of him.

"Of course I did," Olivia said. "I know I was still living in Texas when it happened, but we still texted, checked in with each other. Dan wasn't the type of guy to let friendship die out."

"Did he ever confess his love for you?" I asked, half joking.

Olivia melted a little and finished her wine before answering. "No." A long pause then, her eyes far away. "No he didn't. I don't think he could. He was too sad. I mean, deep down. I don't think he thought he was deserving. You would never know it if you just met him, but I always knew he was hurting. Little comments he would make over text, things like that. He hid it so well though. Outwardly, he was always so cheerful. He'd always tried to make me laugh. To make me feel validated. He watched out for me, in his own way."

Olivia's eyes were turning red and I stared down at the bar, giving her space. I knew exactly what she was talking about. It came out in little ways, but I knew Dan didn't think much of himself. Didn't think he was ever good enough. Didn't think he added much value to the world, despite being such a ray of sun to everyone who got close to him.

The world was worse for losing him. He was a better person than I'd ever be. While I had grown angry and hateful, he had loved. But inside, we were both hollowed out and it was that emptiness that had killed him.

"I'm going home," I said, realizing that my eyes were wet.

Olivia looked at me, her face sympathetic. "Already? You sure?"

I nodded, dragging an arm across my eyes. "Yeah. Thanks for coming, though. Dan and I love you, Olivia. You've always been there for us."

Olivia slid off her stool and gave me a hug, standing on her toes. "We'll talk soon, ok? You ok to get home?"

I nodded and kissed her on the cheek. "Yeah, I'll be ok. You going to stay?"

"For a bit, yeah."

"Ok. Talk soon."

"Bye."

I stopped at the liquid store on the way home and picked up a case of beer. I knew I'd need it tonight. When I was on the road again, I passed a pet store. On a whim, I turned into the parking lot and went inside. After browsing, I left with a box of mice.

I popped a beer when I returned to the highway, drinking half as I headed back to my house. I slowly left the city behind as the landscape turned to rolling hills and woodland, the darkness of night growing.

I pulled into my driveway ten minutes later, eyeing the dark single story ranch I had purchased three years ago. I had no neighbors and no one to bother me. Isolation suited me. I opened my door and stepped out of the car, hauling the case of beer and box of mice behind me.

I paused as I strode across the uncut lawn, taking a moment to breathe in the gentle air. I thought of Dan. I thought of his smile. If he were still alive, I wondered what he'd be doing tonight.

I set my jaw and walked to the front door, unlocked it, and stepped inside.

"Mom, I'm home!" I bellowed into the darkness, locking the deadbolt at my back.

I walked into the kitchen, keeping the lights off, and set the beer and mice down on the counter. I could hear the little bastards squeaking and scurrying inside their cardboard prison.

Half empty beer in hand, I walked into the bathroom. I turned on the light.

Mom was right where I left her, handcuffed to the shower curtain rod, her naked body sagging. In the light, I saw that she hadn't managed to spit her gag out. Her red rimmed eyes were closed and I guessed she had passed out from exhaustion at some point. I didn't blame her.

The hell I had put her through over the past two years would have killed most. I surveyed her in the cold white light, eyes trailing up her battered body. How many times had I beaten, cut, and burned her flesh? How many times had I carefully nursed her back to health?

"You're not dead, are you?" I asked, voice echoing off the bathroom tile. I stepped toward her and splashed beer into her face.

"Wake up, bitch."

Groggily, my mother's eyes fluttered open. When she saw me, her eyes began to tear. She knew what today was. Knew it'd be worse tonight. Last year, on Dan's anniversary, I had broken her elbow backward and left her hanging by her ruined arm for hours while I poured scalding hot chicken broth over her ass and thighs. For the grand finale, I had flogged her with a belt, the buckle tearing at her breasts, pussy, finally shredding one of her ears. I looked at the lump of ruined scar tissue that clung to her head now, reminding myself of all the times she had beaten Dan and I. How many times her ringed knuckles found our soft flesh. How many times those filthy hands groped us in the night.

How many times had she crept into our beds after Dad left and violated us? I couldn't count that high. Dan caught the worst of it.

She was always worse after a night of abuse. She'd blame us for what she did. The accusations that we raped her, sobbing, manic, insane, and then the physical punishment she doled out for her own actions. It was a cycle we had endured for years. The scars she left on my back and legs were nothing compared to what Dan hid under his clothes. At the worst of it, she had squeezed one of Dan's testicles until it burst, resulting in an extended hospital stay that we were eventually punished for because she couldn't afford it.

I truly believed my mother was the devil. When I found her two years ago, it had been easy. She lived in a shit apartment in the city projects, had no friends, no one who checked up on her. She was alone and helpless. It had taken one swing of the bat to get her on the floor, into my trunk, and over to my house.

She had been my guest ever since then.

I walked to the shower knob and blasted her with cold water. My mother moaned as the cold waves poured down on her, soaking her battered body. I wanted her awake and alert. I wanted her to feel everything that was coming.

With the shower still going, I walked to the living room and retrieved Dan's picture from the mantle. I stared at it, while my mother wept in the bathroom, memories of my brother surfacing. My mother's crying reminded me of all the times she made Dan cry. Her fists plowing into his stomach, her fingers ripping at his hair, all the times she had forced him to bed in a drunken rage. She had violated us both, but it was always worse when she chose Dan. I couldn't stand it. I couldn't bear to listen to it. Mom would always lock me in the closet and force me to listen, because she knew how much it bothered me. Sometimes she was quick with him, other times, it was forever.

I remembered the aftermath. A time she had really tore into him. She was beyond drunk and when she unlocked the closet door and let me out, I had rushed to the bed where Dan lay, convinced he was dead. I heard my mother go into her bedroom and lock her door. I had been ten at the time, my father was on a business trip, and Dan looked almost infantile as I scrambled up next to him. He was crying, his nose bleeding, his body naked and aching. I held him to me, both of us sobbing.

"One day, I'll kill her," I cried softly into his hair. "I promise, Dan. I'll kill Mom."

Dan just shook his head, sniffling, chest hitching. He didn't want vengeance. He didn't want to punish her. He just wanted to be left alone.

"I won't let her do this again," I said. "I'll tell Dad this time."

"Don't," Dan whispered. "It would make Dad sad."

"She's going to kill us," I hissed, eyes red.

Dan just shrugged, pulling the covers up around his quivering body.

I held him tighter, my heart a raging coal. "I'm going to *kill* her, Dan."

Slowly, I turned back to the bathroom, eyes watering, the present moment returning. I went to turn the water off, bringing Dan's framed picture with me. I set it on the sink and turned it so Mom had to look at it. I shut the water off and grabbed her swollen face by the chin, forcing her head up.

"Everything I do to you tonight is for Dan," I said in a low voice. "Everything I've done to you over the past two years has been for him." I gripped her face tighter and removed her gag. "I loved him more than anything in the world. What you did to him, what you did to us? There isn't a flame in hell hot enough for you."

My mother looked up at me, one eye blackened and swollen from three days ago. Her cracked lips parted as she spoke.

"Please...I haven't eaten in days..."

I drove my fist into her exposed stomach, her handcuffed wrists clanging against the shower rod as she rocked backwards.

"Don't you fucking speak to me," I snarled. "Every time you make a noise tonight, I'm going to make it worse on you."

I felt heat in my chest, adrenaline coursing through me. I needed to hurt her. I needed to mangle this godless cunt. I opened the sink cupboard where I kept my tools and pulled out a coat hanger. I uncoiled it and set it down on the sink. Next, I pulled out a filet knife. I flashed it in front of my mother and she began to cry.

I had already removed most of her teeth, ripped her fingernails off countless times, broken her toes with a hammer over and over again. Each time they healed they felt the hammer again. It was a cycle I had practiced since her captivity–break, cut, rip, then wait for her to heal only to start all over again. I knew she didn't have much time left. She was dying, her body giving out after years of unspeakable abuse.

But tonight, even if it was her last one, would be special.

I raised the knife point and dug it into the side of her left breast. It was a sagging, veiny mess, the flesh soft and giving. Mom screamed as I poked and dug into her, blood running down my hand as I worked. When the hole was big enough, I made a similar hole on the other side, numb to her screams.

Satisfied, I picked up the straightened coat hanger and threaded it into the hole in her breast. From the other side, I wormed my fingers into the open wound until I felt the tip of the hanger. With a grunt, I pulled it through so that both ends stuck out on either side of her breast. Mom was sobbing, thrashing, her vocal cords so raw and shredded from years of screaming that she sounded like an animal.

"Keep that there for a minute," I said, washing my hands in the sink. As the weeks and months of torture had progressed, I found myself less and less satisfied with the pain I inflicted on her. I felt like a drug addict who needed a bigger and better fix each time I worked her over. It was getting frustrating and I knew the end of my satisfaction was near. I had realized there wasn't enough pain in the world for this woman.

But I was going to do my fucking best.

I wiped my hands on my pants and turned back to Mom. As I did so, someone knocked on my front door. My whole body turned to ice, throat tightening to a point I couldn't breathe. I waited a moment, convinced I had imagined it. A moment later, the knock came again.

My mother heard it too, her eyes going wide. She parted her torn lips, filling her lungs with air.

"HELP M-!"

I slammed my hand over her mouth, panic shooting through me like lightning. I grabbed the dirty washcloth I had gagged her with and crammed it back into her mouth. Then, I tangled my hand in her hair and slammed her head as hard as I could against the shower wall. It had the desired effect and her body slumped as she blacked out.

The knock came again, accompanied by a voice this time.

"Come on, I know you're in there! Your car is in the driveway! I'm not leaving until you open the door!"

It was Olivia.

"Oh hell on fire," I growled, heart thumping urgently. I checked myself in the mirror, ran a freshly washed hand through my hair, and then hurried out of the bathroom, shutting the door behind me. I crossed the living room and unlocked the front door, opening it a crack.

"What the hell are you doing here?" I asked. Olivia stood, swaying slightly on my front stoop, eyes red from crying.

"Hello to you too," she slurred.

"Are you drunk?" I asked.

She snorted. "Isn't that the point, today? I had a couple shots after you left the bar and then decided I wasn't going to just let you wallow alone in misery tonight." She spread her hands in mock celebration. "Surprise!" She nearly fell over.

I opened the door wider and caught her elbow before she could. " I think you had more than a couple shots."

"I had some on the way over too," Olivia confessed, pulling her hair back. "Now, can I come in? You never let me come over."

I grit my teeth, forcing panic away. If Mom woke up and let out a single scream…

"You have to leave," I said firmly.

"Oh stop it," Olivia said, placing a hand on the door.

I blocked the entranceway. "I'm serious. You shouldn't have come over. I just want to be alone tonight, ok?"

Olivia waggled a finger, eyes glassy. "Too bad. We're going to be sad together and tell each other more stories about Dan, ok?"

"Olivia," I said again. "Don't make me be an asshole here. I love you, but I'm begging you. Just go."

Olivia grew frustrated. "Dude, what is your problem? I'm wasted and you really want to put me back on the road?"

"Jesus," I said, clenching my jaw. I could feel a timer ticking down in the back of my head. I needed to get her out of here.

Suddenly, Olivia perked up, her face growing serious. "What was that?"

My heart crawled up my throat. "What was what?"

"I thought I heard something."

And then I heard it too. Mom was waking up.

"Please," I begged, gripping the door. "Just leave."

A thump from the bathroom.

"Wait a second," Olivia said slowly. "Do...do you have company already?"

Mind racing, I nodded frantically. "Yeah. I didn't want to tell you. I was uh...embarrassed."

"Who is she?" Olivia asked.

I could hear Mom's consciousness growing by the second and I knew she'd start screaming around her gag any second.

"Just some old fling," I said hurriedly. "She's no one. We hook up sometimes and I needed to feel...something else tonight. Obviously, I wasn't going to ask you."

"Gross," Olivia grunted, a small smile on her lips now. "No wonder you're acting so weird. Ok. I'm sorry to barge in on you like this. I just didn't want you to be alone."

"Thank you. I mean it."

Olivia turned to go, then stopped. "Can I uh...sleep it off in the driveway for a couple hours? I promise I won't bother you." She touched her head. "I really am wasted right now."

"Sure," I said, "Fine. Sorry to push you out like this."

She leaned forward and kissed me on the cheek. "It's ok. Love you."

I kissed her back. "Love you too."

I closed the door and raced back through the house, feeling like I was going to vomit. I burst into the bathroom, closing the door behind me. Mom was in the process of working the washcloth out of her mouth, her eyes bulging with urgency. She wriggled her naked body in desperation when she saw me, the handcuffs clanking loudly along the curtain rod. Fresh blood trickled down her ribs, the hanger still protruding from the either side of her breast.

I grabbed her by the face, enraged. "Shut the fuck up!" I hissed. "I swear to god, if you try to scream, I'll rape you with a fucking *steak knife* until you bleed to death, you got that, bitch?"

She stopped struggling almost immediately and I saw a familiar hopelessness fill her eyes. That was good. I stuffed the washcloth back in her mouth and thought about what I should do. Olivia was just outside, sleeping the booze off in her car. In the state she was in, I knew she wouldn't hear anything, but the chance, the slightest chance she might, caused some hesitation.

"Damn it," I muttered, heart still twitching. Tonight was supposed to be an event, an excursion in creative torture. Now though, I couldn't afford to drag it out.

I looked at my mother, her ruined body almost unrecognizable after two years of abuse. How much longer could I keep this up? How much longer until I felt her debt was paid?

Never. I could spend a lifetime cutting her up and knew I'd never feel like I had done enough. It was a realization I had slowly become aware of as the months dragged into years. It was a horrible, dawning epiphany, but I couldn't deny it any longer. Nothing I did to her could erase what she had done to Dan and I. And god, had I tried.

I retrieved a roll of duct tape from under the sink and wrapped a couple strips around her face so she couldn't spit out the washcloth. It would also mute the noise. As I cut the strip from the roll, I realized just how tired I was. Exhaustion draped itself around me like a wet coat. How much of my own life had this cost me?

I glanced at myself in the mirror and was horrified at what I found. The singularity in which I had been living my life exposed itself in my reflection. I looked wild. Deranged. Unrecognizable almost.

I turned away, staring at my hands. My voice was low and measured. "What do you say, Mom? You wanna dance with me one more time?"

She began to sob. I didn't understand where she found the energy.

Steeling myself, I gripped the ends of the coat hanger sticking out of her breast and began to pull, gritting my teeth, knuckles going white. With the skin weakened and infected, the scabs and pustules erupted in a gush of yellow fluid and dark blood, I felt the hanger dig through her. I had been curious to see if I could pull it through her entire breast, severing it in half horizontally. Grunting, mother screaming into her gag, I continued to pull hoping to get it all the way through. I finally gave up after a minute or two, dropping the coat hanger with a frustrated growl. I felt a little better when I saw the state I had left my mother's chest in. Blood and pus dripped down her quivering legs, the skin around her breast horribly discolored and stretched.

"Damn shame," I spat. "Would have loved to tear those fucking things off." I could just cut them off, I realized, but didn't feel like I had the energy. I felt extremely drained from the work out. I thought about biting the remainder of her fingers off, one by one, chewing them, crunching them, teeth filled with blood. What would she do if she saw me eat them?

I knew she would just cry and scream--same as she always did. And I was so tired of hearing it. I knew exactly what level of pain my mother was feeling, to the decibel. I had learned, trained my ear to it. I knew when she had more in her before she passed out and when she didn't.

I looked down at the picture of Dan on the sink. I picked it up, chest heavy. He would have been so disappointed in me. I knew this. Knew he would hate what I had done to our mother, despite everything she put us through.

The past two years were about me. And now...finally, I realized with an unexpected amount of relief...that it was time to end this.

"Don't go anywhere," I said, slamming a fist into my mom's ribs. I left the bathroom as she gasped wetly. I went to the kitchen counter and picked up the box of mice. I shook it, listening to the rodents squeak inside. Before I went back to the bathroom, I went to the living room window and peeked through the curtain. Olivia's car was parked at the end of the driveway, dark and unmoving. From where I stood, I could see the outline of her head, reclined in the front seat, fast asleep. My anxiety lessened a little.

I returned to my mother, each step a realization that I was finally coming to the end.

I would be free of her. Forever. Closing the bathroom door behind me, I set the box of mice down on the sink. Mom looked at it miserably, tears welling, the skin around her eyes swollen and red.

"I think this is it," I said, sitting down on the toilet. I looked up at her, her wrists horribly scuffed and scabbed from the handcuffs. Her disgusting, flabby body sagged before me like a sack of wet earth. She smelled like vomit, piss, and sweat, her skin a canvas of filth, infection, and torture.

"I think I realized something tonight," I said slowly. "Though it's been festering in the back of my mind for months now." I stood and tapped the top of the box. "Do you want to know what it is?"

Mom just whimpered.

I gripped her by the hair and yanked her head up so her eyes met mine. "I am so *fucking* tired of wasting my life on you. What you did is unspeakable and I've spent years making sure you knew just how much I hate you for that. But I need to move on now. You're like dog shit that I need to finally scrape off my shoe. You have become nothing to me. I could keep you here for another decade and it would feel meaningless. I don't care how much I hurt you anymore. I don't care how badly I mangle you. I'm exhausted from all of this and I think it's time to send you to hell where you belong."

I gripped her hair harder. "When I'm done killing you, I'm going to cut you up and dump you into a sewer drain. It's the only kind of burial you deserve."

I let her go and roughly tore the tape off her face. I pulled the washcloth out of her mouth and threw it off to the side, my other hand reaching to open the top of the box.

"Please, I'm sorry-"

I slammed my forehead into her nose, breaking it instantly. "I don't want to hear it," I spat, gripping her face with one hand, forcing her mouth open as blood leaked into it from her shattered nose.

With my other hand, I fished out a handful of small mice. I stuffed them into her mouth, feeling their soft, furry body wriggle and squirm in my grip. Mom's eyes went wide as the rodents filled her mouth, their tiny bodies compressed between her teeth.

I pulled out three more mice from the box and crammed them into Mom's mouth. Her cheeks were alive with activity and she fought back a retching gag as she struggled to breath. I grabbed two more mice from the box. I pushed them past her lips, her mouth crammed to capacity as she tried not to swallow the furry, squeaking rodents.

Satisfied, watching my mother's eyes bulge, her throat working furiously, I grabbed the duct tape. Slowly, I wrapped it around her face, her nose, sealing the mice inside her mouth.

Mom bucked and thrashed in the shower, the handcuffs clanging loudly as her face turned blue. She had begun to suffocate. I could hear the mice going absolutely wild inside her mouth.

Crunch.

I sat down on the toilet as Mom began to eat them, desperate to free her airways. Bucking, she sent muffled howls up her throat, her teeth coming down again with another sickening crunch.

But she was losing the race. Her face was dark blue now and I saw trickles of blood leak from beneath the strips of tape. Her jaw tried to work faster, but there simply wasn't time for her to consume them all. Everytime she tried to bite down, the mice went crazy and she would scream again, losing what precious little air she had.

Her eyes began to droop as she lost oxygen. Her mouth was like a hive, her cheeks alive with the nest of mice as they fought for survival. Mom gagged finally and then threw up into her mouth. That was her end. I listened, without feeling anything but exhaustion, as Mom drowned in the vomit and gore. Her chest heaved painfully as her body fought for air, her body jerking violently... then less so...

...until finally...she died.

I expected to feel something when I realized she was finally gone. Some sense of satisfaction or relief. Instead, I felt completely hollow, like the batteries on the remote just died and I resigned myself to just sit in silence.

"What a mess," I finally said. I left the mice in her mouth. They would either wriggle down her throat and die in her chest or die on her tongue. Either way, I didn't care. Gathering my willpower, I stood and went to the garage and got my hand saw.

It took me three hours to cut my mother up. When I was finished, the bathtub was drenched in blood. Body parts oozed across the acrylic surface toward the drain where they crowded like a gory cairn.

I just didn't have the energy to do anymore and so I dropped the saw into the tub, muscles aching from the hours of work, and washed my hands and arms with hot water and soap. I splashed my face, ran my hands through my hair, and then undressed. I tossed my clothes into the tub. I would have to bag all of it up later, but I couldn't bear the thought in my current state.

Naked, I trudged to my bedroom and collapsed. I half expected to lay staring at the ceiling, the gravity of what I had done beginning to sprout roots. Instead, I slept like the dead.

I woke up to a knock at the door, hours later. The sun was just starting to rise, purple and orange light filling the window panes. I rolled my head on my pillow and saw it was just after six. The knock came again and my heart exploded as memory vomited up last night's events.

I bolted up and threw some clothes on, hurrying to the front door. For some reason, I was convinced it was the cops, like they had some radar for dead bodies that had led them to my front door.

I cracked the door open and to my relief, saw it was just Olivia.

"I'm so sorry," she started, face puffy with a hangover and bad sleep. "I have to pee so bad I think I'm going to die. Can I just pop into the bathroom super quick and then I'll get lost?"

I coughed into my hand, heart still sputtering. The image of my mother's body hacked into pieces rose in my mind's eye and I scrambled to put an excuse together.

"Sorry...my uh...guest...is in there right now," I said stupidly.

"Your late night hook up?" Olivia asked, looking desperate, practically dancing from foot to foot.

I nodded. "I'm sorry. She's been in there for like an hour. I think she drank too much last night and has been throwing up. I told her when she felt well enough that she could take a shower and sleep here until she feels better."

"I'm literally going to piss my pants, dude," Olivia stated.

"I can't drag her out of the bathroom, she's really messed up," I said with a little more force than I meant.

Olivia looked around frantically. "Fuck her—ok I'm going to pee in your bushes, pal. I don't even care. Can you at least get me some toilet paper?"

I nodded as she raced to the side of the house. I went into the bathroom, stepping over a huge pool of blood to grab the roll of paper that sat on the back of the toilet. I tore off a couple strips that were stained with blood, tossed them onto the mess that used to be my mom, and went back to the front door. I grabbed my wallet and keys, then slipped on my shoes. I stepped outside, the warm morning air cleaning the stink of blood from my head.

A moment later, Olivia came marching back toward me from the side of the house. She grunted at the toilet paper.

"I used a couple leaves, like some kind of barbarian."

"A true outdoorsman."

"You going somewhere?" She asked, looking at the keys in my hand.

I jingled them at her. "I was hoping you wanted to get some breakfast with me."

She cocked an eyebrow. "What about your little honey in there?"

I shrugged. "I think she's going to be out of commission for quite a while."

Olivia smiled then and it made me feel good. "Ok, but you're buying! Can't believe I slept in your driveway cause you were getting pounded last night. You owe me buddy."

I smiled back at her. "You wanna follow me into town?"

"Absolutely."

"Then let's go."

As we drove away, the pieces of my mother continued to drain in my rearview mirror.

THE NIGHTMARE VIRUS

"Wake up, Mr. Hughes."

Ryan Hughes opened his eyes. It felt like pulling himself from the ocean depths. Fatigue, a symptom of whatever drug he had been injected with, hung around his neck like an anchor. He raised his head, blinking sluggishly, and tried to force his mind to restart.

"You may feel some nausea," the voice continued. "Perfectly normal. Take a moment to collect yourself, please. We have much to discuss."

Ryan scrubbed his eyes with hands that felt swollen and alien. He pushed his memory into compliance and took stock of his situation.

He was sitting on the floor of a barren room, the walls and floor lined with sheet metal. No furniture, a single fluorescent blooming white light overhead. A man stood before him, blue jeans, brown blazer–the gray streaking his hair and the wrinkles around his eyes put him around fifty.

"Where am I?" Ryan croaked, his mouth dry.

The man standing before him shifted his weight, his brown loafers scuffing the floor. "You're in my facility," he offered. "Level B27 to be specific."

Ryan scraped the top layer of his brain, hoping flakes of memory would free. "Why am I here? God, it's freezing."

The man nodded. "Yes. We are quite far below the surface of the earth. These rooms are not heated either. The chill is expected."

Ryan thought about standing, but discovered his body wasn't ready for that commitment. He leaned back against the hard wall and stared up at the man in the brown blazer.

"Who the fuck are you?"

The man's face puckered into a smile. "My name is Richard Pickle. I will be overseeing your stay here. Once you're able to stand," he checked his wrist watch, "in about four minutes, I will begin your sentence."

"Sentence?" Ryan asked. That word pried a memory loose. A fragment of one. He felt his stomach drop.

The man, Richard Pickle, casually slid his hands into his pockets. "Yes. You have been sentenced to my facility to assist in developing the Nightmare Virus."

Ryan gripped his head and squeezed his eyes shut. He willed memory to return. It came in flashes. Horrific, sickening flashes.

He had killed someone. No. He had killed two. A mother and her young child. He had been robbing their house in the middle of the night. They weren't supposed to be there. The mother had been up feeding the kid. A boy. Couldn't have been more than three months old. She had heard Ryan rummaging around in the living room and had come out to investigate the noise. She had been holding the child to her chest.

The gun in Ryan's waistband came out in a surprised panic. Before he knew it, he had fired three shots. Two in the mother's chest and one into the infant's head. The shock struck him like a hundred pound hammer as he watched them both fall to the floor, blood pooling. The sound of the discarded infant thumping against the hardwood floor thrashed around in his brain like a wild animal.

He had never killed anyone before that. No history of violence. The gun was an afterthought, something he brought to the robbery in case he had to scare someone. He hadn't anticipated someone scaring *him*, so much so that he pulled the trigger.

The rest had followed quickly. Arrest. Trial. Sentencing. He pleaded guilty, horrified by what he had done. The kid...the sound of the fucking *kid* hitting the floor...

"I'm supposed to be in prison," Ryan said, finally raising his head. He looked around. "This doesn't look like my cell."

"You've been transferred," Richard Pickle explained. "You will spend the rest of your sentence here. With me."

"What does that mean? Where is this?" Ryan asked, growing frustrated. "Come on, man, stop making me ask the same damn question over and over again."

"I have the luxury of answering however I please."

Ryan rubbed his aching head. "I really hate the way you talk."

"Feeling better, yet?" Richard asked. "Your tongue certainly seems to have loosened some."

Ryan met the man's eyes. "Why am I here?"

"My staff and I are working on a very special program here. Something we hope to integrate you into. I reviewed your file, among many others, and decided you'd be a prime candidate for my project." He chuckled then. "I say 'mine' - a selfish tendency, but there are many dedicated men and women in the facility who have contributed to the evolution of the program."

"What's so special about me?" Ryan asked, feeling more and more uncomfortable. Who the hell was this clown? Why wasn't he in his cell?

Richard leaned down, hands on his knees as if he were speaking to a child. "Why, you're plagued by a guilty conscience. I would imagine it's eating you up, yes? What you did?" he shook his head. "Shooting a mother and baby, shooting them dead." His face changed then in an instance, the smooth surface of his skin erupting into a beat red storm of angry lines and bulging veins. "DEAD DEAD DEAD RYAN!"

Ryan jerked away from him, rattled, but Richard stepped closer, his face continuing to contort. "I bet the stench of that child's blood is stained forever inside your *fucking* nostrils, isn't it? You murdered them. *Murdered* them and for WHAT!?"

So derailed by this sudden change, Ryan could only stare, heart thumping in his chest.

Richard stood back up, his face instantly smoothing, his calm demeanor returning. He ran his hands down his blazer and smoothed his graying hair.

"Ryan," he said, his voice as soft as butterfly wings, "some men are going to come in here soon and take you to Room 1 where you will spend three months. If you make it, then I will come visit with you again and advance you to the next stage. I very much hope to do that. I'm rooting for you. Remember that, when you think you cannot go on any longer." He smiled at Ryan. "I'm rooting for you."

And then he was gone, exiting through the seamless door at his back. Before Ryan could collect himself, three men in dark brown jumpsuits came in and hauled him to his feet.

They dragged him to Room 1.

The journey was unremarkable. Long dark halls full of sheet metal, sturdy iron doors leading off into the unknown, fluorescences lighting the way overhead. It was the absolute silence that chilled Ryan, more than the temperature. Other than the grunt of the three men escorting him, there wasn't another noise to be heard. He allowed them to drag him along, twisting and turning down a series of identical corridors until they got to a long, descending staircase. It plunged down like an open throat, deeper into the facility. With a firm nudge, Ryan began the spiraling plunge, his boots echoing off the metal stairs, around and around and around, down down down.

He was fucked, he knew that much. Whatever shadow corporation this was, whatever hidden government agency he had been sold to, he knew he was in massive trouble. Danger, even. Much of what Richard Pickle had told him meant nothing. Nightmare virus?

He figured the goons at his back wouldn't answer his questions, so he kept his mouth shut. He had known people like them, back before he had been arrested. Strong hands, soft minds. They were here to hit and prod and nothing else.

Finally, they reached the bottom of the staircase, where the floor turned from sheet metal to lined stone. The hallway stretching before him looked ancient, like it was a set piece from a medieval Hollywood set. As he was pushed forward, he realized that the stone was wet, all around him, droplets dripping on his head as he walked. Electric sconces lit the long hallway, barely providing enough light from one to the next. They passed branching hallways that led into darkness, the constant drip of water interrupting an otherwise silent journey.

"Here," one of the goons said, grabbing Ryan's arm, halting him. They stood before a metal door that looked more like a bank vault.

Grunting, two of the men spun a combination lock on the side and cranked the massive door open. Ryan's heart was racing at this point. Nothing about this little trip helped ease his anxiety either. And now the door. He blinked when it opened fully, confused. The door had opened to reveal a blank faced stone wall.

He turned around, "What the hell is this?"

The man holding his arm pointed down. "Get in."

Ryan followed the man's finger and felt his heart skip a beat. There was an opening at the bottom, nothing more than a narrow slot.

"No," Ryan said, heart pounding. "No, no, no, what the fuck is this?"

"Get in."

"NO!"

The three men grabbed him then, a fist was delivered to his stomach, and the fight left him. He was forced to his knees, then pressed to the floor. The wet stone was cold against his cheek as Ryan craned his head to stare inside the small opening. Total darkness.

"Push," the one who had punched Ryan instructed the other two. Ryan, panicking, fought to get to his knees, but was slugged in the back of the head, bouncing his nose against the hard floor. He saw stars and then felt himself being shoved into the opening.

His head barely cleared the impossibly low ceiling and as he was pushed further in, he realized just how narrow the space was as well, his shoulders scraping the walls.

He began to scream, claustrophobia attacking his mind. He couldn't breathe in here, couldn't move, couldn't see, everything was dark and cold and terribly encased. He felt like he was being shoved into a stone coffin hundreds of miles beneath the surface of the earth.

He was pushed the rest of the way in and he felt his head strike the far wall, leaving no space to wiggle or stretch. He could lift his back a couple inches before it hit the low ceiling, but that was the extent of his mobility.

A voice came from the slot, the opening in which he had been shoved into.

"See you in three months."

Ryan's eyes bulged and his screams became howls, which returned to him as the massive door slammed shut, entombing him in total darkness.

It took him a long time to calm down. He felt like there wasn't enough air in the terribly small space. Once the waves of panic exhausted him, he tried to wiggle, move, anything to push back the viscous claustrophobia. He could lift his chin a couple inches off the floor before the back of his head struck the ceiling and he could extend his elbows outward about the same distance.

And the darkness. The darkness made everything worse.

Ryan began to cry.

He didn't know how long he had been in his new prison when a rush of liquid jetted from some unseen tube at his feet by the vault door. Ryan had been dozing in a state of miserable fatigue when his legs were suddenly engulfed in a flood of freezing cold. He jerked awake, banging his head on the ceiling as the tiny space quickly began to fill. He realized that it was water as it rushed up to his arms and then his face. He sputtered, screaming as the spout continued to fill the enclosed prison, the water level rising at an alarming rate.

In a panic, he lifted his chin out of the water and pressed his cheek flush against the ceiling, gasping. He felt his ear submerge and just as it was about to fill his mouth, the spout shut off. Panting, Ryan tried to move again in vain, desperate to keep his airways above the icy waterline. He began to shiver in a matter of minutes, his body reacting to the fridge slosh. His heart thundered as he fought rising hysteria, the total darkness and the sliver of air whittling down the fragile grip he had on his own mind. It wasn't long before his neck began to cramp, his elbows and legs banging uselessly against the stone walls as he fought for a better position. The restriction of movement only fueled his claustrophobia and every time he moved, the water rolled in small waves over his face, momentarily cutting off his airway.

Sputtering, Ryan forced himself to stop struggling. Every small twist and turn only worked against him, drowning him in small doses. The pain in his neck increased, flame turning to fire as each minute passed. The cramping pain worked down into his shoulders and he grit his teeth, his face mashed against the cold ceiling, each breath seeming more hopeless than the last. Finally, he let his head drop, accepting the shock of water around his eyes and mouth in order to relieve some of the agony that continued to build from the forced position.

Time was meaningless. Hours, minutes, years, it was all a pointless statistic as Ryan continued to alternate between the gap of air and the freezing water. His teeth chattered and his body felt as if it was encased in ice. The agony in his neck and shoulders dug into his mental fortitude, a spear of white hot pressure and constricting, spasming muscle. It was the most miserable hell he had ever endured.

And he had no idea how long it would last.

Again, Ryan began to cry. And then weep. And then he screamed for someone, anyone, to help him.

In the darkness, no one answered and the vault door remained shut.

Ryan had reached a point of absolute exhaustion. It felt like he had been in the cold prison waters for days. His mind begged for him to go to sleep, just lower his head and drown. End it. Instead, he had begun to drink the water, hoping it would buy him a little more space to breathe and consequently, lower his head and give some relief to his throbbing neck and shoulders, which now felt like stone slabs.

He had developed a system. Take a deep breath, relax his head until he was underwater, easing the searing pain, and then come up for air. Ten seconds of that. Then he would drink a mouthful of water. Repeat.

In his desperation to change his situation he had overlooked something. He had to urinate now. In the hours and hours of rotating his cycle, his bladder had begun to fill and then overfill from all the water he had ingested.

Now, along with the pain in his neck and shoulders, his penis felt as if someone had shoved a tiny balloon down the length of it and had expanded it until threatening to explode. And he knew it was only a matter of time before he did it. Before he pissed himself and was forced to soak in his own urine.

He held out as long as he could.

And then he cried again, time nothing more than a rotation of pain.

Starvation. It crept up on him and then it consumed him. The hole in his stomach tore at him, reaching a level of hollowness that Ryan could not fathom. He had no idea someone could feel as hungry as he was. But it was a constant misery that he had no answer for.

He couldn't even begin to guess how long it had been since he first pissed in his watery prison, but he had been forced to many times since. Mercifully, he had figured out a way to prop his chin up above the water using his arm, which he rested on and had been able to sleep. The first time he did it, he prayed to wake up and find the chamber drained. Now, when he slept, he prayed he just wouldn't wake up.

Ryan felt skeletal. It felt like weeks since he had been locked in the hole. His raging hunger had faded to a dull numbness and the stubble on his cheeks foretold a miserable length of time that he had been imprisoned. He had been forced to drink some of his piss water, but by the time he caved and did it, he couldn't care less. Dignity was a word in some foreign language.

He was going to die in here. He knew that. Not a single person had come to check on him, feed him, anything. In his constant state of near drowning, his mind had turned to mush. His thoughts weren't thoughts anymore, but rather, washed out images that held no meaning. At first he had reflected on his past, held onto memories to sustain him, but soon his own misery drained any meaning those experiences had. He had lost all hope in his situation. His arms and legs, his entire body had turned into a lightbulb of pain, each day upping the amps. The piss water, in which he marinated in, stank horribly now. The total darkness pressed further into his eyes with every breath, invading his mind. He didn't know why he hadn't just drowned himself yet. He considered it almost constantly now. He had tried it once, just to see how long he could hold his breath and the frantic, chest ripping pressure had left him weeping as he finally pulled his mouth out and gasped for air.

Let me die...

The sound of the vault door opening was so sudden and loud that Ryan jumped from his catatonic state and struck his head on the low ceiling. Through a daze of stars, dull light flooded his tiny prison. The stinking water drained in an instant, escaping through the open door and into the hallway. He heard two men grunt in disgust as it pooled around their feet.

"Oh Jesus, we forgot to drain the chamber."

"I reminded you this morning, idiot."

"God, it reeks of piss."

"Let's just get him out."

Ryan felt hands grab his ankles and then he was pulled from the cell, his cheek scraping along the rough stone floor, and out into the hallway. He raised his hands, shielding his eyes from the light, dim as it was. Every muscle in his body screamed and cramped and writhed at the movement.

Two blurry figures stood over Ryan as he blinked and gasped, trying to acclimate to the sudden change.

"This one's been pickled, hasn't he?" One of the men said. "Come on, get him up. Grab the bag."

Ryan cried out as he was hauled up, his legs refusing to hold his weight. His skull felt like a pinball machine, every movement adding another ball that crashed into the sides of his head. One of the two men held him upright while the other pulled out a black cloth bag. He fitted it over Ryan's head, encasing him in darkness once more.

"P-please..." Ryan gasped, hunger ripping a hole in his guts. "Eat..."

"Take his other arm, we're going to have to drag this one up to Richard," one of the men said, ignoring Ryan's plea.

Hanging limp between the two men, Ryan was dragged away from the vault, the cloth sack filling his world with darkness. Every joint in his body felt like it would dislocate as he was jostled down the halls.

"Elevator," the man on his right said.

They stopped and Ryan heard doors slide open before he was pulled inside.

"You stink," the man on his right said.

"Don't talk to him," the other said sharply. "We don't want to undo everything."

Ryan wished, begged, one of them to put a gun to his head and pull the trigger. He didn't know what hell awaited him next. He began to cry as the elevator ascended.

"Please don't do that," the man on his right said, almost tenderly.

"Shut it," the other barked.

Ryan felt the elevator jolt to a stop and then the doors opened. Despite the warmer air, his teeth were chattering and he felt like he had a raging fever, billows of fire gusting across his aching brain.

He was dragged further, the men's footsteps echoing down a series of unseen hallways. He heard others pass them, their footsteps passing without comment. Surely they saw him? How could they not stop this torture?

The men stopped and a keycard beeped, a door unlatching.

"Sit him here, next to the others," the man on the left instructed.

"Down you go," the other said, lowering Ryan into a hard metal seat with a high back. It was slightly reclined and Ryan's limbs flopped to his sides as they released him.

"Do we shackle him?"

"That's what Richard said."

Ryan felt his arms lifted and locked into place by metal restraints. Something clicked over his legs, binding him to the chair.

A hand touched his shoulder. "Sorry about all this."

"Zip it and let's go," the other man said. Ryan heard them leave, the door closing behind them.

They hadn't removed the bag from his head and so Ryan was left in total black, the fabric around his mouth wet as he sucked in air, his teeth clacking together as the fever filled him in ice.

"Help me..." Ryan cried miserably. He heard machinery whirring all around him, along with a muffled series of low, almost silent groans.

He didn't know how much time passed until someone entered the room, the door unlatching loudly.

"Ryan," a voice said, stopping directly in front of him. "Let's get that bag off you, yes?"

Ryan gasped as the fabric was pulled off his face and the world realigned around him. At first it was a wash of blinding light and color. He felt his eyes watering as he struggled to focus.

"Get him hooked up to the IV while we prep the box," the voice in front of him instructed. Blurred people in lab coats encircled him as he fought to find himself. He felt something sharp slide into the crook of his elbow, while something else was inserted into his ear.

"High fever," someone said. "104.2."

"That'll come down," someone else replied. "Check his pupils."

A thumb pulled his eye open and light blinded him.

"Turn up the heat in here," another voice ordered.

"What about the others?"

"They'll be fine. Up it two degrees."

"Yessir."

Ryan squeezed his eyes shut, willing his vision to come back. Everything was happening so fast. He felt like if he didn't get oriented he would slip further into madness.

"Dry his hair," a voice barked.

A towel dropped onto his head as someone massaged the moisture from his still damp hair. Another pair of hands checked his pulse along his neck.

"We're good here," someone announced, stepping back from Ryan. "Clear for injection."

Ryan finally got his eyes back as a familiar face positioned themself before him, arms behind his back. It was Richard Pickle, the man who had condemned him to the vault.

"Can you understand me?" Richard asked. "Do you remember my name?"

Instead of answering, Ryan rolled his head around, trying to figure out where he was. What he saw tore his guts out of his throat.

He was in a small room with metal walls and floor. Machinery lined the walls, a whirring, blinking, array of tech. The wall behind Richard held a tinted window, blacking out whatever lay beyond. But that wasn't what filled him with gruesome terror.

It was the three others in the room with him. They were sitting to his left, lined neatly in similar chairs. Protruding from their arms and neck were a tangle of tubes and wires that coiled across the floor to the computers and machinery against the wall.

Sitting atop their shoulders, encasing their heads, were black metal boxes. Additional wires sprouted from the boxes like elongated spider legs, humming with electricity. A thick tube sprouted from the top of each metal box, like an external vein that slowly pumped a yellow fluid into the encased heads.

Richard saw Ryan's bloodshot eyes grow wide as he observed this.

"Are you ready to join them?" Richard asked quietly, a small smile lining his mouth.

"W-what...is this?" Ryan croaked, fear strangling him.

Richard puffed his chest out. "This is the next evolution of human punishment. Horrifying to witness, isn't it?"

Ryan didn't answer, his eyes glued to the motionless bodies bound to their seats, the metal boxes obscuring any humanity these people may have once possessed.

"Do you know how long you were in your cell?" Richard asked, as the other lab techs continued to work behind him, prepping something.

Ryan's head threatened to split beneath the feverish headache. "A don't...know. A month?"

"You were only in there for eight days," Richard said, grinning. "Felt longer, didn't it? We had no intention of keeping you in there for three months, but it helps break you down psychologically if you believe it'll be that long."

Richard walked over to the subject closest to Ryan, running his fingers over the box entrapping the person's head.

"We've had to make adjustments to our procedures," he continued. "Ways to make the mind more receptive to the virus. We realized we needed to tenderize the subject's psyche. Break it down, soften it, smash it, pulverize it like you would meat or potatoes. Mush it up. Which is why we put you in the hole. Awful, isn't it? The water was my idea. Creates an exhausting sense of near panic. It helps accelerate things."

Ryan couldn't believe what he was hearing...he had only been in the cell for eight days? How could that possibly be?

Richard turned to the lab techs. "Is his box ready?"

"Almost sir."

Ryan felt a spear of pure panic impale him as he swung his eyes over to the table the techs were huddled around.

"You'll be the twenty-third host of the virus," Richard said, eyes sparkling. "It was my own design. The prototype at least. I've had the help of some very smart minds as we've tweaked it. Made it more sustainable."

Richard reached out and touched the box sitting atop the subject furthest from Ryan. "Piotr here has lasted almost two years. It's absolutely remarkable. I cannot even fathom what the virus has mutated into at this point. I wouldn't dare even to peek at the nightmares plaguing him inside this box."

"Two minutes sir," one of the techs announced.

Richard nodded and returned to stand in front of Ryan. "The Nightmare Virus is what we've taken to calling my work. You're about to get your first taste of it. First, we'll fit you with the box and then feed the virus in through the top where a filter turns it into an airborne mist, which you'll breathe in continuously. You won't feel anything, don't worry. In fact, you may even feel at peace as you drift off to sleep."

Richard leaned forward, placing his hands on Ryan's, his face inches away. "And then the nightmares will begin. They won't be pleasant, but nothing shockingly different from the nightmares you've had your whole life. But with each thirteen day cycle, the virus mutates. It builds upon the last compound, growing your nightmares, over and over and over again. With every mutation, with every thirteen day cycle, your dreams will begin to learn how to grow increasingly traumatic as your exposure to the virus continues."

Richard cocked his head at Piotr, the man at the end of the line. "Can you imagine how horrible his nightmares must be after two years of mutation? How unbelievably suffocating it must be, trapped, as your mind learns new ways to traumatize you every thirteen days, building and building upon each iteration of your darkest fears?"

"We're ready, sir," one of the techs stated from the table.

Richard waved them over as he continued. "The government has tasked me with finding an evolution of punishment for mankind's worst. The worst of the worst. And I intend to find it, Ryan, I intend to give it to them. But what do I know about what traumatizes and haunts individuals? Why don't I let you and the virus figure that out, yes?"

Richard stood up and waved his hand. "Bring it over."

Ryan, in a state of shocked horror, his mind overloaded, began to cry out as the techs wheeled over his own, personal metal box. Richard tapped it with his knuckles.

"I believe in you, Ryan. We've never kept someone alive longer than twenty-eight months before they go into cardiac arrest. But you will be the first to witness the latest strand we've developed. I fully expect you to outlast your companions here. Who knows, maybe you'll make it. Maybe you'll stay alive for five years? A decade? Don't worry about your physical body, we'll keep that running for you. It's the least we can do."

The techs lifted Ryan's box off the small cart, trailing wires as it was heaved up.

Richard crossed his arms as he watched. "I appreciate you listening to my ramblings. I'm a prideful man. My work excites me and it's not often I'm allowed to share." He patted Ryan's arm then. "Goodbye, my friend. May your dreams tear you apart."

Ryan screamed then, as the metal box was fitted over his head. Thrashing, pleading, he continued until the vapor filled his lungs and he fell asleep.

In that place of darkness, the nightmares began.

Hoot

I leaned over the porch railing, listening. I could hear them again. Off in the woods, just past the field before me. The cold night air sliced into my face and I felt my eyes watering, my boots creaking across the old planks. My house stood dark at my back, a dark tombstone in an expanse of empty country.

I was alone, and as I heard the noise once more, I felt an overwhelming isolation. The hairs on the back of my neck stood up and I shivered, wishing I had put my jacket on before rushing outside. The air smelled of snow and the moon was hidden behind a swath of thick cloud.

I stared out at the wall of trees across the field, an acre away from my front porch. I waited for the sound to come again. I had heard it last night, but by the time I made it outside, the sound had faded and hadn't come again. Tonight was different though. There wasn't a shadow of a doubt that what I was hearing was real.

The wind cut through my clothes, turning my veins to ice, and then the noise echoed from the woods once more.

It sounded like an owl. A huge owl, but that wasn't quite right. It sounded like a person imitating an owl. And there was an odd reverb at the end of the call, elevating the sound across the wind.

"Don't like that," I muttered, goosebumps rising on my arms. "Don't like that at all."

I couldn't imagine what the hell was making that sound. After thirty seconds, another call came, a low hooting drawl. I stared at the long row of dense woods. The second call had sounded different.

Like there were more than one in there.

"Screw this," I muttered, turning back to my front door. "Just stay in the woods and away from my house. Whatever the hell you are."

As I went inside and shut the door, the hooting came again, as if in response.

I lay in bed, two hours later, staring at the ceiling, trying my best not to look at the big, dark bedroom window to my left. I could faintly hear the hooting still, coming every couple of minutes. It set my teeth on edge and pushed sleep from the conversation. I thought about calling someone. But who? And what would I say?

Hello, police? There's some weirdos hooting in the woods in my backyard, can you come check it out? Yes, you heard me correctly. Yes, I am aware that owls are a thing. I understand. Sorry for wasting your time.

I turned my back from the window and stubbornly closed my eyes. I told myself to stop being such a baby. I tried not to think about how three people had gone missing from town over the past week. What a stupid thing to be thinking about right now.

"Stop it," I growled, gritting my teeth, squeezing my eyes shut even harder.

I waited for the next noise, bracing myself for it. Everytime I heard it out there, I felt as if my heart was bathed in ice. I just *didn't like it.* But as I waited, fearing the next distant hoot, it never came. Seconds turned into minutes and I slowly felt the knot in my chest begin to unfurl. I didn't dare take a breath, stupidly thinking whatever was out there would hear me. I didn't know why I was so wound up over such a dumb thing, but I couldn't shake the feeling of dread engulfing me.

It's just some dumb animal, I thought. *You've heard a million weird noises in the ten years you've lived here, most of them coming from those woods. Why has this one got your penis curled up into your guts?*

I knew though. And I didn't want to think about it, but I did anyway.

It was because those noises sounded human.

I sat up in bed, rubbing my eyes. My mind just wouldn't shut down. I looked at the clock and saw that it was already past one in the morning. I had work in the morning and I knew I was now doomed to a day of exhaustion.

"Stupid owls, why ca-"

My words died in the air as I stared at the bedroom window. I felt my body turned to liquid and a horrified scream gathered in my throat.

Perched on the ledge outside my window was a naked man. His palms were pressed flat against the window pane and his eyes were locked with mine.

I let out a gurgling howl of terror and scrambled out of bed, falling onto the floor in the process, the figure at the window an all consuming nightmare. In the process of falling out of bed and scooting against the wall, screaming the whole time, I realized something about the naked man at the window.

His eyes were huge and yellow, three or four times bigger than normal. And instead of a mouth, something else jutted out from where his lips should have been. It looked like a dark black beak, the skin around the protrusion an angry, bloody ring of flesh. His hair was long and wild, his mangled face dirty. He looked absolutely rabid, those huge eyes unblinking and massive.

As my eyes traveled down his body, everything happening in an instant, I noticed that between his legs hung a pinkish trunk, like an elephant, ending in an orifice that was slowly opening and closing almost like a lipless mouth. It slid across the window leaving a trail of slime as it searched for seams in the glass.

Before I could stand or make sense of what I was seeing, the deformed man suddenly raised his hands, which I saw were enormous as well, and balled his long clawed fingers into fists. He brought them against the window, smashing it, the noise huge and all consuming. I screamed again, mind a jumble or terror as he stepped off the ledge and into my bedroom, his feet filthy, his toes long and ending in hardened, sharp nails.

He took a step toward me as I huddled against the wall, tilting his head to the side. He cooed at me, the sound a reverbing tremor that matched the horrible noises I had heard from the woods.

"What are you!?" I screamed stupidly, trying to stand. "Jesus Christ, what do you want!?"

Instead of answering, the owl man leapt across the room, the movement shockingly quick. Suddenly his face was leaning down into my own, those massive, round, yellow eyes inches from my own, its head still cocked, its curved black beak almost touching my noise.

I took a wild swing at it, but it twisted its body and I smacked air instead. Before I could ready another punch, the owl man grabbed me by the neck and dragged me over to the window. Its grip was unbreakable and my bare chest scraped roughly against the wood floor. Clothed in only my boxers, the wind gusting in from the window bathed me in ice and I struggled vainly to pull myself free from the owl man.

A clubbed fist thudded into my back, knocking the fight out of me, the air crushed from my lungs. I let out an *oof!* and felt myself go limp, its powerful grip digging into my neck. Gasping, I felt the creature step up onto the second story window ledge, one foot planted on the shattered opening.

And then the owl man tensed its leg muscles, coiling into itself, then shot us out the window like a bullet. The force of our exit was so explosive that I felt my stomach drop like I was in free fall. What little breath I could muster was ripped from my throat as we rocketed through the night sky, the wind screaming in my ears. Blinking wetly through tear filled eyes, I caught a glimpse of my house behind us now, the field whistling twenty feet beneath us.

A thought ripped through my terrified mind like wildfire.

It's taking me into the woods.

And then the branches and trees were all around us, cutting and flaying my exposed flesh like wooden whips. I felt a dozen pain points ignite like fire across my body as I was blinded by darkness, forest, and agony.

The entire flight lasted only a couple of seconds, but the pain and shocking explosiveness of the whole thing made the world blur by in slow motion. The creature's grip on me never lessened as we descended through the thick forest, the ground rushing up to greet us at an alarming speed.

The owl thing landed on its gnarled feet effortlessly and casually tossed me to the ground, its firm hand slowing my momentum by a hair. I rolled across the frozen ground, rocks and dead underbrush lashing me, drawing ribbons of warm blood that splashed onto the dead earth.

Gasping, eyes bulging, I lay panting, every alarm blaring red. I coughed and spit out a tooth, feeling like I had just been run over by a train. I knew I had broken some bones in the fall, could feel the precursor of sharp pain in my side, but the coming pain was secondary to the owl creature before me.

It was staring at me from a couple feet away, its beak opening and closing soundlessly, the worm-like appendage between its legs rising up like a snake to inspect me, the gummy opening like a black hole.

I struggled to half sit and managed to with a whimper. The owl thing looked at me and then let out a long, shrill hoot that made me wince, heart racing. A second later, five more owl creatures dropped down from the trees. They all looked exactly like my captor with their huge yellow eyes, beaks, clawed hands and feet, and that disgusting trunk between their legs.

Six now, the creatures circled me, cocking their heads and hooting amongst themselves like they were talking, deciding what to do with me. I put my back against a tree, pain ripping up my left leg, chest heaving. Panic had rooted deep in my mind as I took in my surroundings, eyes bloodshot and strained in the darkness.

With a dawning horror, I swept my eyes upward and saw three more people, completely *human* people, above me. They were naked as well and hung upside down from the trees, their bare ankles laced and knotted with a thick white webbing, binding them to the branches. They looked dead and their bodies were swollen, horribly swollen, as if they had been pumped with air. Their torsos were puffed and bloated, as if they had comically been stuffed. Their arms and legs looked like broken stubs that jutted from their engorged bodies, the skin across their abdomens and broken chest cavities was torn and ragged, like they could barely hold whatever was fitted inside of them. I could see the white of exposed ribs and torn stomach lining, exposing a sliver of duller white from inside.

Blinking hazily, I realized that these people had been impregnated with something. And from the shape of their stretched, rounded bodies, I had a crazed realization that each of them hosted a giant egg inside their bodies.

With a surprised yell, I felt myself yanked by my ankles toward a tree. Two of the owl creatures were pulling me toward the impregnated hosts.

You're going to be hanging next to those three if you don't do something!

The owl men that weren't dragging me were gathered around the egg corpses, poking and prodding them, the dead bodies swinging from their perch as they were tested. With a horrified shiver, I saw one of the hosts shudder, its bloated stomach quivering. With a sudden pop, a chunk of flesh fell to the ground, exposing the white wall of the massive egg inside the host's guts.

The patch of egg cracked then, a spiderweb of dark lines and then a large finger poked through, pushing the broken shell away. As I was dragged past it, I saw a human face with enormous yellow eyes stare out at me from the dark hole in the flesh.

I was jerked again and felt myself go upside down. The world inverted and I realized I was being pulled up a tree by my ankles.

I felt warmth envelope my feet as I was hoisted higher, my arms dangling in the air past my head.

I looked up and saw that one of the owl men was oozing a thick white web from the fleshy tube between its legs. The trunk of muscle and pink weaved and moved around my legs as the thick white gunk dripped over my bare feet and down my calves.

Before I could kick out, I felt something huge and warm slam into my mouth. I gagged and my eyes went wide, a sickening taste erupting across my tongue and down my throat. Eyes watering, I saw that one of the owl creatures stood before me and had inserted the trunk between its legs down my throat. I spit and gagged, choking horribly as the invasive tube slithered further into me, vomit begging to be released.

It's going to spit an egg into your guts if you don't do something RIGHT NOW.

In an act of desperation, I bit down as hard as I could, while kicking up with both legs. They must not have been expecting the sudden resistance, which was my saving grace. The wet goo flowing over my legs stopped momentarily and the owl men hopped back from my swinging legs, dropping me in the process. As I fell, biting down on a mouthful of owl cock, I jerked my head and ground the flaccid member into my teeth, tearing away the head in a bloody eruption that squirted into my eyes as I hit the forest floor with a thud.

I rolled onto my back as the owl men hooted and screamed, the one with the wounded trunk flopping over next to me as hot red blood pumped out of its wriggling, gored flesh tube. I spit the hunk of owl hamburger out of my mouth with a retching gag and then scrambled to my feet.

The owl creatures were frozen in place, their massive yellow eyes darting between me and their wounded comrade, their curved black beaks clicking and hooting urgently.

I didn't wait for them to finish their conversation. Gritting my teeth, pain shooting up my leg and across my side, I bolted away from them. My bare feet were still covered in the white goo and I felt the substance beginning to harden. I didn't have time to scrape it off as I flew between the trees, the night around me filling with enraged screeching.

I don't know why they didn't come for me. Maybe no one had ever fought back and they saw me as a risk. Maybe they just wanted to help the owl I had injured. Whatever the reason, they never came. As I exploded out of the woods and into the field, my house came into view. It was the most wonderful thing I had ever seen.

I made it to the front porch in a breathless rush, crashing through the front door to get the keys to my truck. I grabbed them from the kitchen counter and then bolted back out into the night.

As I fired up my truck and hit the gas, I knew that I had been unbelievably lucky. I had been moments away from an excruciating death and had made it out alive somehow.

As I roared down the road toward town, toward help, I heard the woods at my back erupt in screams from the owls.

Their new host had gotten away.

MARTY MELLOW

Hugh jumped out of his chair as someone thundered on the front door. What in the hell? No one ever came out this far, and so as he rose from his recliner, he calmed his racing heart. He didn't like surprises or unexpected visitors. He was too old for all that nonsense.

He made his way over to the front door, his bad knee aching, and scanned the floor to ceiling windows that lined his expansive living room, sunlight illuminating the woodland outside.

He had purchased the house thirty years ago for a fraction of what it was worth now, hoping that he and his wife would be able to enjoy a long retirement together in the northern New Hampshire woods, away from all the bustle their professional lives had accosted them with. When Margret had died, ten years ago now, Hugh had wanted to sell the place, but his two kids convinced him to keep it. He was glad they had. The remote area filled him with peace and the twelve foot windows that lined the entire house gave him a constant view of the gorgeous forest that surrounded his slice of the world.

Another round of urgent pounding came from the front door and Hugh grumbled as he continued his trek across the considerable square footage. He figured it was probably some stray hiker who had taken a wrong turn. There was a trail head about a mile down the road that saw foot traffic three or four times a year.

Hugh reached the front door and cracked it open. Warm afternoon sunlight blinded him for a moment and he squinted in the wash of light.

"Please, let me in!" A silhouette begged.

Hugh blinked and saw that a man of about forty stood before him, his face red and sweaty. He had the beginnings of a dark beard and the lines around his blue eyes were deep, as if he had spent his entire life in a state of worry.

Hugh wished he had grabbed his pistol from the kitchen counter, where he left it at all times. It had been his daughter's idea, a way to ease her worry as she wrestled with the fact her father had retired to a massive house twenty-three miles from the nearest town.

Hugh locked his bad knee and kept his foot wedged against the bottom of the door.

"Who are you?" he asked.

"We don't have much time, he's right behind me!" the man urged, putting a hand against the door.

Hugh frowned. "You in some kind of trouble?"

"Yes!" the man yelled frantically. "Yes, but I've done nothing wrong! Please, please let me in! I'll be safe here!"

Hugh didn't like this one bit. He appraised the man again, saw the panic in his eyes, and weighed the decision heavily for a few moments.

"If you let me in, you won't be in any danger, I promise!"

Sighing, Hugh eased the door open. He had been an ER doctor for over twenty years and he still felt an obligation to help someone in trouble, as foolish as it might be.

"Come on in," Hugh said, stepping aside. "Go sit down in the living room and let's talk this out."

The man sprinted into the house as Hugh closed the door behind him, taking a quick peek outside to see if this stranger really was being pursued. He saw no one.

"If you're trying to rob me, I'll have no problem pointing this thing at your head," Hugh said, limping into the kitchen to retrieve his pistol from the counter. With it in hand, he turned to the living room where the stranger paced nervously, eyes scanning the large windows.

"I'm not here to take your stuff," the stranger said, barely noticing the pistol.

"What's your name?"

"Preston."

Hugh leaned against the countertop, taking the weight off his knee. "Ok Preston. What kind of trouble are you in? Who's after you?"

Preston continued to pace, eyes darting across the windows, then up at the skylights twelve feet overhead.

Hugh tapped the pistol against his leg. "Hey, Preston, I'm over here. What's going on?"

"Huh? Oh right…Jesus I know he's out there, I know he's coming."

"Who?"

Preston ran a hand through his dark hair. "Marty. His name is Marty Mellow. He's been after me for years now. Years."

"Why?" Hugh asked, feeling uneasy. He didn't make it his business to interfere in people's problems, but he had a hard time turning those in need away, especially when they showed up at his doorstep.

Preston stepped toward Hugh, a sickly smile plastered to his face. "That's just it! I have *no idea* why he's doing this. Why he keeps me stuck in this endless cycle, why he keeps-"

"Take a breath," Hugh instructed. He was used to taking charge, calming down people at their most frantic. "Look at me, stop looking out the windows. Right here, Preston. Breath. Deep breath. Good. Now tell me what's going on. How'd this start? Who is this Marty Mellow fellow?"

Preston snorted, that horrible smile still twisting his mouth. "Who is he…that's a fantastic question. I couldn't even begin to describe the last three years of my life. You wouldn't believe me because none of it makes sense. There's no one I can talk to about this. They'd think I was crazy. I've been on the run for so long only to get caught and sent away and killed-"

Hugh cocked an eyebrow. "Killed?"

Preston pressed his fingers into his eyes. "Yeah. Killed. Over and over again. Jesus, the things that bastard has put me through."

Hugh checked the windows, a snake of worry slithering in his guts. "You're not talking sense, son."

"I know. I know I'm not."

"Have you gone to the authorities?"

Preston collapsed into Hugh's armchair, arms hanging at his sides. "Yeah, during the first year. They didn't believe me. Not really. I know how my story sounds. I doubt I'd believe it either."

Hugh, sensing no danger, only terror from this strange man, put the pistol back on the counter.

"Why don't you tell me."

"Tell you what?"

"Your story. I've seen a lot of crazy stuff during my sixty-seven years on this earth and I've heard even crazier stories."

"You won't believe me."

"Try me."

Preston looked at Hugh hard, the dark bags beneath his eyes pulling his face down. He nodded slowly.

"Fine. You've been kind enough to let me into your house, I suppose I owe you an explanation."

He opened his mouth to begin when everything changed. In an instant, the entire world outside went dark. It was as if the sun had been snuffed out by a giant hand, smothered in the sky leaving only a complete midnight.

Preston leaped to his feet. "Oh no, NO!"

Alarmed, Hugh felt his heart sputter. "What's happening?"

Preston backed away from the wall of windows, the woods outside now completely hidden. "He's here! He found me!"

"Who!?"

"Fucking Marty Mellow!"

"I thought you said we were safe?"

Preston glanced at Hugh. "I said what I needed to get inside. I'm sorry."

Hugh clenched his jaw and snatched the pistol from the counter top. "Can't stand a liar."

"I'm sorry!"

Hugh limped to the nearest lightswitch and flicked it on. He massaged his knee for a moment and then went into the living room and turned on more lights, bathing the house in a cool yellow hue.

"What's this Marty fellow like?" Hugh asked as he continued to move.

Preston's eyes never left the windows. "He's sick. Violent. You can't reason with him and you can't escape him. If he wants to find you, he will, and he'll continue to hurt you until he decides he's had enough."

Hugh stood by the hallway, feeling more and more unsettled. "You ever try fighting back?"

Preston snorted. "Sure I have. Tried almost everythi-"

A sudden *bang!* on the far window spun both men around. Hugh raised his gun, unsure what he was pointing at, eyes scanning the dark panes for the source of noise. What he saw made him suck in a lungful of air between his teeth.

Standing outside, with both hands pressed against the glass, was a man. He looked to be about thirty, and was completely naked except for a pair of orange gym shorts. His chest and legs were completely hairless and he stood about six feet. Rising from his head, impossibly, were two long rabbit ears. They twitched independently as the man outside the window smiled in at them. His eyes were dark and his body was toned, his short brown hair blending perfectly with the two furry ears sprouting from his head.

Preston screamed and fell onto his backside at the sight of him, but Hugh only stared at the strange intruder. At his near nakedness. At the ears. He had to be wearing a headband, some kind of costume prop...but the way they *moved*...

The man, who Hugh could only assume was this Marty character, laughed when he saw Preston fall over. His voice was muted by the windows, but his glee was pure and almost childlike.

"Whoopsie!" The man, Marty, yelled. "Scared you didn't I, Preston? What are you doing in there? Who's your friend?"

Hugh locked his bad knee and raised the pistol to the window, steeling himself. "I'm guessing you're Marty Mellow, the fella who's been chasing after Preston here?"

Marty snickered, slowly dragging his hands down the window pane. "That's me! Almost caught him too before he barged in and got you mixed up in our little game. Preston is such a goof. What's your name, old timer?"

"Hugh."

"Don't talk to him!" Preston squeaked from the floor.

"Oh hush!" Marty yelled through the window. "Don't you want me to make new friends? After all we've been through, I'd think you'd be *thrilled* my attention was on someone else for a change!" The two rabbit ears on his head twitched again.

"I think you better leave," Hugh said, gesturing with the gun. "As you can see, I'm armed and I'd rather not shoot someone dressed as the Easter Bunny today."

Marty cocked an eyebrow. "Bunny?"

"Those fool ears you got on your head."

Marty rubbed his hands vigorously over his head, confused. "Ears?" And then he stopped, a long smile creeping up his face. "Do...do I look like a bunny man to you?"

"Just leave me ALONE!" Preston wailed, now having crawled to the far wall where he sat in terror.

"*Leave me alone!*" Marty mocked, smiling. "Come on now Preston, don't wet your pants in front of our new playmate. We don't want him thinking you're a little baby man, now do we? Is that what you are? A little baby man who pee-pees in his pants?"

Marty threw his head back, his voice exploding into the night. "PISS PISS PLEASE DON'T MISS!"

"Go AWAY!" Preston cried again.

Marty settled himself and returned his gaze to Preston. "Now now-"

Suddenly the strange man in the orange shorts stopped and spun around, as if he heard something in the darkness behind him.

"Mommy not yet!" He yelled into the void of black. "Not yet, not yet! Mommy just wait a second!" His ears drooped and he fell silent, as if hearing a voice that wasn't there. Then his ears perked back up and he pumped a fist into the air.

"Ok deal!" He yelled. He slowly turned back to the window, grinning, his voice low and barely audible through the glass.

"Mommy mommy, please don't rob me, mommy mommy, make me milk."

"What the hell is he doing?" Hugh asked, completely disturbed. He felt like the whole world had gone crazy and he was the last to find out.

Preston covered his eyes with his hands. "Oh no, oh no, oh no..."

Hugh walked over to the sitting man and grabbed him by the shoulders, hauling him to his feet, shaking him. "Hey! What's he doing!?"

Preston was crying now. "He's going to take us away."

Suddenly, Marty slammed both fists against the windows, his voice a screeching wail of delight. "MOMMY MOMMY PLEASE DON'T ROB ME!" He slammed his fists against the glass again, this time splintering the panes. "MOMMY MOMMY MAKE ME MILK!"

Hugh raised the pistol in a panic, and emptied the clip. As soon as he pulled the trigger, the man in the orange shorts sprang back into the darkness, vanishing from sight. The glass panes shattered as the bullets passed through them, the report of the pistol deafening. Preston screamed and shrank back to the floor, covering his ears.

Click, click, click.

Feeling sick, Hugh lowered the empty gun, the smell of burning metal wafting through the air.

"Did I hit him?" Hugh asked, his voice a rattle.

"It doesn't matter," Preston sobbed. "He's going to take us. He's going to hurt me again. Oh god..."

The dark air outside was cold as it seeped into the shattered windows, colder than the temperature had been mere minutes ago. Hugh checked his watch and saw that it was a little after three in the afternoon. It should be hot and sunny, it was the middle of August for Chrissakes. What in the blue hell was happening here?

From outside, a voice echoed through the trees, coming at them from the wall of darkness.

"Almost ready mommmmmy..."

"Get up," Hugh said, hooking a hand under Preston's arm. "Keys to my truck are on the counter. Grab them while I watch the windows. We're high tailing it out of here. Grab my phone as well, it's right next to the keys."

"It won't work," Preston said, eyes red, as he allowed himself to be pulled up. He hurried to the counter and scooped up the keys and phone.

"It's charged," Hugh assured, keeping his eyes glued to the shattered windows.

Preston shook his head frantically. "No, no, the darkness Marty brings, it'll block out everything."

Hugh snatched his cell from Preston's hands and glanced down at it. "Fuck."

Marty's voice came again, closer this time, drifting from the unseen trees beyond the windows. "I'm going to get youuu...going to get some milk from mommyyyy...". A shrill laugh followed.

Before Hugh and Preston could make it to the door, Marty leapt in through the broken window at full speed. His ears lay flat back against his head and the broken glass sliced his skin and tore at his orange shorts as he exploded into the house, charging straight for them.

"GOT YOU GOT YOU GOT YOU!" He screamed, trailing bloody ribbons.

Hugh raised his arms, shielding himself as Marty dove at them, crashing into the pair with all the force of a locomotive. Hugh felt his knee ignite with pain upon impact, the world spinning, falling, tumbling.

His head struck the floor and the last thing he saw before blacking out was Marty's face, his dark eyes boring into his own.

"Wanna come home with me?" Marty whispered, leaning down.

Hugh lost consciousness.

He awoke to Marty breathing into his face. His whole body felt broken, the ache of the collision pulsing through his skull with every heartbeat. He was convinced his knee had shattered, but wasn't brave enough to move yet. He blinked, the fog clearing, feeling the madman's hot breath. It smelled like digested candy.

"Welcome back, Hugh," Marty said, his face inches from Hugh's. "Sorry about that. Had to get you two out of the house and into the miasma. Didn't see any other way. Do you know what miasma is?"

"G-get off me," Hugh croaked as Marty shifted his weight, sitting hard on Hugh's stomach.

Marty ignored him. "I had to get you home," he continued, "and I didn't think you were going to just waltz into the dark with me. So I had to get you down, knock you out, really smash the lights out of you. Did you know bodies are heavier when they're dead or unconscious? I worked up a *sweat* dragging you two outside that house. Sorry about your windows by the way. You shouldn't have shot at me, though." He waggled a finger in Hugh's face. "That wasn't very kind. No no, it wasn't. Why were you trying to kill me, ya idiot?"

"I...can't breathe," Hugh gasped as Marty shifted his weight on him.

Out of nowhere, Marty suddenly grabbed Hugh by the face, his demeanor changing in an instant. Gritting his teeth, eyes going midnight black, he snarled into Hugh's face.

"Shut the fuck up, you old *cunt*, or I will eat your lips right off your fucking face."

He shoved Hugh away and stood up, stretching his bare torso, running his hands over his long ears. He sighed and looked down at Hugh.

"Sorry. Didn't mean to say all that. We just met and we haven't even started our relationship yet. Honestly though, I can't think of a better way for you to get acclimated with how things are going to work. So just shut up and watch."

Hugh heaved in a couple gulps of air, the world spinning. He grunted and tried to get up, but lances of pain kept him down.

"Stay put, you old bones," Marty instructed. "Let me show you some things and then I can take you to Mommy."

Hugh, trying not to panic, stared up into the sky. It was the first indication that his situation was even more sideways than he anticipated.

The sky was green, vibrant, lime green. A few trees rose around where he lay, the expanse of branches weighed down by some kind of fruit, though it was no fruit Hugh had ever seen. They were long, like a banana, but orange, with sprouts of smaller fruits jutting off like tiny limbs.

"Where did you take me?" Hugh wheezed from his back.

"I told you, I took you home," Marty answered, fiddling with something off to the side.

"Where's home?"

"Just keep your pants on, I said I would show you. I just have to deal with Preston here."

Preston.

Hugh raised his head and saw the younger man leaning against a tree, his body bound to it by some kind of white substance, almost like a spider's web. He was awake and crying silently.

Marty strolled over to him and crouched down, smiling. "Here we are again, huh pal? Seems like just yesterday I had you here. How long has it been? Two, three months? How many more trips do you have in you before Mommy drains the rest of you away?"

"Just get it over with," Preston sobbed, immobile, his chest and legs tightly constrained against the tree by the white substance.

Marty ruffled his hair. "You're always so sad." He reached out and grabbed one of Preston's ears. "Sad sad, don't be mad it makes you bad."

Marty ripped off Preston's ear. The act was so quick and violent that it took Preston a second to start screaming as the pain caught up to mutilation. Blood erupted from the torn stump and ran down the side of his face, dripping from his jaw onto the white substance.

Marty stood and chucked the ear up into the air before catching it in his mouth. He chewed on it slowly and turned to look at Hugh, who was petrified. Marty bounced his eyebrows at Hugh and then winked.

"Leave him alone!" Hugh yelled, now struggling to stand. His knee exploded in pain the second he put pressure on it and he slumped back down into the dirt with a wail.

Marty rolled his eyes and chuckled. "Wah wah wah." He turned back to Preston and grabbed two fist fulls of hair. "You need a haircut, Pres, don't you think?" Then, he braced a bare foot against Preston's shoulder and began to pull. Preston screamed as Marty grunted, face going red with effort. With a great tearing sound, like grass being uprooted, Marty stumbled backwards as the hair came free, along with parts of Preston's scalp. Blood oozed from the exposed patches as Preston howled, tears running down his face.

Marty dragged the back of his hand across his brow and unfurled his fists. "Whoa, we got some skin with that one." He suddenly darted forward and kicked Marty underneath his jaw, the blow cracking his teeth as they slammed together. Stunned, Preston's head snapped back, eyes rolling, his cries cut short.

"Enough with the noise," Marty said. "Just way too much." He strolled over to Hugh and knelt down. He offered Hugh the handfuls of hair and skin.

"You hungry?"

"You're out of your mind," Hugh croaked. "He didn't do anything to you."

"And you're boring," Marty said, his long ears rubbing together. The way they moved reminded Hugh of a fly grooming itself.

"Let us go," Hugh said from his back. "Take us back home. You don't need to do this. We're not a threat."

"You tried to shoot me, you ding dong!" Marty said, eyes going wide. "I'd say that's a pretty big threat! But regardless, you can't go home. Not yet. Not until I take you to Mommy."

"Then where the hell is she?" Hugh demanded, sounding more pressing than he felt.

Marty twirled a finger in the air, smiling. "Don't you want to know where we are first? You want to take a peek at my home? You had to have noticed that this place is a little different, yeah? Maybe it's the smell, maybe it's that green sky overhead, or maybe you noticed the toonie fruit on the tree Preston's tied to? Yeah? Have you started to piece it together?" Suddenly Marty stood up, his ears going stiff as he listened.

After a moment, he smiled. "Oh man, you're in for a treat. Come on, let me show you something. This is going to blow your mind."

He grabbed Hugh by the scruff of his shirt and began to drag him through the dirt. Hugh let out a cry of pain as rocks and roots scraped across his back, his knee throbbing. It felt like a balloon filled with pulsating needles. From his back, he stared up at the green sky as it passed overhead, his eyes watering. The canopy began to thin the further Marty dragged him and the roots beneath him turned to slabs of rock. A cool breeze cooed through the air, smelling like sweet candy.

Finally, Marty stopped, releasing Hugh. Wincing, Hugh propped himself up on his elbow and sat up, catching his breath.

"Look at that," Marty said softly, pointing. Hugh twisted his creaking body and saw that they had come to a cliff, barren of trees or vegetation. It jutted out over a massive expanse, the green sky unfurling before them like an ocean of lime vapor. The world lay far below, an enormous stretch of white plains the color of fresh snow, a flat, barren slab of earth and rock.

"You see them?" Marty whispered, still pointing.

Hugh scanned the horizon, searching. What he saw took his remaining breath away.

Four titanic creatures lined the horizon. They looked like caterpillars, each one the size of a city. They were colored to match the sky, the patterns lining their bloated, rolling bodies ranged across the entire spectrum of green, from light to dark, swirls and dots joining then separating like dyslexia geometry. Their stubbed legs rose and fell along the incredible length of their bodies, back to front, front to back in rolling waves.

Extending from their spinnerets were great coils and long strands of web that trailed behind them like celestial capes. The ends of the web were attached to mountains, sprawling ranges of rocky spires and towering summits.

And the caterpillar creatures were *pulling* the mountains, dragging them like cargo across the barren world. Even from this distance, Hugh could feel the vibration of rock and earth as it was shifted, transported, across the alien realm.

"Should see your face," Marty smirked. "Cool huh? They're called Poolies. They move the world around when the seasons change. In about two weeks, you'll see more coming from the other direction, but they'll be towing rain forests and great lakes instead of mountains. They shift things, like puzzle pieces being relocated, as the temperature changes, as the rain and snow comes and goes, as the sun heats and cools. Neat, huh? Can't believe you got to see the Poolies. Maybe the next time I take you, you'll be able to see more. You should see it when they shift the oceans every couple decades. WOW. I don't think you'll make it that long, you probably only have three or four trips in you, but we can hope!" Marty slapped the dumbfounded Hugh on the back, causing him to gasp in pain.

"But enough sightseeing," Marty said, "I'm getting sidetracked here. This isn't a pleasure cruise, we got work to do and mommy to feed. Mommy mommy please don't rob me. Mommy mommy make me milk."

Marty, having apparently seen enough, grabbed Hugh roughly and dragged him back to Preston who still lay bound against the tree, head bleeding. He was groaning and in a state of semi consciousness as Hugh was discarded to the side, his cheek scraping in the dirt.

"Ok you sick puppies," Marty said, clapping his hands together. "The finale approaches. It's time to go see Mommy. Preston, you're a seasoned pro at this point, you know what to expect, but this will be very exciting for Hugh." Marty began to effortlessly claw away at the webbing that held Preston, tearing it away in great white globs.

"Preston, you know we usually have time for a little more fun, but I'm excited to introduce your friend here to mommy. She encourages me to play with my food and we usually have so much fun, but I'm just too jittery today for any more of that. SO! Enough with all this, let's go!"

With Preson now free, Marty grabbed him by what hair he had left and dragged him limply over to Hugh who he secured with his other hand. With great ease, he began to pull them through the woods, in the opposite direction of the cliff face.

The strange, chartreuse sky slid over the alien trees above as Hugh and Preston groaned and struggled, their bodies abused by the contours of the earth. Hugh felt as if his bones were coming apart, the rough treatment slamming his aged joints with every root and rock. Marty hummed to himself as he pulled them along, his stride quick and confident.

Mercifully, the journey wasn't long.

"Hi mommy!" Marty called to something Hugh couldn't see. He and Preston were tossed aside as Marty released them.

"Brought a new friend with me today!" Marty continued. "He's old but he should be good for a couple cycles."

"You ok?" Hugh whispered, his voice ragged as he assessed Preston from his place in the dirt.

Preston just closed his eyes and wept, his head wet with blood.

"Talk to me, what the hell is all this? What's going to happen?" Hugh begged.

"We're dead," Preston sputtered, curling up into a ball. "We're dead dead dead, oh god..."

Marty was suddenly over them again, hauling Preston up with seemingly limitless stamina. "Come on, you're up. Mommy's hungry, let's get you set."

Preston began to scream as he was dragged between the sparse trees, the toonie fruit branches dangling indifferently between neon glow of the open sky. Hugh twisted his aching body as best he could, a vain hand outstretched to help the poor man.

But when he saw where Preston was being led, his hand dropped and his heart crammed itself up his throat.

Hanging between the trees was an abomination.

"Come ON, Preston, quit struggling!" Marty complained, smiling, as he led the thrashing man to the base of the trees.

Mommy. This had to be her. Hugh felt his face go numb with terror.

Suspended by white webbing, as if calcified in place, was an enormous creature. It looked like some kind of rabbit, its light brown fur spotted with black. It was about twenty feet long, its body fat and bloated, like a hairy worm, its huge paws nothing more than stubs jutting out from its rolls of flesh.

Eight massive utters hung from the belly of the creature, swollen and pregnant with fluid, stretched and strained, inflamed red veins nearly bursting from the engorged sacks. The head of the creature was far too small compared to the rest of its hulking girth. Two black eyes sat embedded in a snouted skull with two huge teeth jutting out from its lower jaw. Strands of white drool dripped from its thin lips and fell lazily onto the webbed strands that hosted the enormous beast, the supporting trees bending beneath the weight. Two long ears extending from the top of its hairy head, each one splitting halfway up to reveal nests of wriggling worm-like creatures that seemed to infest the stalks.

Hanging above the gigantic creature were four fleshy shapes each the size of a coffin. To Hugh, they appeared to be external organs, covered in dead patches of hair and thick veins. These too were held up by strands of webbing attached to the towering boughs overhead. Three of the pink, seemingly alive organs were in constant rhythmic motion. The sides compressed, giving the horrible biology a momentary concave look, only to release a moment later like a breath of air. Pink flesh tubes ran from these breathing organs, like uncircumcised penises, and disappeared into the monster's ear canals, as if directly supplying its brain with oxygen or blood.

Marty kissed one of the bloated utters as he approached the beast, as he approached mommy.

"Sorry I was gone for so long," Marty said lovingly. "Preston here thought he could outrun me. Isn't that funny? Marty Mellow Marty Mellow he's the quickest fellow." Grunting, Marty bent his knees and then leapt up onto mommy's back, Preston in tow, his feet sinking into the fatty fur as he balanced himself.

"You look thin," Marty pouted, observing the beast. "Don't worry, dinner is coming. Marty will take care of you, don't you worry. You must be starving."

Mommy opened its tiny mouth and a horrible hissing sound escaped, like steam releasing from the bottom of a rotting bog.

Marty nodded sympathetically and then reached up to the singular unbreathing organ, rubbing his hand along its broad, sickly surface.

"Open up, mommy, come on."

The other three suspended organs increased their rhythm, as if excited. The fourth organ beneath Marty's hand, seemed to pucker for a moment and then a portion of it opened. It looked like a sphincter retracking, a sickly pink maw, hungry for an offering.

"No no NO!" Preston screamed as Marty hauled him up over his head, raising the man as if he were weightless.

"In you goooooo!" Marty cackled. Preston thrashed and screamed, but it was useless. Marty shoved the hysterical man into the fleshy organ, which accepted him like a hungry mouth, the skin closing and seemingly gulping the offering into itself, a few inches at a time.

Horrified, watching the spectacle, it reminded Hugh in a sick way of a noodle being slowly sucked through gluttonous lips.

Hugh could still hear Preston screaming from inside the organ as his feet were sucked through the puckering receptacle. The orifice closed behind Preston, the rubbery skin smoothing out once more in a seamless shudder. Hugh could see the shape of Preston's body pressing desperately against the interior of the organ as he fought viciously to escape his wet, sickening prison. A hand pressed outward from inside and Hugh could see all five fingers, Preston's muted screams now becoming a full throated howl.

Marty wiped his hands and jumped back to the ground, landing next to Hugh. He smiled at Hugh and offered him a sly wink.

"You're lucky mommy is still digesting the others," he said, pointing to the other three organs suspended next to the one Preston had just been shoved into.

"You'll just have to wait your turn," Marty said, "but that's ok. I'll find you when the time is right. And who knows, maybe once mommy has fully consumed Preston, the two of you can find one another again, back in your world. Team up. Try to come up with a plan to stop me." He giggled. "Wouldn't that be fun?" His ears twitched and he rubbed his hands down his naked torso. "Oh that would be fun, I think."

"He's dying in there," Hugh hissed miserably, watching, listening, wishing he couldn't.

"Obviously," Marty said, squatting down. "But don't worry. In a couple days he'll be consumed, his body broken down, melted into a slurry so mommy can drink him up. And then he'll be back! POP!" Marty clapped his hands loudly by Hugh's ear. "He'll open his eyes, back in your world, ready for another round of hide and seek. I like to give mommy's food a little time before I hunt them again. Let their anxiety build, knowing I could come at any time. Must be torture, huh?"

Marty sighed. "I think he has at least one more round left in him, one more squeeze before his meat is too used up." He grabbed Hugh by the ear and pinched it, hard.

"That's the magic of mommy. She's very considerate, isn't she? If you could, wouldn't you put a fish back in the ocean after you ate it? Return a cow to its field? An egg to its mother?"

Marty shook his head in awe. "She can use the same food source for years, letting me hunt the same prey over and over again until she requires something fresh. Something new. Until every last ounce of meat and bone and blood is too processed to recycle. Amazing, isn't she?"

Marty gazed lovingly up at the creature, his voice filling with reverence. "One day, I'll be mommy. I just got to take care of her until then. Until I'm ready. Until she's ready to give me more of herself." He gripped Hugh's ear harder. "But you'll be long dead by then."

He suddenly slapped his forehead with the palm of his hand. "Oh my gosh! I almost forgot! We gotta kiss!"

Before Hugh could move, Marty bent down and pressed his lips to Hugh's, a sickening scent of decayed candy filling his head. Hugh tried to scream and squirm away, but Marty held his head firmly between his hands.

Hugh gagged as he felt something enter his mouth and then slide down his throat, two, then three, then dozens of them. They felt like worms, vomited into the back of his mouth, balling and forcing their way down into his guts where they wriggled and squirmed.

With a sucking sound, Marty pulled away and wiped his mouth. "Whew. There we go. That's so I can find you again. Those little guys will keep you alive too. No use trying to kill yourself, they'll just bring your systems back online, even if you're ash.

They'll rebuild you and it will be agony, so I don't advise it. You're preserved now, salted, seasoned, all packaged up until I come and pluck you off the shelf for mommy."

Marty finally released Hugh's ear and stood up, the ever present sound of Preston's slow death still thundering through Hugh's senses.

"But enough about me and mommy. Sorry. I tend to run my mouth sometimes. It can get pretty lonely, even with mommy."

He slowly strode over to the great suspended monstrosity, running his hands over mommy's utters. He looked up into the grotesquely small face above him.

"Can I have some milk now, mommy?"

The fat beast creaked its jaw open and let out a hiss, a gurgling, wet sound that sounded like drowning.

Marty smiled greedily. "Thank you, mommy."

He cupped an utter in his hand and then slowly accepted a teat into his mouth, filling it. The act looked almost sexual in nature, the way Marty closed his eyes in ecstasy. He began to hungrily suckle down great gushing mouthfuls of white liquid, the release from the teat so forceful that streams of it gushed from the corners of Marty's mouth. He gulped and drank, slurping, sucking, his eyes rolling into the back of his head as his belly filled.

When he finished a few moments later, he detached from the teat and let out a gasp, his tongue mopping his lips.

"Hooooooo…" he breathed, exhaling. "Oh mommy…mommy…"

Slowly, his chin and neck wet with milk, he turned to Hugh. "There's nothing like it. Nothing in all the worlds."

Hugh said nothing, the hell of this place turning his mind to madness.

"I think it's time for you to go now, though," Marty continued, his voice serene. "But don't worry. I'll come find you soon once mommy is hungry again." Marty leaned down and stroked Hugh's cheek. "This isn't goodbye, just see you later. Now go."

And then all at once, a darkness emanated out of Marty Mellow. It was as if he had turned himself into black hole, sucking in all light and sound. It pulled the world inwards, into a singular point, until there was nothing but black.

The last thing Hugh heard before waking up in his kitchen was Marty's gentle voice in his ear.

"Get on home now. I'll find you in the clover fields."

ROLLING THUNDER

The man walked toward the farm house with bad intentions. His hulking frame passed through the cornfield, his thick, meaty hands brushing the tops of the waist high stalks. The morning sun was at his back, casting a long shadow ahead of him. Birds fluttered by, their song sweet and indifferent. The rain from last night still clung to his clothes, the air filled with the scent of wet dirt. The sky was an ocean above him, blue and clean and without corruption.

The farmhouse was a hundred yards away now, a two story white monolith with a cherry red barn at its back. A green tractor was parked outside the barn, as vacant as the sky. A dog barked somewhere in the distance.

The man saw that the house was open, a simple screen door the only barrier keeping the bugs at bay.

He continued his linear march, death in his wake, as if wading through the streets of Gomorrah. His size fourteen boots churned the damp ground, an earthy breeze descending from the heavens to sweep the strands of greasy black hair away from his dull brown eyes. He could hear voices now from inside the house. Children.

It did not matter. He continued forward.

The night had been unkind and he had spent the entirety of it walking through the woods, onward, always onward. The rain had soaked him as he plowed through dogwood and sassafras, as he trod over moss and lichen, as he trampled fern and geranium.

He continued onward.

His mud clogged boots thumped loudly up the front steps of the porch now, thunderfalls announcing his presence. The voices of the children grew louder as laughter echoed from inside.

The man pulled open the screen door and went in, ducking his head as he went so he wouldn't hit the frame. His dirty scalp practically scraped the ceiling as he strode down the hallway, into the kitchen.

A man of about forty, dressed in blue jeans and an old green t-shirt stood by the stove, cooking a skillet of eggs. Two young boys of about three sat at the breakfast table, their eyes huge as they saw the man, his presence shattering their morning innocence.

The farmer at the stove turned in surprise, his face a mix of shock and confusion as the giant strode forward.

The big man grabbed him by the throat before he could speak and slammed his face into the countertop. Teeth clattered to the floor like bloody dice. The children at the table screamed, absolute terror.

The man pulled the farmer up by his hair and punched him in the jaw. The blow sounded like a sledgehammer connecting with an Easter ham. The farmer went down in a spray of broken cartilage. Standing over the dazed farmer, the man brought his boot up and then rearranged the man's face with it, the skull finally giving way after three murderous blows.

The man turned to the stove and retrieved the pan of eggs. He took it to the table where he sat and greedily shoveled the steaming hot breakfast into his mouth. The children continued to weep, shrieking as their dead father's blood lapped at their chairs.

The man looked up, the eggs only half eaten. The children were small. Their faces red and stained with tears. Mouths open in great wails.

The man stood, his chair scraping loudly across the wood floor. He grabbed the two boys, one in each hand. He went to the oven and pulled it open. With a boot he kicked out the wire racks and then he shoved the children inside. They were too big to both fit. They were screaming, screaming so loud. The man grabbed the smaller of the two and inverted the child's elbows, then snapped his legs at the shin as if he were breaking apart dried firewood. The man shoved the broken boy into the oven next to his squealing brother. He had to use his boot to get him all the way in.

He closed the oven, flipped the lever to lock it, then set it to broil.

The man finished his breakfast as the boys cooked.

He was back in the woods, staying off the roads. The food had closed the hole in his gut. He needed to sleep, but he would not succumb until dusk. Squirrels and birds chitted and cooed, filling the soaked canopy with life. The warm morning sun continued to heat the world, turning the air humid. The man was sweating and he wiped a calloused hand across his brow. He had no destination in mind, the crunch of the underbrush blazing a trail with no end.

He walked. In the distance he heard the hum of cars along a road. His arm ached from where it had been struck by a wooden chair two days ago. Another meal, another litter of mutilated dead. He thought of nothing as he went, his mind a haze of unfocused images that meant little to him. His dirty shirt had dried from the night's rain, but was now wet and clinging with his foul stench. The jeans he wore were crusted with dirt, the blue denim faded and thin. The stubble along his protruding jaw had grown into a full beard, now beaded with sweat.

A chipmunk crossed his path, a few feet ahead of him. It paused, frozen, staring. The man stopped and stared back. He slowly crouched, watching it, mouth open, exhuming fetid breath. Their eyes locked, equally empty. The man said nothing. The chipmunk scurried away. The man stood and continued on.

The sun was setting. The man was in a field, surrounded on all sides by wide, spaceless green. He sat, staring at the sun. It dipped toward the horizon, plunging into a pool of watercolor. Orange swirled into pinks and purples, tides of brilliant, electric clouds catching the light. He no longer heard the road. The woods were hours behind him. He lay on his back, still staring at the somber sun. It was a brilliant thing, an artist that painted the world without asking anything in return.

As the air cooled, the man closed his eyes and slept. When he woke, it was still dark. The moon had replaced its celestial counterpart, a thick wedge of white glacial ice. The stars were few and far between, dim dots of snow melting into asphalt.

The man stood. He was horribly thirsty. Lit by the moon, he began to walk again. Lightning bugs lit the field, blinking like slumbering traffic lights. They expanded before him, dancing in the wild flowers and reeds whisking between his long strides.

His tongue felt bloated, like the corpse of a dead boar beneath an African sky. His throat was raw as if the Atacama had filled his mouth as he slept. He tore reeds from the earth as he walked, sucking on them, his large teeth crushing and tearing, extracting any moisture they could.

Despite the hour, it was still humid and within minutes, he was sweating again. Hydration leaving the body. Within the hour, he heard the hum of the road again. He walked toward it. Eventually he saw headlights, lonely white eyes, pulled wide, traveling along the long tongue of blacktop. He descended, the earth tilting now, almost tumbling him toward the road.

A gas station sat nestled against the backdrop of night, about two miles away. A white sign rose high above the rundown building, displaying prices, illuminated by hot sodium light. The man walked toward it. Another car snaked into view, passing by the shadow in the hills above it, completely unaware of the abhorrent the darkness hid.

The man reached the gas station, his towering form breaching the boundary of white light. There was a lone car parked along the side of the building. The man passed the pumps and pushed his way inside, a wash of temperature regulated air cooling him instantly.

An attendant was at the counter, a rather bored looking man in his twenties. When he saw the hulking figure of the man, his face went white. His intuition became that of an animal, a deer frozen in the path of danger. He said nothing, his jaw tight as the man went to the coolers.

The man retrieved a bottle of water and drained it. He dropped the empty plastic to the floor and drank another. Finished, he took a third and shoved it into the pocket of his jeans. He turned and walked the isles, snatching at food, tearing the packages open with his teeth, and then consumed it all without etiquette.

His beard now stained with sugar powder and crumbs, he ceased his caloric pillage. He looked at the attendant who stood like Lot's wife behind the counter. Their eyes met. The man lumbered over to him. He stood, with just the register dividing them, and gazed into the terrified attendant's face. He placed his hands on the counter, palms flat. The attendant backed away, throat tight, his back hitting a wall of cigarettes, sending a few tiny white packs tumbling to the ground.

The man continued to stare at him, heavy breath heaving through his enormous chest like waves that crashed through his smeared lips. The man curled his hands into fists, knuckles cracking.

And then he left, the small bell above the door jingling at his departure.

He walked along the road with the sunrise at his back. He needed more sleep. His joints ached from his long journey, the muscles in his legs were weary and used. A car passed him by every couple minutes, but he paid them no heed. They were anomalies. They existed on the fringes of his focused purpose. For he had developed purpose now, an amalgamation of need that had come to him, forming and coalescing into a singular drive. This drive fueled him, churning the pistons of his body onward.

He came to a trailer park. It was set back from the road down a dusty turn off. There were about thirty trailers, run down and weather blasted. The cars parked beside these trailers were rusting, dented, at the end of their life, as were all things of age. The man waded into the park, passing plastic chairs and toys strewn about, bicycles and grills, lawn chairs and unmowed grass. The park seemed to sleep for he didn't spot a soul as he walked.

He picked a trailer at random. There was no car parked before it and the white paneling was filthy with dust. He went to the door, uncaring if curious eyes watched him, and tried it. He found it open, as if inviting chance into the small residence. The man pushed through and shut the door quietly behind him. The interior was neat and simple, furnished in a financially stunted attempt to make the space pleasant. A small living room greeted him, a couch on the far wall, a tv, a couple potted plants and a few emotionless paintings that hung on beige walls.

The man went for the bedroom. The door was closed and when he opened it he saw an elderly woman asleep, alone, her dentures in a glass of water on the nightstand. The man gently laid down next to her and closed his eyes. The pillow smelled of lilacs and honey.

He woke up a few hours later to the old lady staring at him. She sat in a small chair next to the bedroom window and the sunlight filtered through her lush white hair. She had her teeth in. She smiled at him. He did not move from the bed. He watched her and she watched him back. Outside, a car passed, bumping down the dirt road on the way to work or school or perhaps something sinister.

The woman attempted to stand, steadied herself, and then beckoned wordlessly for him to follow her. She moved slowly, but kindly, as if the arrival of a guest, no matter how strange the circumstance, had filled her empty day with purpose.

He stood and went after her, ducking through the doorway.

Sitting on the modest kitchen table was a spread of pancakes, bacon, eggs, and a large, frothy glass of cold milk. Again, the woman wordlessly gestured to the man with a smile. The man's face remained impassive as he sat and began to eat, bacon grease dripping from his fingers. The woman took a seat across from him and studied him curiously. She did not speak, her voice perhaps awaiting her in the next life.

She seemed pleased to watch him eat, her eyes dull with years, but endearing in their decay and filled with motherly comfort. She did not partake, but instead sat with her knuckled hands folded before her, as if in prayer.

When the man was finished eating, he drained the glass of milk, little streams escaping from the sides of his glass and into his beard. He wiped his face, setting the glass down. The old woman beckoned to the fridge, as if to offer him another kindness. The man just stared at her, his bulking frame filling the entire side of the table.

The old lady stood shakily and began clearing the dishes from the table. A picture hung on the wall above the sink. It showed a much younger version of the woman, smiling a pretty smile with her arms wrapped around a handsome man with dark combed hair and a pearly grin. A snapshot of a time when life seemed eternal. As the old woman set the dishes in the sink, she stared at the picture for a moment, almost ritualistically.

The man rose from the table. He went and stood next to the woman at the sink as she washed the residue from the plates. She looked up at him and smiled and part of her younger self broke through, emerged from the wrinkles and liver spots, a snapshot of history long gone.

An array of kitchen knives sat embedded in a wooden block, atop the counter, beside a jar filled with flour.

The man took one of the knives and stabbed the old woman in the throat. Her eyes opened in pained shock, a plate dropping mid-wash to shatter on the floor. Blood ran over the man's knuckles as he slid the knife from her flesh. He took the woman by the throat, lifting her, gurgling now, off her feet. He pressed the tip of the knife into her eye, slowly, puncturing the soft jelly. She was howling now. She sounded like a dog screaming as someone ripped its ears off, boot to throat.

The man punctured her other eye. Then he tossed her to the floor at his feet. She lay on her back, blind and shivering, croaking those pained dog noises. Blood filled the kitchen floor. She would not be spared death. She knew this. She was alone and would die as such, wishing Abraham would plead mercy to God's ear.

The man stepped over her and left.

He could no longer smell the lilac and honey.

He walked along the road again, the sun a charred slice of lemon. Cicadas droned and the air smelled of heated blacktop. His big boots were beginning to come apart and the man knew he would need to replace them soon. Cars droned past at a lazy, infrequent clip, paying no mind to the huge man striding toward town.

It was around three in the afternoon when he reached the suburbs. He had passed a couple motels, auto shops, a market, and a few mom and pop joints, the landscape evolving into a domesticated community. He noted a few signs of recently developed neighborhoods as he walked, sideroads leading to wooded cul-de-sacs and wealthy housing. He turned off one of these side roads.

The neighborhood he found himself in, about an hour later, was one of many he'd seen before in his travels. Generous plots, big five bedroom houses, manicured lawns, sprinklers, a sense of cleanliness reserved for larger wallets. The cicadas continued their summertime choir, the world infused with the scent of recently cut grass and wet fertilizer. Most of the houses he passed looked empty, their driveways barren, garage doors closed. He passed these by.

He got to the end of the street, a cal-de-sac, and noted the singular house set back against a sprawl of lush woods. It was removed from the others, further back, the privacy inviting. There was also a car in the driveway, a red SUV that looked freshly waxed. Inside the open garage he saw children's toys.

The man slunk off the road and into the woods, feeling the rest of the neighborhood vanish behind him. He circled through the trees toward the back of the house. He heard voices. Splashing. Laughter.

This was good.

A large inground swimming pool came into view. The man watched from the trees. A teenage boy leapt into the water, cackling. A younger girl, about eight, screamed as her brother's airborne body exploded next to her, creating a great spout of splashing water.

A man, probably the father of the two children, rose from his reclined chair. He yelled at the teenage boy. His body was flabby but hairless, coated in a ghostly film of white sunscreen. A woman lounged in the chair next to him. Sunglasses, bikini, toned. The man was not interested in her.

The little girl was crying, having been splashed, and was now climbing out of the pool. She trailed water along the concrete as she went to her mother who folded her small frame into a towel. The teenage boy was still laughing as his father continued to yell at him.

The man stared. Watched. He did not move. Three hours passed.

The family had retreated inside by the time the sun set. He had watched the father cook dinner on a chrome grill, the scent of meat and propane mixing with chlorine from the pool. The sun, veiled by the trees overhead, tipped toward the horizon and night spilled its ink across the heavens. The man remained a piller, his eyes glued to the father as he cooked, then went in to feed his family. The cicadas had given up the stage to crickets and croaking frogs. The air grew cool, the humidity dropping. The lights from inside the house slowly winked out as the hour grew late until all was dark and still and silent, save for the critters and rumble of breath in the man's chest.

He moved. He did not hesitate now. He strode confidently across the concrete encircling the pool, reaching for the sliding glass door. They had forgotten to lock it. Or perhaps, so confident in their bubble, they had deemed it an unnecessary precaution.

The man opened the door and stepped inside to find a darkened kitchen. He went to the fridge, the house smelling of cleaning products. Inside the fridge was a plate of leftover hamburgers and hotdogs. He took the plate to the dining room table where he sat and consumed the cold meat. He stared at nothing as his jaw worked the overcooked meal. The house was silent above him where the family slept.

When the food was gone, he went back to the fridge and retrieved a half empty jug of sweet tea. He stood in the glow of the fridge and drank deeply. He dropped the empty jug and it clattered loudly at his feet. He turned, movement in the corner of his vision.

The teenage boy stood frozen by the dining room table, his eyes huge, two polished marbles. Bathed in light from the fridge, the man met his gaze. Held it. The boy turned then, jerked almost, screaming for his father, scrambling back toward the stairs.

The man took three steps, grabbed one of the chairs from the table, and threw it with tremendous force, one handed, at the boy. It struck him squarely in the back, shattering and dropping the youth. But the alarm had been raised. The call for help, sent. Dazed, the boy lay on his stomach amid a ruin of shattered wood.

The man opened a kitchen drawer and selected a meat tenderizer. His thumping boots brought him to the boy. He flipped him onto his back, another scream rising in the young man's throat. The meat tenderizer landed like an asteroid in the boy's face. A crater of cracked bone and cartilage formed where the nose had been. Another blow deepened the impact, blood spraying, teeth scattering. The boy gurgled, one eye burst, the other bulging from its socket, partially dislodged. The man hammered the boy's face one final time, the sharp crack of skull finalizing death.

Standing, the man let his weapon drop to the floor. He heard movement from upstairs. He walked to the staircase and looked up, staring directly into the confused face of the father, one slippered foot teasing his descent down the stairs.

The man climbed and the father barked a shriek, retreating into the shadows of his bedroom once more. He was yelling for his wife to get the kids, get them out of the house, that there was an intruder. The man reached the top of the stairs only to grunt as the wife thumped into him as she ran for her daughter's room. She went sprawling at his feet, a scream rising as she stared up at the filthy giant.

The man grabbed her by the throat and threw her down the stairs, as if discarding a piece of trash. As she crashed to the ground floor, he turned his attention to the father. He found himself the target of a small pistol clutched in the father's shaking hand. His figure, trembling in the bedroom door, was only a few feet away, the gun dancing in the dark. The man advanced.

The gunshot was loud and the impact of the bullet took the man in the gut. He grunted and went to one knee, the father screaming as he pulled the trigger, as if shocked he had actually fired. Before he could get another shot off, the man stood again and grabbed the gun from the father's hands. He then brought it smashing into the father's forehead, dropping him instantly.

Panting, the man felt pain in the form of fire spreading inside his guts where the bullet had lodged itself. Blood leaked from the wound. The man tore his filthy shirt off and tied it around his body, tight, to prevent further blood loss.

Righting himself, he went to the daughter's room.

The parents were still screaming. The man had found a bin full of bungee cords in the garage and had them bound, back to back, in a sitting position on the living room floor. The young daughter, who had wet herself, screaming as he took her from her bed, sat on the couch, paralyzed with fear.

The man wasted no time. The pain in his bleeding stomach was growing worse and he was sweating profusely. With the parents secure, he took the daughter by the hair and dragged her over to the dining room table. One handed, he lifted her and slammed her down on her back, the legs of the table screeching. Staring directly at the parents, he throttled the child. She made horrible gagging noises, eyes wet with tears, tiny hands clawing at his arms as he applied pressure. A moment before she passed out, he released her. The parents howled, thrashing, bound, helpless as they watched. The little girl, sobbing, rubbed her throat and coughed violently.

The man pushed her back to the table and then severed her head with a meat cleaver. Blood fountained onto the floor, the head thumping and rolling off the table to rest against the fridge. The parents went hysterical.

The man breathed heavily, his intestines feeling as if they held jet fuel. He sat, panting, watching the blood continue to drool off the table. He swatted the headless body of the girl away and it tumbled to the ground where it thumped limply. Blood soaked through the compression around his stomach. It was getting harder to breathe. He stared down at his hands as the parents screamed. His eyes lazily rolled over the floor to the severed head. He stared at it. The eyes were open.

The clock on the wall showed that it was almost midnight. The man stood, like a monster breaking the surface of a bog. He looked at the parents as they thrashed, immobile, spittle flying as they wept and screamed. He went back into the garage, leaving them momentarily.

The man returned holding a red gas can. He upended it onto the parents, soaking them, filling the house with sharp, acrid fumes. Gasping now, one hand pressed to his abdomen, the man retrieved a lighter from a drawer.

Wordlessly, he lit the parents on fire. They went up instantly, the explosive wall of heat caused the man to take a step back. Their skin cooked and blackened, their hair reduced to ash, their mouths wide in blazing screams.

The man watched them for a few moments and then turned, leaving.

A storm had split the night open. Great booms of thunder shook the sky, like some biblical war drum. Lightning cracked the darkness, electric spiderwebs that blinked viciously. The rain had come without warning, a droning downpour that soaked the man as he walked toward town. The suburbs vanished at his back, his stomach aching with wet fire. His blood diluted in the rain and his breath was labored. Police sirens filled the far distance. A call had been made, something seen or heard or some intuition claimed.

The man's long, stringy hair clung to his paled face, his mouth open as he fought to choke another lungful of air. And yet he walked, onward, always onward.

He approached a truck stop. The dead of night blanketed the gas pumps and service center. The parking lot was mostly empty save for a few semis parked off to the side, their drivers presumably asleep or inside the center, catching a shower or lonely meal. The man headed for one of these trucks, a large white rig, parked away from the others.

The rain drove him forward, great lashing sheets that did nothing to chill the heat in his wound. Water ran down his back and dripped from his chin as he reached for the door handle. Locked. He stood for a moment as thunder pounded the late night sky, his eyes focusing on nothing. Someone yelled. He turned and saw a trucker, perhaps the owner of the rig, trotting toward him, a hand raised in a vain attempt to shield his face from the rain.

He was shouting angrily and pointing toward the truck. When he approached the man, the trucker slowed, the size of the bleeding form dulling the blade of anger in his voice. The trucker told him to get lost, keeping his distance, a hand already reaching for his cellphone.

The man grabbed the trucker's wrist and broke it, sending the phone clattering to the pavement. The trucker opened his mouth to scream, but the man pulled him close, compressing him against his chest, and placed a mammoth hand over his parted lips. He felt the scream vibrate against his palm.

Keeping one hand smashed against the trucker's mouth, he placed his other hand on the back of the man's head. And then he squeezed, his tired muscles contracting and bulging, the roar of the rain all around them.

The front of the trucker's face gave way after a few moments of immeasurable pressure, the bone cracking, the nose inverting, eye sockets shoved inward toward the brain. Bone fragments lacerated the important parts, the vital parts, the crucial parts, and as the man's face caved in, a gush of blood erupted outward and onto the parking lot.

The trucker died instantly, his body going limp. The man let the body fall and then stooped, retrieving the keys. His breath hissed between his teeth as a knife of pain stabbed his wound. Standing, lightning illuminating the world in a flash bulb instant, the man saw another trucker in the parking lot, frozen, a witness to what had just transpired.

The man unlocked the truck, unrushed, and climbed in with a grunt. The trucker who had seen him was now on the phone, the glow of the screen pressed against a rain streaked face. The man started the truck and noted the proximity of the police sirens. They were closer.

The man shifted the truck into gear and gunned it, the great wet rig jerking violently as it was called to life. The man on the phone took a step back, alarmed, and dove to the side as the snarling vehicle jetted forward.

He didn't clear the wheels. The rumbling rig ran him over, the huge wheels compressing his chest, crushing it, gouts of blood shooting from the trucker's mouth and eyes and ears, his body popping like a caterpillar beneath a child's thumb.

The man swung the rig out onto the road, shifted gears, and pressed onward. The headlights cut white cones through the night and the wipers swept the rain from the windshield in great whooshing strokes.

Up ahead, a few minutes after clearing the truck stop, the first police car came into view. Its lights were on, red and blue neon that swirled like twin scoops of summer sherbert. Its path would take it past the rig and the bleeding man inside, headed for the service center or perhaps the house with the pool, the bodies of the parents now embers.

The man watched it approach, his eyes half lidded, knowing it would pass him in the opposite lane, pass him to assess what he had done. At the last second, the man jerked the wheel and rammed the cop car head on.

The crunch of metal and shattering glass was monumental. The man jerked forward in his seatbelt as the collision shuddered through the length of the rig, his teeth clacking loudly at the moment of impact. The police cruiser folded like origami and the officer inside shot out of his windshield as if he had just learned flight. His head and neck hit the grill of the rig and then the rest of his body followed. At the speed the truck was going, the impact was explosive and the officer's body came apart like a piñata stuffed with bloody organs.

The huge truck pushed aside the ruined police car as if it were a snowplow discarding a drift, leaving it and its ruined occupant in its tracks. The man shifted up again, gathering speed, cranking the wipers, leaning forward, adrenaline and pain clashing in his veins.

More sirens came. He checked the rearview mirror and saw a swirl of police vehicles. They were still some distance off, but they were gaining and would continue to gain. Once they saw the ruined police cruiser, they would be on him.

The man shifted once more, the speedometer rising. He placed a hand on his gut and it came away soaked with blood. He checked the rearview once more and then rolled down his window. Rain poured into the cab with the force of a hurricane.

The man casually hung his arm out the window, his hair whipping wildly about his head. The hole in his stomach continued to leak. He could feel a haze beginning to settle in his mind, a numbness coming to his limbs. The man could see a motel in the distance, just off the road. The police cars continued to grow closer, almost urgent now in their pursuit.

But the motel was closer and the parking lot was full. He aimed for the building, accelerating once more, the rig like rolling thunder.

His bloodied, outstretched hand caught the rain and left a trail of red in its wake.

ELIAS WITHEROW is a New England-based author with a passion for writing that can only be matched by his love of the mountains. He hopes to create stories that stir the darker side of imagination while bringing a fresh perspective to the horror genre. Elias can usually be found muttering over his keyboard or inspecting his lawn. If you ever run into him, he'd love to talk horror.

Twitter @EliasWitherow
Facebook.com/FeedThePig

MORE FROM ELIAS WITHEROW

THOUGHT CATALOG BOOKS

The Worst Kind of Monsters

The Black Farm

The Third Parent

The Worst In Us

The Last Tower

Return To The Black Farm

Final Sky

Outlast Your Gods

Vagabonds

Memories of Monsters

THOUGHT
CATALOG
Books

THOUGHTCATALOG.COM